LENNY'S BOOK OF EVERYTHING

LENNY'S BOOK OF EVERYTHING

KAREN FOXLEE

Pushkin Children's

Pushkin Press
71–75 Shelton Street
London WC2H 9JQ

The right of Karen Foxlee to be identified as the author
of this Work has been asserted by her in accordance with the
Copyright, Designs & Patents Act 1988

Original text © 2018 Karen Foxlee

Lenny's Book of Everything was first published in
Melbourne, Australia by Allen & Unwin in 2018

First published by Pushkin Press in 2019

9 8 7 6 5 4 3 2 1

ISBN 13: 978-1-78269-238-6

Offset by Tetragon, London
Printed and bound by CPI Group (UK) Ltd, Croydon, CR0 4YY

www.pushkinpress.com

For Mum

Perfectly Normal

7lbs. 3
20 inches
1969

Our mother had a dark heart feeling. It was as big as the sky kept inside a thimble. That's how dark heart feelings are. They have great volume but can hide in small places. You can swallow them with a blink and carry them inside you so no one will know.

"Something's not right," she said, when she brought baby Davey home from the hospital.

She rubbed her fingers over her chest and looked at him sleeping in the crook of her arm.

"I have a feeling," she said.

She was good at knowing the wrongness of things, sadnesses and sicknesses, and, in the park, she could always find the pigeon with one leg. She knew when Mrs. Gaspar was coming down with a wheeze before she wheezed. She knew my thin hair was caused by some undiagnosed malady. Some days were more wrong than others. Whole days. From the moment she opened her eyes, "Something's not right," she said.

"Does it hurt?" I asked her. I looked at my new baby brother and he was perfect as a walnut in its shell.

"No, it doesn't hurt," she said and she took my three-year-old hand and put it to her heart. I could feel her ribs through her nightdress. "It's not a hurting kind of feeling. Just a something-will-happen feeling."

"A good thing or a bad thing?" I asked.

"It might be good or bad or somewhere in between," she said. "We'll have to wait and see."

Davey was born six days after Neil Armstrong took his famous step and everyone was still crazy with moon walk fever. Mother liked to tell the story if she was in a lying-on-the-sofa mood. An untying-her-hair mood. A tickle-my-feet-and-I'll-tell-you mood. We knew all her stories by heart, word for word, so that we could have told them ourselves if we needed to. The story of the day her father died from a heart attack after blowing out his birthday candles. The story of her friend, Louis Martin, who was struck by lightning when he walked home from school in the rain. The story of the river and how she nearly drowned in it when she was seven, of the first dress she ever made, which her mother forbade her to wear because it was cherry red. The tale of the UFO she saw beside the highway when she ran away with Peter Lenard Spink.

"It was a perfect summer day when you were born," was always how the Davey story started.

She must have noticed all the perfectness from the bus window because she couldn't afford the cab fare: Second Street, glinting and shimmering in the heat, and ponderous summer clouds sweeping their shadows over the sunbaking cars, the marigolds growing in the park, children eating ice-creams.

I was left behind with Mrs. Gaspar in number seventeen. She had two Pomeranians with marmalade-coloured coats named Karl and Karla. The apartment smelled of them, and also ashtrays, filled with white cigarette filters, each decorated with a ring of peach lipstick. Her apartment was a kaleidoscope of tan crocheted doilies and pumpkin-coloured throw rugs; even Mrs. Gaspar's orange beehive, which sat a little askew on her head, matched the decor. Her hand-knitted clothes were unravelling and her pom-pom slippers had the dishevelled look of something she had fished out of a trash can. She liked to bless me when my mother wasn't looking. She drew crosses on my tiny forehead and whispered in Hungarian.

"Yes, it was a perfect summer day," said Mother. "And I knew you were coming. I knew it and I hadn't had a single contraction. Not one. But something told me I had to go to the hospital. Something said, *Cynthia Spink, get to that hospital this instant.*"

"What was the something?" I asked.

"Hush now," she said.

But I wanted to know. She was thin with worrying, our mother. She combed out her long fair hair with her fingers, closed her eyes. She was made almost entirely out of worries and magic.

"Was it a voice?" If it was a voice, it would sound like dry leaves.

"I said hush, Lenny, it's my story. I took you across the hall to Mrs. Gaspar's and then I caught the number twenty-four. The voice said, *Get on that number twenty-four, Cynthia, because it doesn't do the loop to Safeway. It goes all the way down Second with only five stops.*"

I tried to imagine a voice like whispering leaves saying all that. I rolled my eyes at Davey but he ignored me because he loved his sudden-arrival story.

"You were a week late already. I sweated on that bus. I must have sweated a gallon. Then I stepped off that bus, down onto the sidewalk near that hospital and wouldn't you know it, I get a contraction that bends me in half and then another one just a minute later. And I get two more and I haven't even made it to the hospital front door, Davey. And there were people running from everywhere but I had you right there on the doorstep with everyone walking past."

"Holy Batman," said Davey.

But it wasn't like we hadn't heard the story before. He knew there was more to come.

"But the thing was," she said, "when you were born, they told me you had a true knot in your cord. A true knot, pulled tight, and that's why you came out so quick, because my body and your body knew you'd run out of air and blood if you didn't."

Air and blood. I always repeated that part in my head. *Air and Blood.*

"Gee," said Davey.

"You almost might have never been," said Mother.

"I'm glad you got the number twenty-four," said Davey.

"You were a beautiful baby," said Mother.

"Was I?" asked Davey.

"So beautiful," said Mother.

But she didn't mention the dark heart feeling to him, not ever, not once. That was always our secret. That was never in the story. She never told him how she asked Dr. Leopold if everything was fine.

"Why, he's a perfect bouncing baby boy," said Dr. Leopold.

"Are you sure?"

"Why, he's perfectly normal," said Dr. Leopold on the perfect summer day.

So she smiled and agreed.

"Father's name?" the doctor asked. He was filling out the birth certificate.

"Peter Lenard Spink," said Mother. "L. E. N. A.R.D."

"Will Mr. Spink be in tomorrow to see his boy?" asked the doctor.

"Yes," said Mother. "Yes, he will be."

When I was older I liked to say his name in bed. *Peter Lenard Spink. Peter Lenard Spink. Peter Lenard Spink.* His name rolled off my tongue like a punctured wheel. I said it until, in the darkness, Davey told me to be quiet. But it was a name that needed saying.

He did not come that day or the next. Whole weeks passed. Davey slept and my mother worried and fussed over his sleepiness. She worried and fussed over his poor appetite. She worried and fussed over his boy-ness. She worried over the bills and how she would pay them and who would look after us when she went back to work.

The weeks were sunshiny but sorrowful. Mrs. Gaspar came daily and tended to Davey and sang him mournful lullabies. Each afternoon thunderstorms came and washed the streets clean but they could not wash Peter Lenard Spink from our mother.

Until one night the key turned in the lock and Peter Lenard Spink appeared. He stood very still, as though he wasn't sure he was in the right place. He smiled his small whiskery smile. He'd been working. He'd had to take the work. He'd had to work construction a long way south. The reasons were offered up in various ways but Mother shook her head at all of them. She nodded to us.

"Little Lenny," he said, dipping his head to me.

"And baby David," said Mother.

Still we waited for the thing to happen. Mother's dark heart feeling did not go away. It found a tiny crack and climbed inside her. It took up residence. She carried it around with her, alongside Davey on her hip.

"Something's not right," she said. Sometimes when she fed Davey his cereal. Once when she watched him crawling behind me squealing through the small nest of rooms that was our home, crawling so fast he skinned his baby knees. When he took his first perfectly normal steps.

Sometimes it wasn't mentioned for months.

Sometimes ten times in one day.

"Something isn't right," she said quietly.

"What is it?" I asked. I put my hand on her heart the way she liked me to do. I knew it soothed her. I felt its beat beneath my fingertips.

"I just don't know," she said.

Peter Lenard Spink sat at the kitchen table turning the pages of the paper slowly.

"You worry too much, has always been your problem," he said. "There's work in Pensacola. What about this? Immediate start. Meals provided."

He read out the newspaper advertisement. That's the way his goodbyes began. I kept my hand on my mother's chest. She smiled at me but beneath my fingertips her heartbeat quickened.

Davey pulled himself up beside us using fistfuls of Mother's skirt. He smiled and it made us smile in return, it couldn't be helped. Baby Davey had the happiest smile in the world.

Peter Lenard Spink went to Pensacola. He went to Tuscaloosa. He went to St. Louis. He went to St. Marks and St. Cloud. He went north and south. He went east and west. Sometimes we were allowed to look from our bedroom window down at the Greyhound bus station when he went. He would wave up at us, just a small raise of his hand.

But other times Mother said, "No."

She said, "Don't you dare look from that window."

Peter Lenard Spink left and the door clicked and Mother went and lay very still on her bed like a stone princess on top of a tomb.

Peter Lenard Spink was a tan figure hunched over shoelaces. He was sideburns and a nervous smile. He was leaving sounds: rusty suitcase clasps and zippers. He was the belt-buckle jangle. He went to Marietta and Blacksburg and as far away as Buffalo, Wyoming. He gave me a sticker from there. I didn't stick it anywhere. I kept it pristine and unstuck in my jewellery box and Davey coveted it for many years.

Davey grew up. He tottered. He walked. He said his first word which was *Dada* and it made Peter Lenard Spink's small whiskery smile quiver. First birthday, second birthday, third birthday, fourth. Nearly his fifth ... Mother got dressed each day in her pink uniform. She tied up her fair hair in a fountain on her head. She went to work at the Golden Living Retirement Home. She deposited us with Mrs. Gaspar and Karl and Karla. Mrs. Gaspar said, "My little dumplings," and took us in. My mother wore her happy Cindy Spink smile but we both still waited for the thing to happen.

"He'll come back," Mother said each time Peter Lenard Spink left.

"He'll come back," she pleaded with no one.

The last time was no different from the others. The sound of him peeing, the faucet, a match strike, keys. A suitcase sound. A small cough. A belt-buckle tinkle. He whispered out of our lives at dawn, unlatched the door and clicked it behind him, and never came back again.

Davey turned five the very next day. There was a small cake and a cowboy shirt and a blue toy tractor that he adored. At the end of the day he had a tantrum. He bellowed and stamped his feet and threw himself to the ground over nothing. Mother said everyone always cried on their birthday when they were small, but it was a lie because I never did, not once. Davey bellowed for no reason and wore himself out to sleep and it was while he was sleeping that the thing happened. The thing we'd been waiting for. When Mother saw it in the morning, she made a noise like she had seen a ghost.

"Davey," she whispered.

But then she sat down, plonk, on the sofa, as though she was glad it had finally arrived. She let out one long breath.

"What's happened to you?" she said.

Swedes

5 and a half years
4' 3"
DECEMBER 1974

E ach morning Mother woke us early in the dark. She said goodbye to us as the sun was coming up, a pale wash of light lifting on the green walls. It rose, that light, before my eyes as we waited for Mrs. Gaspar to open her door.

"What?" said Mrs. Gaspar in her shaggy tangerine bathrobe. "He is growing more?"

"No, he's just the same," said Mother, laughing. "He's just the same, Mrs. Gaspar."

But Davey *was* taller than me and I was a third-grader. Standing in the corridor, we could see his new pyjama pants were already knickerbockers again.

"Cyn-thi-a," said Mrs. Gaspar, each syllable registering her disappointment. "Mrs. Spink! He must go to the doctor. This is not normal!"

"Oh, no," said Mother, "he's just big, there are big people in the family, my mama always said it, they came from Sweden."

Mrs. Gaspar shook her head. She patted Davey's head where his hair surged upward like prairie grass. As soon as Mother was gone to work, she blessed us like a round orange pontiff, very solemnly, her beehive wobbling on her head. Mrs. Gaspar had a very large Jesus painting in a frame above the television.

This smiling Jesus had red cheeks and wore robes the colour of a pastel Easter egg. Light beams shone from his fingertips. He looked friendly enough but was a little off-putting when we tried to watch cartoons. We ate our cornflakes beneath his benevolent gaze.

We prayed with Mrs. Gaspar. She made us close our eyes and hold her hands, one hand for Davey and one for me. I didn't like to close my eyes but she said, "No peeking, dumpling," like we were about to do something fun. Her hands were puffy and cool and slightly damp.

Mrs. Gaspar prayed for us. For our mother to be kept safe travelling to the Golden Living Retirement Home on the number twenty-eight bus, for the return of our wayward father, for my hair, for her wheeze, for her long-ago parents, for Karl and Karla, who meanwhile sat at our feet watching with shining black eyes. And she prayed for Davey to stop growing.

We ate breakfast in her little kitchen that was a shrine to Apollo 11. There were newspaper articles cut out and stuck all over her fridge, coloured *National Geographic* pages taped around the kitchen door with a triptych of the astronauts Buzz, Neil, and Michael up top. Davey was sad every time I was ready to go to school, as though it had never happened before, this business of me donning my jacket and clipping my schoolbag shut. He said, "Len-neeeeeee," long and slow. He grabbed me and pushed his big blond head into my stomach and cried all over my clean shirt.

He stayed with Mrs. Gaspar and they would watch *Days of Our Lives* together. "Like sands through the hourglass," Davey said, "so are the days of our lives." "Good boy," said Mrs. Gaspar. She would make him pray three times a day, on his knees, and he would do it, very good-naturedly. But he'd have tantrums too. He didn't like Mrs. Gaspar's soup. He didn't like the tea she made him drink to slow down his growing. It was exactly the same bitter yellow tea she gave me for my thin hair. "Drink it," I whispered after school, "just drink it." She wheezed when she was agitated. She said we were ungrateful. Where would we be without her? Would we stay with Mr. Petersburg in number sixteen? Would he make us breakfast? Would he make us hearty soup? "Just drink it," I said, "it's got nothing in it." My hair was still thin. But he wouldn't. He closed his eyes and opened his mouth and I waited for his bellow.

Davey bellowed like a wounded bull. Davey's bellows shook the walls.

Mrs. Gaspar raised her hands to the ceiling and said a silent prayer. Karl and Karla hid under the sofa.

"I'm too old," said Mrs. Gaspar to Mother. "I love my dumpling, but this crying. It makes it hard for me to breathe. There must be a kindergarten."

All the way to school I tried not to think of him. Second Street, Grayford, Ohio was long and straight and its buildings were almost entirely the colour of moon rock: light grey, dark grey, and occasionally a strange light green. I knew this because Neil Armstrong had brought some rocks home to Earth and they'd shown coloured pictures of them on the television. I told Mother once that I thought Second Street looked like it was made out of moon rock.

She said, "I like that about you, Lenny, you always see the good in the bad."

Moon rock smelled like spent gunpowder.

Second Street smelled like diesel exhaust and pigeon poo. It smelled like the popcorn at the entrance to the movie theatre and the rotten fruit at Mr. King's "King of Fruit" Fruit Store and the cool gasping sliding-door breath of the bank, which had the aroma of suits and dollar bills and perfumed ladies.

I walked past the Greyhound bus station. I walked past the grocer's and Mr. King's "King of Fruit" Fruit Store. I walked past the movie theatre and the bank. I went past the Three Brothers Trapani, tailors, and Miss Finny, the seamstress. I went past Mr. Kelmendi, the shoemaker. Each day he said, "Aren't you too small to walk to school alone, young lady?" and each day I frowned at him and said, "No," which made him laugh so hard that the pigeons exploded into the air.

I went past the park where the trees shivered their grey fingers at the winter sky. I breathed out my foggy breath, puffed it in front of me like a dragon. All the way I could feel the ghost of Davey's big hands upon me and smell his tears.

My third-grade teacher was Miss Schweitzer and her name sounded like the swish of a rag across a dirty table. She was tall and frostily blonde and her bell-bottoms were ironed with a crease. She made us sit tall, she pulled our ponytails into line, and she inspected the handkerchiefs in our pockets each day.

My mother said, "That Miss Schweitzer has too much time on her hands if handkerchiefs are all she worries about."

But I worried about handkerchiefs incessantly. I worried about their cleanness and pressed-ness. I tended to the floral handkerchief collection, which my nanny Flora thankfully had sent me for a birthday present, like my life depended upon it. Matthew Milford had been shamed for having a handkerchief several days old and dried hard in places with snot. Miss Schweitzer discovered it during handkerchief inspection. She asked him what it was.

"It's a handkerchief," said Matthew Milford, although it took a lot longer than that on account of his stutter. He was on the *It's* for a good minute and then, between the *a* and *handkerchief*, he jerked for an eternity. We all waited patiently. Matthew Milford had a big mole on his cheek. Hairs grew out of it. I liked to count them when he wasn't looking. There were always five.

"No, Milford," said Miss Schweitzer, "it's not a handkerchief."

Matthew looked confused. He stared at the handkerchief, which Miss Schweitzer held up as an example of what was not to come to school. Matthew Milford had a stutter and a mole *and* a terrible haircut so he didn't need any more bad things to happen to him.

Apart from Matthew Milford there was a girl called Frankie Pepelliani who could tap dance and everyone coveted her tap shoes. There was a girl named Tara Albright who looked exactly like a doll. She was so shiny and her eyes so glassy and her hair so neatly tied back in tails that it made you want to poke her just to see if she was real. These were just a few. There was also a girl called CJ Bartholomew and CJ Bartholomew was my best friend.

CJ Bartholomew didn't sound like the name of a girl in third grade. It sounded like the name of someone who wrote books about dentistry. CJ stood for Cassandra Jane which conjured up images of girls in long dresses in green gardens, but Cassandra Jane wasn't like that. CJ was a small wild slip of a thing. She had a blast of fair hair that wouldn't stay in the bunches her mother tied. Sometimes she had just one bunch left by the end of the day, like the handle on a teacup.

CJ Bartholomew got dirtier than other kids. Her eyes watered in the sunlight. She wiped at them with her palms so that two dirt trails formed on her cheeks like cheetah tear lines. She had a permanently snotty nose. She was Miss Schweitzer's worst nightmare.

"Bartholomew, go and wash your face!"

I liked her from the first. CJ ate her triangular sandwiches upside down, crust first, point last. She pushed her wobbly teeth in and out with her tongue. She screwed up her nose at things, squinted her eyes. CJ had five sisters and she recited their names to me until I could remember them: Bonnie-Anne, Nancy Jane, Lorelai Marie, Susan Louise, Josephine Claire.

"I only have one brother," I said. "He won't stop growing. Mrs. Gaspar said we should take him to the doctor. No schools will have him. But my mother said he's just big and that happens sometimes. There are Swedish people in our family."

"Like with Jack and the beanstalk, he just kept growing," said CJ.

"The beanstalk kept growing," I said.

"Yeah," said CJ, who was very wise, "but it's the same thing."

Davey had been to one nursery school for ten minutes. It was called the Sacred Heart Mary Street Nursery School, which was a very long name for no good reason. I had a bad feeling about the place before we even went there. I could tell Mother did too. She spent forever slicking down Davey's hair with hair cream like it was his biggest problem. She used so much cream he said his head felt heavy with it. He didn't like his scratchy new pants either. His new brown shoes were too squeaky. I could tell he was just plain scared. We walked along Second—all of us, a cloud of dark feelings. It got so bad I stopped still on the corner of Charlotte and Second because I knew it was wrong. We couldn't take Davey to some place and just leave him there.

My fear sucked all the sound out of the day. All the cars and buses and trucks stopped making noise. The pigeons burst into the air without volume. The winter sun winked from behind a cloud. It sent a semaphore message. It said, *DON'T GO.*

Davey frowned at the winking sun too.

"What on earth are you two doing?" said Mother to us, stopped still, staring at the sky. "We'll be late."

Inside the Sacred Heart Mary Street Nursery School it was hushed, like the inside of a church. Sister Agnetha met us at the door. Sister Agnetha smiled and looked for our five-year-old. She looked behind us like he might be there. She looked over the top of Davey's head. My mother showed her Davey. His hair held down with a gallon of Brylcreem. His scratchy pants and his new brown shoes shining. Sister Agnetha's smile vanished.

"He's too big," she said.

She was the first one to ever come right out and say it.

It wasn't *He's VERY big*. It was *He's TOO big*. He didn't fit. And the worst thing was we'd never tried to fit him anywhere else. It was our first attempt. It jolted two tears right out of my mother's eyes.

"He's just big for his age," whispered Mother.

"How can he play with children when he is twice their size?" asked Sister Agnetha. *Twice their size* was a stretch. He was approximately fifteen inches taller than the average five-year-old. Sister Agnetha tried to salvage her smile. Davey, who always smiled, didn't smile in return. He knew meanness when he saw it. He grabbed a fistful of Mother's skirt.

"It's just I wasn't informed of his size," said Sister Agnetha. "It isn't right. It might be dangerous."

Now my brother was strong. If my mother needed heavy furniture lifted he could do it, but he would never hurt anyone. The other children had stopped doing what they were doing at the word *dangerous*. Building with blocks and painting on easels and reading on beanbags. They were staring at Davey.

"I filled in all the forms," said my mother. "He *is* five. He *was* with me. They saw him. They would have said if there was a problem."

Davey's hands went around Mother's waist. My ears went numb with a feeling that something bad was about to happen.

I tried to hear. Sister Agnetha was saying something. She looked like she was trying to cover up her meanness. It was a patchwork affair and parts of it showed through. There was some kind of deal being struck. Her lips were moving but there was no sound. Then Davey had his tantrum.

His mouth opened up into a dreadful lopsided oval. The sound turned back on. It was a roar. His roar. Sister Agnetha leaned backwards, shocked. The glass, high up in the windows, rattled.

"No!" he bellowed.

"Don't be silly, Davey," said Mother into the brief silence that followed. Children's paintbrushes wilted in their hands. A pile of blocks fell to the floor.

She tried to prise him from her waist. He gripped harder. She peeled his fingers backward and he reapplied them with more force. Sister Agnetha backed away. Her hand reached out for the red telephone on the wall. I watched it all unfold, as though I wasn't really there, just the ghost of Lenny Spink.

My mother succeeded in removing Davey from her. She jumped back from him.

"Quickly," she said to me and he looked at her with such desolation. She sobbed back at him with such despair.

Davey took off running. He ran in a great galumphing arc around the classroom. He overturned two book stands, hurling them to the ground, he reached out one arm and tore a painting from an easel. He picked up a beanbag and tossed it up to the ceiling. He splattered paint and crashed right through the teacher's chair. His Brylcreemed hair came unstuck and rose in two gelled horns upon his head, his face grew red, hot tears streamed down his cheeks, and glittering snot poured from his nose. Children screamed and cowered.

Davey completed his lap of infamy. He rushed back into my mother's skirt. He wept and bellowed into her lap at the terrible thing that he had done and the thing that had been done to him.

"Please leave," said Sister Agnetha, the red phone in her hand. "Straight away. Take your mon . . ." She didn't finish the word. "And leave."

I think she wanted to say *monster*. I was almost certain she wanted to say *monster*.

"He's not a monster," I cried, and my words were loud as cymbals, and it was much, much worse for my saying them.

But we left. We sat on the steps outside until Mother could walk. Her legs were shaking so. She held Davey to her and she held him like she would never let him go.

"How's Davey doing at school?" asked Nanny Flora.

It was raining. Icy rain falling past the window and all the pigeons shivering. The whole city was grey and my sadness flower had opened up inside my chest.

"He's not going," I said.

"Not going?" said Nanny Flora.

"They wouldn't let him because he was too big," I whispered. I didn't want Mother to hear. It still ruffled her. It made her spiky. It made her slam down our meatloaf. It made her say, "Too big?"

"Well, he's certainly that," said Nanny Flora on the phone.

Mother had sent her a studio photograph. In the photograph I was seated on a small cane chair with my feet daintily crossed and my white socks pulled up high. My yellow dress had turned my complexion the colour of canned franks. Beside me Davey looked as though he had stepped off a Viking ship. He was blond and huge, his feet planted apart in a sturdy stance and the buttons on his new red cowboy shirt straining over his tummy. He was grinning and I was frowning.

Nanny Flora lived far away and neither Davey nor I had ever met her in person. She spoke on the phone, once a month on a Sunday, twelve Sundays a year. She was an official regular event. There was a picture of her on the china cabinet, a tiny woman with a golden bowl of tight curls on her head and very white teeth. She wore a blue coat and she looked very clean, like someone from an antiseptic advertisement. On the phone she spoke down from somewhere high above, a cloud perhaps, perfectly white and sanitized.

"But there are big people in the family, you know?" she said. "Swedish people. In fact he looks a lot like Uncle Gus and he was from that side."

I imagined them, a family of Swedish giants, with hands the size of dinner plates and jagged gap-toothed smiles.

"How'd you like those handkerchiefs?" asked Nanny Flora from her sanitized cloud.

"I loved them, thank you," I said.

"Did you like the flowery blue one?" Nanny Flora asked. "Or did you have another favourite?"

I really hadn't paid much attention to the patterns, just adored their stiffness and cleanliness and resolved to never blow my nose into them.

"I liked the blue flowery one," I said.

"What about the yellow one?" asked Nanny Flora. "I thought it was very pretty, did you?"

It was like being interviewed by the secret handkerchief police. I wondered if she was trying to trick me. Maybe there wasn't a yellow one. It seemed like the kind of thing her voice might do.

"The blue one is the best," I said.

There was a small silence.

"So too big, you say?" she said finally, then "Well, tell me, how are you doing?"

It was a difficult question to answer. She didn't know me. She didn't know the holes in my stockings. She didn't know my ratty toothbrush. She didn't know the three warts in a triangle on my left knee that I called my holy trinity.

She didn't know how I pretended I was a dragon the whole way to school.

"Good," I said, heart beating fast.

She didn't know how sometimes rain made me want to cry, like there was something deep inside of me—the sadness flower that opened up when rainy days came, and blossomed inside me until I couldn't breathe.

"Tell me something new," she said.

It was a little threatening. I bored her.

"We entered a competition," I said, remembering. Oh, the

relief was sweet. I leaned against the wall, phone pressed to my ear, breathed.

"Really, now?" Nanny Flora said.

"For an encyclopedia set. A whole set. Completely free. If we win it."

"Well, now," said Nanny Flora from her cloud. "That would really be something now, wouldn't it?"

"It sure would," I said.

"Put your mama on," said Nanny Flora, so I did.

Mother turned her back to us, cradled the phone against her neck. Ever since the Sacred Heart affair, her magic had been leaking out. She was made entirely of worries now. Her legs were thin, her arms too. She was worried thin. She worried about Davey's constipation. She worried about whether I needed glasses. "How can I afford glasses?" she asked me, even though I didn't need them and no one had even looked at my eyes. She worried about the box of oranges she brought home from Mr. King's "King of Fruit" Fruit Store, and if she should have accepted them.

"I know," I heard her say to Nanny Flora.

"I know, but . . ."

"Yes, I'll take him to the doctor . . ."

"Mama," we heard her say. "I don't want to hear about Uncle Gus from Sweden right now."

January 5, 1975
Apartment 15, 762 Second Street
Grayford, Ohio 44002

Dear Burrell's family,

Welcome to the Spink family. My name is Cindy and I have two children, Lenore and David. Their father died nearly a year ago. I raise them myself by working shifts as a nursing aide at the Golden Living Retirement Home. We get by, we have enough food and a roof over our heads. My children are the Love of My Life. They are both beautiful although Davey is very big for his age. I've taken him to the doctor and they are going to figure out why. Lenore is so good to her brother and so very smart in third grade. She reads very well. We're hoping for the encyclopedia set so that we can always have THE GIFT OF KNOWLEDGE in our humble abode.

Yours sincerely,
Mrs. Cynthia Spink

February 3, 1975
Burrell's Publishing Company Ltd
7001 West Washington Street
Indianapolis, Indiana 46241

OUR GIFT TO YOU IS
THE GIFT OF KNOWLEDGE

Dear Mrs. Spink,

*Congratulations! We wish to inform you that you are
one of the lucky winners of the* Burrell's Build-It-at-
Home Encyclopedia *set. Our gift to you is THE GIFT OF
KNOWLEDGE. Each issue is delivered direct to your front
door and with this letter we are happy to include your first
three issues. You'll have the A volumes built in no time! If
at any time you choose to speed up the building of your set
please contact our sales team, there are a range of payment
plans available.*

Yours sincerely,

Martha Brent

General Sales Manager

A

African Civets
and the
Abominable Snowman

4' 5"

FEBRUARY 1975

🦅

My mother lied with gay abandon. She lied from the first sentence, *Welcome to the Spink family*. No one ever visited us except Mrs. Gaspar and Karl and Karla. If someone knocked at the door, our mother would be suspicious. She would peer through the peephole angrily. She would mutter to herself, "Who could that be?"

She lied about taking Davey to the doctor. She hadn't taken him once, but only mentioned it, instead, every day.

"I'm taking you to the doctor," she threatened, as though that would stop him growing.

"What will he do?" Davey asked.

"He'll give you a needle to stop you growing," said Mother.

"But I don't like needles," wailed Davey.

On the subject of our beauty, it was true, Davey *was* a handsome boy. He had blue eyes and long lashes and a dreamy gaze. But already he was leaning to the right. He'd grown as tall as a fifth grader and he was only five, but he was beginning to bend, just slightly, like a weed wilting in the sun.

I wasn't pretty, there is no denying it. There were pretty girls at school. They had pretty hair and pretty faces and pretty dresses. They skipped easily, squealed easily, smiled easily.

They had names like Tara or Tabitha or Mary-Lynne. None of them had names like Lenny.

In that letter, my mother lied about Peter Lenard Spink.

Peter Lenard Spink. Peter Lenard Spink. Peter Lenard Spink.

I whispered it in bed at night to remember him.

Peter Lenard Spink had nicotine stains on the first two fingers of his right hand. His skin was hard as a hide there, cracked and bright yellow. He was good at string tricks.

"Come over here, little Lenny," he sometimes said and I knew he was taking the string from his pocket. It was an old frayed string. I knelt before him to watch.

I wanted to.

I didn't want to.

I wanted to.

I didn't.

He made a butterfly, quick, looping that string around his fingers and then he snapped it away. A cup and a saucer, a star, cat's whiskers.

"Meow," he said.

"Do you remember his string tricks?" I asked Davey in the darkness of our bedroom.

"Of course I do," he said.

"No, you don't," I said to ruffle him.

Witch's hat. Broomstick. Church steeple. Spider's web.

"Put your hand in, little Lenny," Peter Lenard Spink said.

I never wanted to. I wanted him to slow down so I could see how he did it.

"I can't slow down, the magic stops working," he said. "Put your hand in."

It was always the last trick. The end of the show. I put my little hand in through the spider's web and he went to catch me, but in one flick the web was gone, leaving just one gaping ring.

"Peter Lenard Spink," I whispered, as though it might stop him from vanishing.

"Stop it," said Davey. "Mama, Lenny's scaring me."

"Go to sleep," she shouted from the living room.

"Peter Lenard Spink," I whispered in a scary voice.

In that letter my mother lied about me.

"Mama, she won't stop it," shouted Davey.

"Don't make me come in there," called Mother from the living room. "Whatever you are doing to scare him, stop it, Lenny. You'll wake Mr. Petersburg."

Mr. Petersburg was our neighbor in number sixteen. We hardly believed he was even real. No noises came from his apartment. None at all. I'd only ever seen him twice in all my years and on those occasions he was tall and pale and wore a suit. Quiet and whispery, he had glided up the stairs like a ghost. That's what I told Davey, who had never seen him.

I liked to remind him.

"Mr. Petersburg the ghost," I whispered.

"I'll tell," he said.

"Let's watch the buses," I said to stop him tattling.

His bed was near the wall but mine was near the window. At night the traffic slowed down but never really stopped. It hummed away below us, punctuated by the garbage trucks and the street sweepers and the truck that delivered fruit to Mr. King's "King of Fruit" Fruit Store. All night the pigeons cooed on the ledge outside. Davey had named those pigeons Frank, Roger, and Martin. I told him for sure one would be a girl but he didn't agree.

Davey crept into my bed, beside me. We knelt and looked out past Frank and Roger and Martin at the Greyhound bus station across the street. We must have watched a thousand goodbyes from our bedroom window, Davey and I, maybe more. Small farewells and big farewells. Paltry farewells and grand farewells. Some people just couldn't leave a place without everyone they ever knew coming to see them off: aunts and uncles and grandmas with canes and every cousin and friend, girls in good dresses and boys in ironed pants. All the thronging and hugging and kissing and waving that went on. The faces made from the bus windows. The frantic gesturing. Other people just got on. They had nothing but the ticket in their hand. They climbed the steps and didn't look back to wave at anyone.

And we saw countless arrivals too, crumpled weary travellers ejected out onto the night streets. We watched them and wondered about where they were going and where they had been. Some had people come to fetch them, others no one. I searched the faces for him, each and every bus, even if I pretended not to.

"Do you even remember him?"

"Of course I do," said Davey. Up close to me he smelled soapy and clean and his eyes shone.

"No you don't," I said.

There were many interesting things that began with A. Aardvarks and aardwolves, albatrosses and African civets. African civets appealed to Davey in a way we couldn't understand.

"I love those cats," he said, between us in Mother's bed.

"It's not a cat, Davey," I said.

"It looks like a cat," said Davey.

"It's an African civet. It makes musk and they want to catch it and make perfume from it."

"Don't talk about that," said Mother. Her hair was out and her face scrubbed clean. "Please."

She didn't like sad things or hard things or mean things.

"They keep them in cages," she said. "Little wild things kept in cages."

"I'd keep one in a cage," said Davey. "For a pet."

"Hush, Davey," said Mother. "Let's read albatrosses instead."

Davey was sad to see the African civets go.

"Look at these birdies," said Mother. "'Albatross,'" she read. "'A sea bird of the order Procellariiformes and the family Diomedeidae, closely related to storm petrels and diving petrels.'"

She spoke these words carefully and with her shining clean face she looked like a girl. Something in the way she spoke about albatrosses quietened Davey. I closed my eyes and listened. I saw storms and birds diving.

"'Some albatrosses have wingspans eleven feet across and once the birds fledge some never see the land again for several years.'"

"Imagine that," she said. "Nothing but flying for years and years."

"Where do they fly to?" I asked.

"Oh, here and there, I expect," she said. "All over the world."

"'Albatrosses pair for life,'" she said and then stopped reading.

She was quiet but her thoughts filled up the room the way they often did.

Peter Lenard Spink did a trick with a coin as well. He twirled a dime between his fingers, then he disappeared it up his sleeve. He brought it back again behind my ear.

"You're too serious, like your mother," he once whispered to me.

Maybe if I'd laughed more he might have stayed. Or maybe it was that my hair was too thin. He mentioned it once. He said, "You've got that bad Spink hair, Lenny." He smelled like cigarettes and toothpaste and hair cream.

He smelled like belt buckles and bus stops and newspaper ink. His cough was wet. He spat, spat, spat into our bathroom sink. I was glad he was gone and I wanted him back.

"Davey is asleep," Mother said at last and closed up albatrosses. "And it's way past your bedtime."

My brother would not stop growing. Our mother measured us against the kitchen door frame. Me on one side, my brother opposite. She squished down Davey's hair with her hand and drew the line in marker pen.

"Davey," she demanded. "Slow down."

"But I can't help it," he said.

Mrs. Gaspar wheezed into our apartment and sat on our sofa. Her beehive looked untended. It listed. She brought her own tea in a little silver canister and handed it to Mother.

"Stand up please, David," said Mrs. Gaspar.

We were on the floor looking at the abominable snowman. The abominable snowman was our favourite entry so far in the *Burrell's Build-It-at-Home Encyclopedia*. Two new issues arrived each Friday in the mail and Davey and I rushed down the stairs, bumping each other to get there first, but we returned again and again to the grainy black-and-white image of the abominable snowman.

Davey stood up.

"Yes, it is true, then," said Mrs. Gaspar. She slumped back into the sofa. "I had a dream last night."

Mother returned with Mrs. Gaspar's tea.

We loved Mrs. Gaspar's dreams. They were colourful and wild and full of warnings. In her dreams birds spoke and the sea washed into the city streets and Mother got married in a blue wedding dress. Once Mrs. Gaspar even dreamed she went to the moon on Apollo 11. "I flew the spaceship," she said, and it made us giggle so much, the thought of her sitting in there with Neil and Buzz, in her pom-pom slippers and her shaggy tangerine bathrobe, that even Mother started to laugh as well.

"What did you dream?" asked Davey.

"I dreamed you got taller and taller," said Mrs. Gaspar.

"Mrs. Gaspar," pleaded Mother.

"Cyn-thi-a," pleaded Mrs. Gaspar back.

"You grew and grew until—bang—your head hit up on the ceiling," she whispered.

"Please," said Mother. "You'll scare him."

We loved Mrs. Gaspar's dreams but sometimes she went too far.

"I'm not scared," said Davey. He looked down at his feet.

"Anyway, I'm taking him to see the doctor next week," said Mother.

"Good," said Mrs. Gaspar and she took a long sip of her special tea.

I wanted to ask what happened next in the dream, after Davey's head hit the ceiling. I wanted details. Mrs. Gaspar's dreams were always lush with details. Clocks that called out her name and secret rooms and white horses thundering through the streets. Dream magical stews made with dream mushrooms she found on dream Second Street. But I knew I'd have to ask her later, when Mother wasn't there.

"You can sit down, David," said Mrs. Gaspar, now that she'd caused enough trouble. "What are you two dumplings looking at?"

"The abominable snowman," said Davey.

"Pah," said Mrs. Gaspar, and she waved her hand as though we bored her. "I saw him once when I was walking home from school in Hungary."

A
Ants and Amphibians

4′ 6″

APRIL 1975

Hungary was nowhere near Mount Everest. We knew this because a complimentary atlas arrived with issue ten. It had buoyed our interest momentarily. There were only so many times we could look at African civets and the abominable snowman. We still bumped and bustled our way down the stairs each Friday, but we'd become bogged down in abscesses and abstract art and the two John Adamses. Acne, amoeba, adding machines, and adenoids. All credit to the ancient civilization of the Aegean, but we did not believe it deserved a two-page spread. We were getting bored and the first volume cover had only just arrived. It was olive green, its skin rippled. We fastened the first fifteen issues into the volume cover, *A to Ampersand*, with a satisfying click, but we didn't much care.

"I knew it," said our mother. She was irritated by our boredom.

As though she had bought the encyclopedia herself.

"I knew it!"

As though she hadn't lied to win it. As though she hadn't said our father was dead.

"I knew it," she said and she took *A to Ampersand* and put it in her bedroom as a punishment.

But then issue sixteen arrived with three pages of glossy colour plates on amphibians. Frogs and axolotls and salamanders. The mountain yellow-legged frog. The blue poison dart frog. The golden frog. Northern leopard frogs. Horned frogs. American bullfrogs. Our favourite, the African goliath.

Included in each description was the sound that the frog made, so we spoke frog language at the dinner table. Davey spoke African goliath. I spoke blue-eyed bush frog.

"Enough," said Mother. "Enough is enough. Honestly, I've had a long day."

But as soon as she was gone into the kitchen to start the dishes, I did the song of the fire-bellied toad.

"I'm not kidding!" she yelled from the kitchen.

Our mother had a strange high-pitched yell, like someone playing on a tin pipe.

"Don't push me," she piped. "Last warning, Lenore Spink."

Which was exactly what Miss Schweitzer said to me at school, only she dropped the *Lenore*. "Last warning, Spink," she said when I was daydreaming about the abominable snowman and if he belonged to a family. If he was a father. If he had two children and a wife.

"Spink," said Miss Schweitzer. "I can't imagine what it's like inside that brain of yours. I bet it's a jumbled-up mess like a junk sale."

She was right. It was filled up with the Arctic and Africa and several colour plates on ants. I thought about the ants a lot. Army ants and Argentine ants, bulldog ants and crazy ants, pharaoh ants and honeypot ants. My head was filled up with ants that could kill you if they stung you and ants that could launch themselves out of trees and glide to the ground without wings. I smiled at Miss Schweitzer and wished I could tell her how bad it really was.

But you couldn't tell Miss Schweitzer things like that. She wouldn't like to hear about the abominable snowman even though she was frostily beautiful. I disliked Miss Schweitzer, yet I touched my handkerchief in my pocket, to check that it was pristine, because I still wanted to impress her. It was a strange and powerful conundrum.

"Don't you leave that iron on and burn the whole place down," said Mother when I ironed my handkerchiefs.

Sometimes I imagined it. I'd be at school and I'd smell smoke. I'd hear the sound of fire engines and I'd know. Everything would be gone. All our clothes. My glow in the dark sandals. My *Bambi* LP. Davey's cowboy shirts. Davey's big brown shoes. The photograph of Nanny Flora. That would sizzle and burn. The *Burrell's Build-It-at-Home Encyclopedia. A to Ampersand.* The issue with the amphibians. All the colour plates of ants.

"That Schweitzer has too much time on her hands if handkerchiefs are all she worries about," I said to CJ in the playground.

"What's the point of a handkerchief if you can't blow your nose on it?" replied CJ.

"Don't you agree?" I asked Matthew Milford who was nearby. I pushed my perfectly ironed handkerchief deeper into my pocket. He looked at me as though it might be a trick question. I crumbled up my cookie and fed it to the ants in the playground and smiled at him to show I was friendly. He crumbled up some of his sandwich. We took turns seeing what the ants could handle.

"I thought you liked amphibians," said CJ.

"I do," I said. "But I like ants too."

I could tell she was anxious that Matthew Milford might become my new best friend. I asked her to be the Ant Olympics crumb-lifting judge and it settled her.

"Did Davey go to the doctor yet?" she asked. She was dreadfully biased. She had ruled three times in favor of my ant crumb-lifting team.

"No, we go on Saturday morning," I said.

"Wh-wh-wh-wh-wh-wh-hat's . . ." started Matthew Milford.

"Nothing is wrong with him," I said.

It was a long walk to Dr. Leopold's office. Second Street, all moon-rock-coloured, stretched forever and I wondered sometimes if it ever even ended.

We went past Mr. King's "King of Fruit" Fruit Store.

"Hello, Cindy," shouted Mr. King.

Mr. King was short and he wore his hair like Elvis, but he had a bristly moustache as well. He had sparkly black eyes and they danced all over Mother. "Where are you all going on such a beautiful Saturday?"

Mr. King had the trace of an accent and black stubble on his chin like Fred Flintstone.

"We have an appointment for Davey at the doctor's," said Mother.

"Oh, you don't look sick, mister," said Mr. King. "When you are bigger, you can come and lift boxes for me?"

No one ever wished Davey was bigger, so it took him by surprise. His smile was huge.

"Can I, Mama?" he asked.

"When you're a lot older," said Mother.

"In a few years," said Mr. King.

Mr. King had no idea. His eyes shinnied up and down over Mother again.

"We better be going," she said. "It's a long walk."

"I will drive you," he said.

"No," said Mother, and then kinder. "We have errands on the way."

"I will stop at every errand," said Mr. King. "Errands are no problem in my Ford Gran Torino."

He pointed to his blue Ford Gran Torino parked in the alleyway.

"Can we, Mama?" asked Davey.

"No," said Mother.

We walked past the movie theatre. We walked past the bank. We walked past the Three Brothers Trapani and one of them came out and sang Mother an opera song that she studiously ignored. We walked past Mr. Kelmendi, the shoemaker. Mr. Kelmendi asked after Davey's shoes.

"They're just fine," said Mother and she didn't stop.

It was a spring day, but not a beautiful one. It was hot and the sky was filled up with black clouds. Davey said his legs hurt.

I said I had heat stroke. Mother shouted, "Would you stop complaining! Would you look at that, now it's going to rain, I just know it!"

Miss Finny, the seamstress, smiled through her window.

It started raining at the intersection of Second and Mary. It was sudden, like someone emptying buckets of water on top of us. It was heavy and cold and we were wet through in minutes. I thought Mother would get angry at the rain but she didn't. She looked up and smiled and held out her hands. A bus went past and sprayed us with water. Davey got mud all over his pants.

We passed the park and the Sacred Heart Mary Street Nursery School and we refused to look at it. We passed the intersection by my school. The moon-rockiness of the buildings looked pretty after the rain but that next part of Second Street was not as tidy as ours and there was trash everywhere now and scowling women pushing strollers. Dr. Leopold's office was beside a grocers. We went inside dripping wet and the receptionist scowled as well.

Dr. Leopold's name suggested a physician in a white coat rushing through corridors with a shining stethoscope, but he had a large belly that spilled over his belt and his breath smelled of mints. He didn't like to get up from his chair much. He opened the Spink file.

Our wetness and the rain falling past his window in a curtain and the day grown dark had caused the sadness flower to open in my chest. I felt worried in that office. My nose started to run. I wished I had a handkerchief, but it was the weekend. I sniffled and Mother scowled at me just like everyone else.

"Well," said Dr. Leopold. "Mrs. Spink. Very good. Sit down."

Davey sat on Mother's knee. It might have seemed wrong to an outsider but he was only five.

"What can I do for you then?" he asked.

"I've come about David," said Mother.

She never used the name David. Never. It shocked Davey and me. Davey stared at me from Mother's lap, his blue eyes round.

"What seems to be the problem?" asked Dr. Leopold.

"Well, it's just about his height," said Mother. She was trembling all over, like someone owning up to a very bad thing. "He's grown very tall."

"I see," said Dr. Leopold. "He is a big boy."

Big was such a small word. "If I had a nickel for every time someone said Davey was a big boy, I'd be rich," was what my mother always said.

"How old are you again, David?" he asked. "Eight?"

We thought he was joking. I giggled.

"Davey is five. I mean he's nearly six," said Mother. Her trembling was worse. Davey vibrated on her knee.

Dr. Leopold inhaled deeply like the big bad wolf.

"Well, I'll be," he said.

In Mrs. Gaspar's dream, Davey didn't just grow. She told me in her Apollo 11 shrine of a kitchen. She waited until Davey wasn't listening on Monday morning before school. She called me into her tiny kitchen and made me sit at her table and she lit her white cigarette.

"Listen," she said through a cloud of smoke. "I will tell you."

I listened.

"I told you he grew and grew, yes, but this is not all. It is how he came to be, Lenora."

Mrs. Gaspar liked to call me Lenora when she was being mystical. I tolerated it for the sake of hearing her dreams.

"He came out of an egg," she said.

I wasn't expecting it.

I might have gasped.

"A big egg. Heavy. Black," Mrs. Gaspar said. "Your mother carried it with her for many years. On her journeys. I saw her. Then one day, crack, she heard it break and out came the baby Davey."

"Where was I?" I whispered. What journeys? My mother hadn't really been anywhere except for when she ran away with Peter Lenard Spink and saw the UFO. Mrs. Gaspar put her finger up to her lips.

"He grew and he grew and grew from that egg. He grew bigger and bigger and bigger until bang, his head hit the ceiling."

"But Mother took him to the doctor," I said. "He said not to worry. Just to keep an eye on him. It's normal if there are very tall people in the family and he doesn't have any headaches. Uncle Gus was very tall. Dr. Leopold said he'd slow down soon."

Mrs. Gaspar shook her head.

"She tells me this. And this is why I tell you my dream."

She stubbed out her cigarette.

Karl and Karla watched us, shining black eyes expectant.

"What does this egg mean?" she asked and stared at me through the remaining smoke, thinking.

"I don't know," I whispered.

"Can I have some more pretzels please, Mrs. Gaspar?" asked Davey, wandering into the kitchen.

"Of course, my little dumpling," she said.

He leaned against her while she filled his bowl. They were tight, Mrs. Gaspar and Davey. He knew the Holy Rosary. He knew the entire cast of *Days of Our Lives*. He knew all the ingredients in goulash. They watched *Starsky & Hutch* together every Tuesday when Mother worked the late shift. Side by side they ate pretzels.

"And did someone mention something about scrambled eggs?" he said.

B
Beetles and Birds

Nearly 6

4′ 7″

EARLY SUMMER 1975

🦅

The *B* issues began arriving on June 20. We knew they were coming. We waited for them. We longed for them. We checked the mailbox each day just in case they came early. We whispered to each other in bed at night about what those pages might contain. *B* is such a dowdy overweight letter but we built those *B* issues right up inside our brains.

"There'll be barracudas," said Davey.

"And bagpipes," I replied. Bridges, batteries, bees, baseball, and hot air balloons, but nothing prepared us for the true fabulousness when they finally came.

Bats for starters: fringe-lipped and spear-nosed and bonneted. Leaf-chinned and bulldog and vampire. Bacteria: four kinds. Badgers and baobab trees. Several coloured pages of birds, which were brilliant. On each page, we chose and ordered our favourites. Then we chose our top seven from all the pages. My ultimate favourite was the meadowlark because it reminded me of open places. Davey's ultimate favourite was the golden eagle and it figured; it was a grand bird with huge wings that shone all burnished bronze. In its illustration it was hunched, its wings curving, as it came down to catch its prey, its great talons ready. Davey stared and stared and stared at that picture.

Mother said, "If you keep looking at that page, Davey, you'll wear a hole in it."

But Davey didn't stop looking at it.

"I really want a golden eagle," he said.

"Well, you'll be lucky if you get a goldfish," said Mother. "No one has an eagle for a pet."

"I'd call it Timothy," said Davey.

Mother shook her head.

"Davey, Davey," she said.

She was ironing her new shirt for her new extra job. Mother needed an extra job because the rent went up and Davey ate a lot. Although she was almost certain his growing was slowing down, she still had to buy him new pants and new shoes because he kept busting out of them. The new job was at Mr. King's "King of Fruit" Fruit Store and the new shirt was apple green with a banana embroidered on the pocket. Sometimes Mother worked at the fruit store in the morning for four hours, then changed and caught the twenty-eight bus to the Golden Living Retirement Home.

"Pah," said Mrs. Gaspar. "That man is a wolf. Beware, Cyn-thi-a. His apples are bad and his bananas never ripen."

"Oh, he's not that bad," said Mother.

CJ told me she saw Mother at school on the very last day before summer break.

"It wouldn't be Mother," I said.

"It sure looked like her," said CJ. "Same hair, same shirt with a banana on the pocket. She was near the office talking to Principal Dalrymple."

"Principal Dalrymple?"

I didn't understand. My handkerchiefs were in good order. It couldn't be my jumbled-up junk sale brain. I got good grades.

Maybe it was the ants. Miss Schweitzer had pulled me aside once after class and told me it wasn't nice for girls to play with ants. I'd stared blankly at her as though I didn't know what she was talking about. As if I'd be involved in such disgusting behaviours. Yes, maybe it was the ants. Or beetles. I'd started hunting for beetles at school since the *B* issues began arriving. Matthew Milford and I discovered a black beetle in the brick fence beside the playground. Maybe we'd been spotted watching it. Mother had been summoned to the school about my insect-leaning tendencies.

Mother didn't say anything at home, which made my suspicions worse. I asked her gingerly, carefully.

"You weren't at school today, were you?"

"I certainly was," she said cheerily.

It was the ants. I knew it. Or the beetles.

"I went to enrol Davey," she said. I swear my feet lifted off the ground with the relief. Then I plummeted back to earth.

"At school?" I said.

"You know as well as I know that Davey will go to school," said Mother and she looked disappointed with me. Of course, I'd always known he was going there. I'd known it and refused to think of it. "There's nothing wrong with his brain. He's just big and leans a little. You know that, Lenny."

— 49 —

"What did the principal say?"

"She said, 'Well, we'll see Davey on the first day of school,'" said Mother.

"Did she actually see Davey?" I asked tentatively.

"I told her his dimensions," said Mother, like he was a piece of furniture. "I told her there were big people in our family. You need to think less about yourself, Lenny, and think about Davey and what it must be like for him. He needs to be with other boys his age. You need to grow a hide. There'll be staring. I know there'll be staring, but you need to think less about yourself."

Because now suddenly she could also read my mind.

"Okay?" she said.

"Okay," I said.

She raised her eyebrows.

"Okay," I said loudly.

"What's okay?" said Davey from the living room.

"Nothing," we both said.

It was a summer of beetles and birds and endless hot days. We languished on Mrs. Gaspar's sofa beneath pastel Jesus's friendly contemplation. We drifted slowly in and out of rooms touching her things from Hungary. Little carved wooden bears. Her precious cutlery wrapped up in a dusty yellow cloth. A little silver clock with its hands stopped on eleven minutes past eleven the day her parents died.

We sweated as we stared into the *Burrell's Build-It-at-Home Encyclopedia* issues, the *A*s neat in the first two volume covers, the loose mysteries of the *B*s. We examined and re-examined the colour plates on birds. We re-perused bathyspheres. I ran my finger over the colour plates on beetles, hesitated, then turned the page. Beetroot. Beirut. Belgium. Bell, Alexander Graham. Bellini, Vincenzo. The Bering Sea Controversy.

Mrs. Gaspar opened up her windows and let the sounds of the city in, all the trucks and Greyhound buses, pigeons cooing, and policemen's traffic whistles. She wore a tea towel around her neck and her perspiration washed away parts of her drawn-on eyebrows. "Mrs. Gaspar," said Davey, "you're disappearing."

"I'm melting," Mrs. Gaspar agreed. "Soon there'll be nothing left of me."

At night, a hot moon rose and we caught crickets on the windowsills in upturned cups.

All the while Davey grew. He didn't slow down despite what Mother said. He grew in the heat like a plant in a hothouse. I stayed the same, but he shot up another inch so that he was exactly as tall as little round Mrs. Gaspar. His yellow hair gushed upward. His shoes split and his toes poked through. His pants strained and complained across his thighs.

"Davey," said Mrs. Gaspar. "This is not right."

He stood in front of her in his ankle freezers.

"Sorry, Mrs. Gaspar," he said apologetically.

Beetles. I went back to those pages again. I tried not to. I hovered over bark, baroque painting, Beethoven, sliding my eyes to the side.

"What are you looking at, dumpling?" said Mrs. Gaspar.

"Nothing," I said.

"What are you looking at?" asked Mother, on the nights she wasn't working the evening shift.

"Nothing," I said.

But I was. I was looking at the perfectly polished hemispheres of the ladybug. Scarlet beetles, emerald beetles, beetles in striped pyjamas. Beetles with anodised shells like cheap Christmas baubles. Armoured beetles. Beetles in war paint. Beetles dressed up in furs.

"What's Lenny looking at, Davey?" Mother asked.

"Beetles," said Davey.

"I am not," I said, flicking back to the coloured chart on beef cuts.

"It's all she ever looks at," said Davey.

"You can't talk," I said. He had birds open on page 642, plate four, featuring the golden eagle—the birds of prey. But I sensed more disappointment in my mother's silence.

I looked at those beetles that summer. I couldn't help it. It wasn't just the trickery of colour; I loved the plainer beetles too. The dowdier American beetles, the skunk beetles, the acorn weevils, and the carrion beetles. I counted the notches on legs. I examined the mandibles on stag beetles. I fumbled my tongue around Latin names. The mystery of antennae, precisely beaded, feathered, saw-toothed. The simple fact that beetles had wings but they hid them away.

Nanny Flora phoned. She said, "How's those books of yours coming along?"

"They're okay," I said. "We're nearly up to the Cs."

"The *C*s," said Nanny Flora. "What if you need some information on something starting with *M*?"

I shrugged.

"Don't shrug, your nanny can't hear a shrug," said Mother.

When it was Davey's turn, I heard him say, "All she looks at is the beetle pages."

Now, I knew clean disinfected Nanny Flora wouldn't like that. I'd once asked her if she owned a cat and she'd said, "I don't care for vermin."

"Mother, Lenny's looking at beetles again," said Davey one evening. There was nothing malicious in it. He was just a champion tattletale.

"Well, she's going to stop that," said Mother. She stormed in, tiny and wild in her pink Golden Living Retirement Home uniform and her hair in a fountain on her head. She took the beetles issue from where it lay in front of me and stamped off with it into her bedroom.

"Holy Batman," said Davey.

"Peter Lenard Spink," I said in the dark that same night. There'd been an evening thunderstorm and we lay sticky with sweat in our beds listening to the rain. The sadness flower was fully bloomed inside my chest. It made me feel empty. It made me feel full. It made me feel like all the glittering wet Grayford streets were inside me. All the lost kittens and sad old ladies waiting at bus stops and pigeons with broken legs.

"Don't," said Davey.

"Peter Lenard Spink," I whispered.

He was faded. I had no photograph of him. Just pieces of memory. Once, he had slapped my hand at the dinner table for reaching out for a third piece of bread. That was a bright flash of a memory. His handwriting, in Mother's blue fountain pen, big letters, very square.

"He'll come back," said Davey.

"Don't be a fool," I said.

"Mother, Lenny called me a fool," shouted Davey.

"Hush up, the pair of you, go to sleep. You'll wake the neighbors up."

There had been no further mention of the confiscated beetle issue. No mention of the Great Living Room Encyclopedia Ambush. She had talked to me after that as though it had never happened. As though all those beetles never existed. She'd pretended to be perfectly normal at dinner, talking about Mrs. Gaspar's lungs, when really she was a pink-clad witch.

"Peter Lenard Spink," I whispered.

Mrs. Gaspar would still be awake. She'd be watching *Kojak*. I didn't know what the elusive Mr. Petersburg would be doing. Probably writing letters. He got letters from all around the country. They filled up his mailbox and spilled on the floor. If you picked them up you saw they were from the Mississippi State Penitentiary and Attica State Penitentiary. Mother said, "Put that down," as though just touching them could end you up in jail.

"Peter Lenard Spink," I whispered.

"One day he'll come back," whispered Davey.

"What makes you think that?"

"I just know," said Davey.

"Where do you think he is?"

"He's in Alaska."

Davey loved Alaska, pages 217 to 220.

I traced my finger over the embroidered ballerina on my bedspread. Nanny Flora had sent it to me for Christmas, further proof she didn't know me at all. I imagined Peter Lenard Spink in Alaska. His tan pants and his sallow skin. His greasy hair and his pockmarked face. It was wrong. He was bear meat if he was living in the wilds. I imagined Davey walking through the woods, smiling at the blue sky. Davey, I could see.

"We should run away," I said.

A silence.

"Where to?"

"Alaska," I said. I knew it would entice him.

An even longer silence. I could tell he was excited.

August 14, 1975
Burrell's Publishing Company Ltd
7001 West Washington Street
Indianapolis, Indiana 46241

OUR GIFT TO YOU IS
THE GIFT OF KNOWLEDGE

Dear Mrs. Spink,

Our records indicate you recently won a subscription to the magnificent Burrell's Build-It-at-Home Encyclopedia *set. We hope you are enjoying your prize so far. We wanted to inform you that you can increase your knowledge for only $2.99 per week and receive three issues instead of two. Your encyclopedia set will then be ready at the end of twenty-four months. We have generously provided you with the first two stunning volume covers free of charge. To receive more please subscribe to the* Burrell's Build-It-at-Home Encyclopedia *set today.*

Yours sincerely,

Martha Brent

General Sales Manager

"It's a ransom note," said Mother. "That's exactly what it is. It's a ransom note."

She had her tin-whistle voice on. She slammed down our dinner on the table.

"There is no way on this good earth I'm going to send them money," said Mother. "I won that prize fair and square."

It was trickery. It was treachery.

I held up the olive green volume cover.

"I wouldn't exactly call it stunning," I said.

"Stunning or not, I'm not paying a cent for it!"

She wrote Martha Brent a letter in her good blue fountain pen, in her high school handwriting.

August 15, 1975
Apartment 15, 762 Second Street
Grayford, Ohio 44002

Dear Martha Brent,
Thank you for your recent correspondence dated August 14th.
I am writing to remind you that I won a competition. The prize
was a complete subscription to the Burrell's Build-It-at-Home
Encyclopedia *set. I will not pay a cent to get this set faster nor*
will I pay for the covers. If it is a build-it-at-home set why then
you must give me the tools to build it with. There will be no
further discussion on this matter.
Yours sincerely,
Mrs. Cynthia Spink

She licked the stamp and slapped it onto the envelope.

"That'll teach them," she said.

C
Canada

4' 9"

LATE SUMMER 1975

No volume covers arrived but the *C* issues did and they contained countless curiosities. The colour plate of cabbage varieties, undersea cables, the cackling goose. Cairo, calculating machines, cameras, and California. The history of chewing gum, clothing (ten colour plates), and clocks. The glorious entry on clouds.

On long summer days, we walked to the park. Mrs. Gaspar pretended to be anxious. She said, "Lenora, you do not let this boy out of your sight, not even for one second." It would be difficult to lose sight of Davey; all four feet and nine inches of six-year-old him. I knew that no one, despite what Mrs. Gaspar said, would want to steal him.

And I knew she was secretly glad to see us go. She needed to sit quietly without us and smoke her cigarettes and read her magazines. She needed to draw glasses on Jackie Onassis and a moustache on Elvis. She needed to close her eyes and think of Jesus and Hungary.

We passed Mr. King's "King of Fruit" Fruit Store on the way and Mother came out to see us. She gave us a change to buy an ice-cream. She gave me all the same warnings that Mrs. Gaspar had. *Don't turn your back on Davey. Hold his hand when crossing the street. He's only six, you know.* Mr. King smiled from the back of the shop. "Give them an orange each," he shouted. "It's a beautiful day for an orange."

"No thank you, Mr. King," said Mother. "They're just fine."

I took my eye off Davey on the way just to see if he'd vanish. He didn't. He loped along beside me, hands in his pockets, his imaginary golden eagle Timothy on his shoulder. I knew the eagle was on his shoulder because Davey kept looking there and smiling. It made me prickly.

"Timothy is a stupid name for an eagle anyway," I said.

"No, it's not," he said.

"It is," I said. "The stupidest name ever invented."

"Len-neeeeeee," he said. "It's a great name for a golden eagle. Say it is."

I ignored him altogether while I searched for beetles.

I searched like a real-life coleopterist. I lifted up stones and twigs and overturned leaves. I prised bark loose. I examined the pond water for ripples. I found a tiny black water beetle and a pond skater near the fountain. I found a leaf beetle that was perfect but it leapt away before I had it.

It was a ladybug on a rose that I caught in the end. "Are you going to tell?" I asked when I had it in my matchbox. I snapped off a rosebud covered in aphids, because I knew that was exactly what ladybugs ate.

"No," he said. "I'd never tell."

I knew he still felt bad about the confiscated beetle issue.

"You know I wouldn't," he said.

On the way home, we stopped to see Mother again and she was unpacking bananas from a box. Mr. King said, "Well hello, the wanderers have returned safely!"

Wherever Mother was in the shop, there was Mr. King. He was always supervising the unpacking of bananas or the packaging of cherries. He was always watching her work with the raspberries.

"They certainly have," said Mother and she seemed flustered and nervous.

"Have an orange, kiddos," he said.

"No, they're just fine," said Mother because she didn't like to take any kind of gifts or charity.

All the same, I smiled at her brazenly with the matchbox in my pocket. I could feel Davey's conscience groaning under the weight of this secret, but he didn't tell. At home, I fashioned a bug house out of a glass jar. I punctured tiny holes in the plastic wrap lid and then carried out the dangerous procedure of relocating the ladybug into its new abode. Davey watched all of this. He watched it as though he was witnessing the crime of the century. He was an accessory after the fact. He grimaced and made uncomfortable noises.

"She took the beetles issue, Davey," I said.

"I know, Lenny," he said.

"Are you going to tell?" I asked again.

"You know I wouldn't."

That night Mother said, "So what did you do in the park?"

I could tell he wanted to say. I burned him into submission with my death stare.

"We just played," I said.

C contained Canada. I traced my finger over the US border into Saskatchewan and Davey lay down on his stomach beside me. We traced a line up into the Northwest Territories.

"This is where we should go," I whispered, pointing to a patch of water.

"Great Bear Lake," he whispered back. Alaska was immediately forgotten.

I drew my finger around Great Bear Lake and shivered. Davey felt it too. The Keith Arm, the Smith Arm, Grizzly Bear Mountain. Canada was airiness and wildness. We would have to walk for weeks and weeks through trees but we'd have air in our lungs and fish in our bellies. We'd make a fire each night and above us the Milky Way would blaze.

"Now what are you two looking at?" asked Mother.

"Canada," I said.

"'O Canada,'" sang Mother as she went into the bathroom.

I threaded my finger back down the page, over the border, off the page.

"Where are we?" Davey whispered.

"Far away," I said. "We'd have to hike for months and months."

"We could catch a bus," he said quietly and raised his eyebrows in a way that made me giggle.

"A bus?" said Mother. "Where are we going?"

"No bus," I said.

I named my ladybug Lady and I examined her with a magnifying glass. I examined her glossy black pronotum and her hard-spotted shell. I turned her on her back and examined how perfectly her six legs curled inwards. I knew from the confiscated beetle issue that she could smell through both her antennae and her feet.

I kept Lady in her jar behind the curtain on the windowsill, but if Mother was in a tidying mood, I hid her in my underpants drawer. I needed to find a fresh supply of aphids each day and I thought she was happy. Each night Davey sat on my bed and said goodnight to the pigeons. *Good night, Roger. Good night, Martin. Good night, Frank.* We could hear their soft cooing.

He sat on my bed in his striped pyjamas and said, "I don't think I can sleep."

"You haven't even tried."

"Lenny," he pleaded. "Len–neeeeeee."

"What do you want to talk about?"

"Canada," he said. No hesitation. He meant *imagine it for me.* I was the chief imaginer.

"Okay, picture this," I said in the dark, and I could hear Davey's breathing shorten in anticipation. "We go to the train station and we stow away on a train. We take some food and some clothes."

"What about the books?" asked Davey.

"We can't take them with us," I said. "That's just ridiculous. You can't run away and take encyclopedias with you."

"I only mean the one with the African civets and maybe birds," he said. "We should take Canada."

Basically, it was every volume we owned so far.

"Okay, I'll think about it," I said.

"And I'll have Timothy," said Davey.

I bit my lip in the dark. Davey hadn't told Mother about Lady, so I tried not to make fun of his imaginary golden eagle.

"We could take a balloon," he said.

"You mean fly in a balloon?" I tried to keep the scorn from my voice.

"Yes," he whispered.

But then I pictured it. Davey and I clambering into a balloon basket, unhitching the anchor, the sudden uplift, rushing us into the golden morning sky, the city flushed pink below us growing small.

"Where would we find a balloon?" I asked. I was the practical one. The sensible one in our running-away stories.

"Maybe they are somewhere," said Davey. "They have to be. People have to park their balloons somewhere."

We took a balloon that night. In the darkness of our room.

I said, "So we find this balloon and we climb into it and off we go. Feel it lift? Up, up, up we go, higher and higher and higher, over the fields and the towns and the cities, all day. And we have our sandwiches and our juice at midday and keep on flying until we reached Great Bear Lake."

"We'd have to come down sometimes," said Davey. "For more food. Or for the bathroom. You always need the bathroom, Lenny."

"Hush," I said. "Don't ruin it."

"Has Mother found us gone yet?"

That jolted the story. We imagined her piecing it together. The sandwich-making crumbs, the missing adventure-type clothes. *A to Ampersand* clearly vanished from the shelf. *Amphibians to Aztecs*. The bird issue gone. The balloon faltered in the golden morning sun. Great Bear Lake gleamed far away as perfect as a postcard photo but our balloon snagged itself on a power line. Davey never wore a fur hat. He never strode through the forest with his golden eagle on his shoulder.

It was all talk, but that's how things start.

On the first day of school it was my job to brush Davey's hair. He had to sit on the living room floor and I had to sit on the sofa with the hair cream. It was an operation that took concentration. I'd get one half down and the other half would be starting to spring up again. "You need to learn to brush your own hair," I whispered.

"Can you believe I've got Miss Schweitzer?" he whispered back. "What's she like really?"

"You better have a clean ironed handkerchief in your pocket," I said.

Then I felt bad because I could tell he was scared. I knew my brother. I knew his jiggling leg. I knew his breathing. I knew when he talked too much about Timothy, his imaginary pet eagle.

"Whatever you do," I said to him on the walk to school, "do not tell people about your eagle. Do not tell Miss Schweitzer about your eagle."

He looked crestfallen. His shoulders slumped. He looked to make sure Timothy hadn't slid off.

"Davey," I shouted at him.

"Stop your shouting at him," shouted Mother, who was walking with us.

We walked slowly, delaying the inevitable; even Mother was delaying the inevitable. She kept saying, "Look at you, Davey, you look so good with that backpack." "Stop for a minute so I can look at you." "Look how handsome you look." "I wish I had a photograph of you." "Stand up tall, Davey." "That's my boy."

So much talking. Too much talking.

Summer had released its hold on the city. The green grass was withering. There was a cold wind blowing brown leaves and rattling tin cans. Everything was grey. We were a small nervous cloud drifting through the streets.

"He grows and he grows," shouted one Brother Trapani after us as we went.

"Shut up and leave him alone," shouted Miss Finny.

We nodded and smiled but we crossed the road to get away from them.

"Tell me about the bombardier beetles again," Davey said.

So I did. So we would both calm down. We felt skittish, coltish, like we might bolt. Mother or not, if we saw a parked balloon, we'd be out of there. Bombardier beetles squeezed hot fart juice out of their bottoms to harm their enemies. It was a fact I remembered from the confiscated issue, and the fact that it was still confiscated made me prickly right there on the street.

"If I had a superpower that would be my superpower," said Davey. "I already have the farting part, I just need the juice."

"Hush now," said Mother. "Don't you talk like that at school."

We were nearly at the gate. There were kids everywhere. *There'll be staring*, Mother had said, but I just wasn't prepared for how much staring. All the staring made me even spikier. It made

— *67* —

me want to spit and curse. I wanted to shout at everyone, *What you all staring at, you big lot of rubber-neckers?* But I kept all the cursing inside of me. My mother raised her chin. She held Davey's hand. She looked calm, serene even, in her pink Golden Living Retirement Home uniform. She left all the spikiness to me.

I felt as if I was walking to the gallows. That's what it felt like. And I was an innocent. We were all innocents. Well, maybe not my mother, because it was her idea to make Davey go to school. To make him go to first grade when he was bigger than a fourth grader. It was a great injustice. Especially now that Miss Schweitzer had moved down to first grade. That was some extra evil in the horror of it all. We took him to his classroom. I tried not to look at the staring faces. Davey said, "Hi," to a couple of people as we went.

At his classroom door, Mother said, "Run along now, Lenny, he'll be okay."

But I lingered. Davey looked at me, pleadingly and made the squelching noise of a bombardier-beetle fart.

"Can I eat lunch with you?" he asked.

"No," I said.

Miss Schweitzer had seen him. Miss Schweitzer, who didn't like anything dirty or snotty, who liked order, who liked neat rows of first graders with ironed handkerchiefs. There would be four neat lines of first graders and then Davey. There would be Davey poking out at the back of the class like a weed, Davey with his hair that sprang up from his Brylcreem, Davey who talked loudly and laughed loudly and walked loudly and leaned into people and breathed his hot breath on them.

I looked at Miss Schweitzer looking at Davey. My mother hovered beside me at the door like a nervous bee. Miss Schweitzer looked at me like there might be something I could do to help. But there wasn't. I just left him there squelching like a bombardier beetle.

What *could* I do? What *could* I say? *He can read pretty well. He's great at counting. He likes to talk a lot about eagles. He's really smart, just very big. He's just really big for his age.* I'd be pleading by then. *Don't be too hard on him.*

I knew it would go badly.

"Are you okay, Lenny?" asked CJ when I got to my classroom.

"Yes," I said.

"It's just you're all red," she said.

"No, I'm not," I said.

"Y-y-y-y-y-y . . . yes you-you are," said Matthew Milford.

"Shut up, Matthew," I said.

And he looked genuinely hurt.

"So," asked Mother, "how was it?"

"Great," said Davey.

"Miss Schweitzer okay?"

"She's so beautiful," said Davey and his eyes misted over behind his thick dark lashes.

When I'd picked him up in the afternoon at the coat rack outside of his classroom, everything was not as I expected. Davey was standing beside Miss Schweitzer's desk and he had the blackboard eraser in his hand.

THE HALLOWED ERASER.

Davey and the eraser and the clean blackboard. He'd obviously just cleaned it. It was almost too much to bear. When he saw me, he smiled. Miss Schweitzer waved pleasantly. No one got to do erasing unless you were Miss Schweitzer's absolute favourite. Tara Albright had been Queen of the Blackboard Eraser. Perfect Tara, sweet and shiny as a candied apple, whose handkerchiefs had a perfect crease.

"Well, I am so glad to hear it," said Mother and she put her arms around his neck at the dinner table and gave him another serving of pie.

I was still speechless over the eraser affair.

"And it was so funny," said Davey. "There was this kid named Fletcher and he wet his pants."

"Oh, no," said Mother.

"Yeah, poor Fletcher. There was this boy named Teddy and his grandpa has a Ford Golden Jubilee tractor."

"No kidding," I said.

"No kidding, Lenny," said Davey. "He got to ride on it. On his farm."

"No kidding."

"Stop saying *no kidding*," said Mother.

"No kidding, Lenny. I drew him a picture of it and he said, 'Yep, that's my grandpa's Golden Jubilee.' He said maybe one day I can go on vacation with him and ride on his grandpa's tractor."

"No kidding," I said.

"Last warning, Lenore," said Mother.

"It was the best day of my life," said Davey. "But poor Fletcher. It wasn't just like a little pee, Mama, I mean this was just so much piss, like an elephant, it just hit the ground splatting everywhere."

Miss Schweitzer must have had the worst day ever.

"Do not say that word," cried Mother. "Do you hear me? I will wash out your mouth with soap. Where'd you learn that word?"

"So much piss," said Davey, shaking his head, when Mother was in the kitchen.

I blew juice out my nose.

September 15, 1975
Burrell's Publishing Company Ltd
7001 West Washington Street
Indianapolis, Indiana 46241

OUR GIFT TO YOU IS
THE GIFT OF KNOWLEDGE

Dear Mrs. Spink,

Thank you for your recent correspondence. Unfortunately, I must inform you that your prize subscription to the Burrell's Build-It-at-Home Encyclopedia *set does not include the volume covers. The volume covers are considered an extra, and all subscribers must pay for these after the first two complimentary volume covers. The covers are available through our easy order system and are of course available COD.*

Yours sincerely,

Martha Brent

General Sales Manager

September 27, 1975
Apartment 15, 762 Second Street
Grayford, Ohio 44002

Dear Martha Brent,
I am writing to inform you that I will not be paying for the
volume covers for the Burrell's Build-It-at-Home Encyclopedia
set. It is a sad day in the Spink household. I have two children
and I must provide for them both. I wrote about this in my
letter to win the competition you will kindly remember. My
younger child, Davey, has a condition, which makes him much
bigger than other boys his age. Our family doctor said it was
just in his genes but the school nurse says I must take him to
the doctor's again so he can have blood tests. My children get
hours of enjoyment from the encyclopedia set and now we will
not be able to build it. When we have visitors, rest assured,
I will tell them of the horrible service we have received from the
Burrell's Encyclopedia people who, it seems, do not give the gift
of knowledge after all.
Yours sincerely,
Mrs. Cynthia Spink

C
Coleopterist

4′ 10″
OCTOBER 1975

"How's Davey doing at school?" Nanny Flora asked me. She'd heard Mother's version. *Well, he's just fine. You should see his writing. He's got some little friends. One's named Teddy and one's named Fletcher.*

She'd heard Davey's version. *I like it a lot, Nanny Flora. Sometimes I get to be the class monitor. I check that all the bags and coats are hung straight. I am the best at drawing in the entire class.*

I figured she wanted a different version.

"He had to go to the school nurse," I said.

"Why's that?" asked Nanny Flora.

"He had some bad growing pains," I said. "He gets them sometimes but he never had them at school before. The nurse said he needed to have his blood tested."

"Give me that telephone," said Mother.

"What?" I said.

"Give it to me," said Mother.

"No, it's nothing to worry about," said Mother to Nanny Flora when she had the phone back out of my hands.

But there was. Sometimes I imagined I could hear Davey growing at night. I could hear his bones stretching. I could hear the hair growing on his head, a soft rustling sound.

I could hear his fingernails and his toenails and his teeth. In the dark, I lay and listened. I willed him to stop but he was an unstoppable thing.

"Yes, I told the doctor all about Uncle Gus. Yes, and the nurse too."

My sinking feeling grew.

The school nurse's name was Sandy Strachan and she was full of sunshine and dazzlingly bright. "Well, hello, honey," she said when I got to the nurse's office and saw Davey lying on his side moaning. He was moaning the way Davey moaned, as though he was about to die, as though someone had stabbed him with a knife.

"Hush, Davey," I said. "He's just got growing pains, ma'am. Mother just gives him some aspirin."

"Well, I've called your mom, honey, and I've given him some. And she's coming from work right now."

"Hush now, Davey," I said.

"Len—neeeeeee," he bellowed.

"It's just that he grows all of a sudden," I said.

I wished I had a reason. Nurse Sandy smiled at me, her mauve lipstick parted around her very white teeth, while she waited for the reason.

"For no reason," I said. "It'll stop soon. Hush now, Davey."

"You're a tall boy, all right," said Nurse Sandy. She stroked Davey on the cheek and I saw him open his big blue eyes at her. I could tell he was secretly enjoying it.

"And so clever," Nurse Sandy added. "He knows everything about tractors. Every different sort there is. Pretty good for a city boy."

Of course Nurse Sandy would fall in love with Davey. *Everyone* fell in love with Davey. I crossed my arms and felt aggrieved.

Davey smiled at Nurse Sandy and then moaned for good measure.

Mother came in like a grass tornado in her green "King of Fruit" Fruit Store shirt with the banana embroidered on the pocket. She came in wild, like Davey had been hit by a motorbike and he was lying half-dead on the street.

"Davey!" she cried and in response he bellowed like the knife had been stuck in farther.

"It's these growing pains," said Mother.

"He's been to the doctor you know," she said. Now she was an excuse tornado. She couldn't be stopped.

"The doctor said it's just in his genes," she said. "But he gets these pains from time to time."

Nurse Sandy listened and smiled.

"Well, he's just gorgeous," she said. Not once, *He's too big.* "But I think you should take Davey to the doctor again."

Mother went to start up again. She went to say, *There are tall people in our family,* but Nurse Sandy bulldozed right over her, smiling.

"I think there are probably some things that need checking. Growth hormone is one thing I'm thinking of. Sometimes a kid might have too much and sometimes not enough. I think Davey needs his blood tested."

"The doctor said I worried too much," said Mother.

"Well, you need to find another doctor, sweetie," countered Nurse Sandy, and I don't know what was more shocking, calling Mother *sweetie* or the hug she gave her straight after. Nurse Sandy grabbed Mother by the shoulders and hugged her while she was speaking. A sudden hug. A big out-of-the-blue squeeze. An ambush embrace. "Everyone is entitled to a second opinion," Nurse Sandy finished.

It was outside that Mother started to cry. She put her head in her hands and sobbed and tried to recover herself but sobbed again. She wiped furiously at her eyes, enraged at her tears that wouldn't stop. Davey hung his head.

"People shouldn't just go hugging you for no good reason," I said, enraged myself.

"Hush," said Mother, and she hiccuped and tried to get herself under control which was straight up and down and skinny with a frown. She closed her eyes and I closed mine. The sun was warm and bright against my eyelids. Davey did a smallish disgruntled bellow so we didn't forget him.

"Okay," she said.

"Okay," I said.

"You have a good day now, Lenny. Go back inside. I'll get this boy home." She smiled and wiped her face. "Everything is going to be fine."

"Yes, everything is going to be fine," I said.

I walked back toward the entrance and they walked out toward the gate, and then through the gates, and then all the way to where the twenty-eight bus stopped. And I turned to check them several times, just to see that everything was still fine.

That day in class I counted the notches on a Goliath beetles' legs in my head. I imagined them and I counted them and it calmed me. I thought it must be like Mrs. Gaspar and her rosary. Mr. Marcus was our new fourth-grade teacher and he was nothing like Miss Schweitzer. He had a bristly moustache and sometimes he gave up teaching us and took out his guitar and sang us "Kumbaya". My handkerchiefs were already a crumpled mess in my underpants drawer. It was Davey who had to worry about handkerchiefs now.

Goliathus goliatus, I repeated, again and again in class that day after Davey went home with growing pains. *Goliathus goliatus. Goliathus goliatus. Goliathus goliatus. Goliathus goliatus. Goliathus goliatus. Goliathus goliatus.* Biggest beetle in the world.

They were words. And words felt good and solid.

Goliathus goliatus. I said it at recess beside Matthew Milford and CJ. I described that beetle to them in detail until their eyes glazed over, until CJ said, "Can you please shut up already about Goliath beetles?"

So I told them about the African leaf beetle that could kill you by paralysing you. I told them about the rhinoceros beetle, lesser cousin to the Goliath. I explained to them the life cycle of the cicada. Matthew Milford listened smiling.

"Beetles, beetles, beetles," said CJ, sighing loudly.

I ignored her.

"First it was amphibians. Then ants. And now beetles."

Amphibians seemed a long time ago. Amphibians seemed like something a baby would like.

"All you ever talk about is beetles," said CJ. "When you sleep over at my house on Saturday, I think I better find my bug catcher."

It was to be my first ever sleep-over away from home and I was excited and terrified. Even if I just imagined saying goodbye to Davey, a pointy lump formed in my throat.

"You have a bug catcher?" I asked, trying not to think of the goodbye.

"I certainly do," said CJ. "A really big bug catcher."

The first of the *D* issues began to arrive. Our mother felt the packages for volume covers but was disappointed each time. In fact, the *D* issues were for the most part a disappointment. Dairy farms. Dallas. The Dakotas. Dolls, deafness, and the history of dancing. All the drudgery of daffodils, Delaware, five pages of dogs, daddy-long-legs, dams.

"Look here, Lenny, there's dressmaking," said Mother. "That might be a nice thing for you."

"I'm not that interested in dressmaking," I said.

We flipped aimlessly. David killed Goliath. He killed lions and bears as well. We tried feeling sad for the lions and bears but it was a listless attempt; the *Burrell's Build-It-at-Home Encyclopedia* provided no satisfying detail.

Even death.

Death was the end of life. Death occurred when vital organs, the lungs, heart, and brain, stopped functioning. Death sat between Dearborn, Henry and death adder on a lonely page. There was no illustration or diagram to accompany the death entry. There was a photograph of a death adder just below.

"Look at it," said Davey. "Don't you think they should have a picture of a dead squirrel or something?"

"Shush," I said.

"Or a dead death adder," said Davey. He thought he was pretty funny.

Those two death paragraphs seemed so clean and clinical. Empty.

I turned the page.

The park gardener had come and snipped the roses down to nothing, just brownish sticks. Now there were no aphids left, not even a chance of finding an aphid. When the aphids disappeared, I hadn't known what to feed Lady. I'd tried honey. I'd tried raisins. I tried little snippets of lettuce, but she ate nothing. She went up and down the wall of her glass jar prison. Up and down her sticks, searching and searching, and searching. She grew slower and slower.

She died.

We had taken her little body wrapped in a handkerchief and buried her near those snipped-down rose bushes in the park, the place where she always should have been. I'd felt sad for stealing her from those summer days.

I couldn't tell Mother about her death. It was my own small grief. I told Mrs. Gaspar, though, and she nodded her head and closed her eyes while she listened.

"Did you try jam?" she asked.

"It was too late for jam," I said.

"Well, then, you tried good," said Mrs. Gaspar. She said *goot* for good. "You tried your very best."

"I don't know," I said. I was despondent.

"I will tell you my dream," said Mrs. Gaspar.

She never asked permission. I went to call for Davey because he liked her dreams too, but she put her soft damp hand on mine.

"In this dream we were walking, you and I. We were walking on Second Street. And I was just a girl like you."

I needed to picture it, a young Mrs. Gaspar.

"What were you like?"

"Long hair, roses in my cheeks," she said.

"Red hair?"

"Like fire," said Mrs. Gaspar.

I had it.

"We were walking and walking and then we found a field," said Mrs. Gaspar. "A big field, covered in pink morning dew, because we were walking and the sun had only just come up."

"Whereabouts was it?"

"I do not recall, Lenora, but in this paddock there were two white horses."

Oh. I don't know if I said it. The *oh* may have been silent. I loved Mrs. Gaspar's horse dreams, but I'd never featured in one.

"They were shining in the morning sun," said Mrs. Gaspar.

"Did we ride them?"

Sometimes Mrs. Gaspar rode her dream white horses. She once rode a dream white horse all the way to Safeway and then right in through the front door and up and down the aisles, picking up canned corn and canned franks and dill pickles in a jar.

"We did not ride them," said Mrs. Gaspar. "We flew them."

"What?" I shouted.

"What?" said Davey from her little living room.

"Nothing," I said.

"We went toward them and they were frisky. They stamped their hooves and took off running and we chased them around that paddock," said Mrs. Gaspar. "And as they ran their wings opened up. Great wings, white wings! And as they ran, their hooves lifted from the ground. We ran after those horses and you had one first and you were on its back as it flew up into the sky."

"Did you catch one?" I asked breathlessly, like I'd actually been running.

"Yes, I caught one."

"Did you fly too?"

"Yes, I flew, and when I looked down it was not here but Hungary and I saw my mother and father in front of their little house, waving up at me."

I imagined it. It was a good dream. The best one yet. After Mother and her black egg, it felt much better.

"What does it mean, Lenora?" Mrs. Gaspar whispered, as

though I might know. As though I might have such knowledge inside me.

"I don't know," I whispered back.

That night Mr. King came to our apartment. Our mother let him in. She let him in because she was expecting him and when I knew that, I realized why she had been so long in the bathroom putting waves in her hair, and why she kept smoothing down her denim skirt and looking at herself in the mirror.

Mr. King was as short as my mother, who was small. I got my smallness from her. Mr. King had a little round belly like he'd swallowed a baby. His satiny shirt strained over it. His Ford Gran Torino keys jangled in one hand. He held a bunch of bananas in the other. He looked at my mother like he could suck her up through a straw, just like that, and she would be all his.

"Hello, children," he said.

I was having difficulty comprehending. Mr. King of Mr. King's "King of Fruit" Fruit Store. In our living room. Holding bananas.

"This is Lenny, you've met her, I know," said Mother, all fluttery and soft and nervous. "And Davey, you've met Davey."

Davey was looking at Denmark. In Denmark, nearly everyone rode a bicycle. Davey sorely wanted a bicycle. In his daydreams, we both rode to Great Bear Lake. He was utterly impractical.

"Hello, sir," said Davey. He stood up and he smiled, the way

Davey always smiled, very good-naturedly, leaning to one side a little, squinting his left eye.

Mr. King put his keys in his pocket and shook Davey's hand.

"I bet those are the keys to your Ford Gran Torino," said Davey.

"Sure are, boy. Do you like the Ford Gran Torino, Davey?"

"No, I like tractors," said Davey. He was only six.

"I'm just nearly finished cooking," said Mother. "What can I get you to drink?"

What. Can. I. Get. You. To. Drink.

We only ever had water or milk in our house. Mr. King didn't look like a milk kind of man. His black moustache was terrible. By *terrible*, I mean I didn't want to look at it. By terrible, I mean I couldn't stop looking at it. I looked at it and looked at it all through dinner. I watched the food going into the little red opening beneath it. The pot pie we always ate on Fridays. The milk droplets hanging onto the bristles.

"Whatcha been doing at school, Lenore?" he asked.

He had a big gold chain around his neck. Back to the black moustache. There was a little piece of pastry caught in one corner.

"Nothing," I said.

"Don't be rude, Lenny," said Mother.

Mr. King's pants strained over his plump thighs. He was all sausage meat inside his shiny pants. Back to his bristly moustache. Mr. Marcus's moustache had nothing on Mr. King's moustache.

"What?" I said.

"I'm in first grade," said Davey.

"You're a mighty big first grader," said Mr. King.

"He's big for his age," said Mother. "There's very tall people in the family."

"From Sweden," said Davey.

There was a flicker of confusion on Mr. King's face like a faltering light. I enjoyed watching it.

"Well, this is mighty fine pot pie," he said, to cover it up.

"Who is this man, who comes up the stairs and knocks on your door?" said Mrs. Gaspar, but she knew all too well. She wheezed in and lit her white cigarette. Mother pushed an ashtray, kept especially for Mrs. Gaspar, toward her. Mrs. Gaspar trembled slightly with her agitation. She'd drawn her eyebrows on hastily, you could tell.

"Please tell me, Cyn-thi-a," she said. "Please tell me, Mrs. Spink. It is not Mr. King."

"He only came for dinner," said Mother.

"He drives a Ford Graaaaannnn Toriiiiiiiino," said Davey slowly.

"Hush," said Mother.

"But he is not right," moaned Mrs. Gaspar. "To look at him, you can see. For you it is from the frying pan into the fire."

"It was just dinner," said Mother. "That's all. No harm in that."

She was getting her Cindy Spink whistle. I saw her nostrils flare. But she needed to be careful. Mrs. Gaspar was our evening sitter when Mother worked late shifts and nights. We spent many nights on her sofa by the soft glow of *Kojak* and the benevolent smiling Jesus.

"Just dinner, that's all, Mrs. Gaspar," Mother said again for good measure. Even though Mr. King was gone, she'd stayed a little fluttery. She kept touching her curled hair in a way that made me feel worried.

Davey tapped me on the shoulder. He had the Canada issue in his hand.

"Great Bear Lake," he whispered and smiled slyly under his long lashes at me.

In bed that night, we made a list of things we'd need to run away to Great Bear Lake. A sleeping bag each, warm clothes, some money. We had to work out a way to earn money for the bus fare.

"Maybe . . ." Davey began, then stopped.

"Maybe what?"

"Maybe we'll meet Dad on the way." He kind of mumbled it.

"Maybe," I said.

I went to sleepover at CJ's house. A real house with a porch and a chair swing. Mrs. Bartholomew had picked me up in her real Ford sedan with CJ beaming from the window. There were six Bartholomew daughters but there always seemed to be many more girls than that in the house. There were girls on the stairs and girls on the phone and girls lounging in front of the television. There were sisters and sisters' friends and friends' sisters and cousins who came to stay to go to school, a shifting tide of girls. That house was in constant flux with the front door forever opening and feet thundering up and down the stairs. The air was full of hairspray and Charlie perfume. Somewhere, always somewhere, there was the sound of a hair dryer, like a lone bagpipe.

Mr. Bartholomew somehow survived in the middle of it all. I liked to watch him, although I pretended not to. He worked for a security firm and he wore a neatly pressed uniform with epaulets on his shoulders. He was tall and permanently exhausted-looking.

The girls liked to creep in under his arms while he watched television and just rest there for a while with his arm slung over them. Or if he was waiting for his coffee, one would come lean against him like he was a post, and CJ lay on him sometimes like he was a rock and she was a lizard, just briefly, and then she was on her way.

He knew most friends by first name.

"Hello, Lenny," he said to me.

"Hi," I whispered. I wanted to lean against him too, just to see what it felt like. I don't think I'd ever leaned against Peter Lenard Spink. Not once.

Mr. Bartholomew's gaze was like a spotlight. My face burned. He looked at me as though he was interested. Like there was no one else in the room. I saw him do it with the others too. He looked at them all like they were the only girl in the world.

He said, "And what grade is that brother of yours in? I bet you he plays football, right?"

I said, "He's in first grade."

"Oh, you have two brothers," said Mr. Bartholomew.

"No sir," I said, and then left him standing there looking confused.

CJ shared a room with JC. Josephine Claire was three years older than us. She had her whole life mapped out. She was going to be a nurse like her mother and her two oldest sisters. Then she was going to get married and have six babies. She knew their names already. JC was really into babies.

CJ rolled her eyes when JC wasn't looking. CJ would never talk about such a thing.

"Where do you think your father is?" she asked straight out, as soon as JC was asleep. Like she'd been wanting to ask it forever.

"I have no idea," I said.

"Do you miss him?" She must have seen me looking at her father. My cheeks flushed so hot in the dark that I thought she might see me glow.

I tried to choose my words carefully.

"Not really," I said. "It's different than missing him."

"Tell me," she said.

"I just don't want to forget him," I said.

There was no way to explain it to someone who didn't have a father fading like an old polaroid photograph. Peter Lenard Spink was all in parts, he was oily hair, he was a belt buckle, he was a nicotine finger stain.

We lay in silence for a while, both of us thinking.

"Guess what, Lenny?" CJ said at last. "I have something mysterious to tell you."

"What?" I said. I hoped it was about the bug catcher.

"Sometimes I can hear music everywhere, even in my heartbeat."

"Really?" I said. It *was* mysterious.

"I'm going to be a drummer," she said. "When I grow up."

"Huh?" I said.

Everyone in CJ's family was a nurse or going to be a nurse. CJ's mother was a nurse. CJ's grandmother was a nurse. Her two oldest sisters were nurses or training to be nurses. Her three middle sisters wanted to be nurses. She belonged to a great nursing dynasty.

"I'm going to get a junior drum kit for Christmas," said CJ.

CJ was already in the school band. She was the youngest member. Mr. Marcus had encouraged it because she was always tapping her feet. She played the triangle with fierce concentration.

"You can get brown or blue or orange," she said.

"Wowee," I said.

"Phew," she said. "I thought you wouldn't like me."

"Of course I would like you," I said. "I'm going to be a coleopterist."

"A whaddy-whoody?" said CJ.

"A beetle expert," I said.

"Oh, now I understand," she said. She exploded out of bed and was down on her knees. I thought she was praying and she was.

"Dear Lord, help me be a drummer and help my best friend Lenny not forget her father and be a bug expert," she said, but she was rummaging too, scratching under the bed. She pulled a box out and I heard a sound like marbles hitting the floor. "And, dear Lord, let my junior drum kit be blue. Amen."

She leapt back into bed and thrust her bug catcher into my arms.

It wasn't just an ordinary bug catcher. It was the Rolls Royce of bug catchers. It was so big I could keep a whole darkling-beetle farm inside it. I don't know how someone who didn't even like beetles ended up with such a thing. By the glow of her night-light, she smiled her CJ smile, a wrinkled nose, too much gum. It was very good to have a friend like CJ.

December 13, 1975
Apartment 15, 762 Second Street
Grayford, Ohio 44002

Dear Martha,

I'm writing in regard to my letter dated September 27th to which I have not received a reply. I won a prize and that prize was a Build-It-at-Home-Encyclopedia *set. Now I cannot build it because I do not have the volume covers. My son Davey has had blood tests to check his hormones. They want to find out why he is growing so fast. We might even have to go see a special doctor in Chicago. All this and I'm raising two children alone. Davey loves the birds entry but he sure is looking forward to the eagles entry even more. I look forward to your speedy and honest response regarding a resolution to this matter and I know you will do the right thing, Martha.*

Yours sincerely,

Mrs. Cynthia Spink

E
Eagles

6 years 5 months
5′ 1″
DECEMBER 1975

I t was a pretty honest letter, considering she was a profession-al letter-writing liar. Davey did love the birds entry but he was more excited about eagles, which would be coming soon.

Davey did go to the doctor again. He did have his blood tested. We went in Mr. King's Ford Gran Torino. Mr. King had been to dinner five times. Meatloaf, pot pie, spaghetti, and meatloaf again times two. Mr. King must have thought we lived on meatloaf. But he always said, "Cindy, you make the best meatloaf in the world."

I didn't like the way he said *Cindy*, like my mother's name was a lollipop and he was rolling his tongue around it. I didn't like the way he said *meatloaf*, like it was a delicacy from a far-off land that he stuffed in under his bristly moustache.

I didn't like the way he looked at our encyclopedia issues, stacked high and volume-coverless. "They always scam the ladies," he said about our encyclopedia. "They will do anything to make a buck." He asked us what letter we were up to. We were still lost in the drudgery of the *D*s, but there was a hint of *E* on the wind. We lay awake in bed at night listing the wondrous things *E* might contain. Emerald pythons, for instance. Electric eels. Eclipses. Eagles. There was no point explaining it to Mr. King.

Mr. King's name was Harold. Mother called him Harry when we weren't there. I heard her when I was in my bed. We had to go to bed straight after dinner when Mr. King came for meatloaf. Mr. King couldn't wait for us to go to bed so he could pop his eyes out all over our mother. They stayed up in the living room, talking and laughing and calling each other by their first names. He said *Cindy*. She said *Harry*. It sounded stupid.

They stayed up and watched *Kojak* and we lay in bed listening until we heard the front door and the goodnights and then Mother in her bedroom making her normal Mother noises, brushing her teeth and her long fair hair. When Mr. King was gone, I could breathe easy again.

Pot pie and spaghetti and three times meatloaf and now the Ford Gran Torino. Davey and I sat in the back among the various jackets and paper bags. Davey smiled at me.

"How fast can this baby go?" he said. It was a line from *Starsky & Hutch*.

"Hush, now," said Mother. Outside snow fell. We puffed out our breath in front of us while Mr. King tried to start his car. I concentrated on the grey sidewalk trees, strung with icicles. The engine roared to life and made Mother jump. Mr. King did go fast and Mother got dreadful anxious and told him to stop so we could get out and walk. I hoped more than anything that no one saw me in Mr. King's Gran Torino. It would be the most embarrassing thing in the world. He dropped us right in front of the doctor's office, and when we got out people stared, especially at six-year-old Davey, nearly as tall as a teenager, his pants sitting just above his ankles, his hair slicked down, leaning to one side, smiling.

Mr. King didn't come in with us. He didn't offer. He couldn't wait to get away in his Ford Gran Torino. Davey waved at him. He said, "Do it!" which was another line from *Starsky & Hutch*.

"Stop it right now," said Mother. She was in a prickly mood. She was ready to do battle with Dr. Leopold.

"I just don't want to be told I'm worrying over nothing," was the first thing she said, even before hello. "You said he'd settle down and he was big for his age but I couldn't get a kindergarten to take him and now he's in first grade and has to sit right at the back so he doesn't block anyone's view. There might be big people in my family tree but quite frankly I don't care. The school nurse said he should have a blood test. That's what she said. That's why I'm here."

Mother could have washed Dr. Leopold out the door and down the street with her flood of words and there was more, I knew it.

"And he is nearly five two and that is just not right. And every time I turn around he's grown some more and there must be something wrong somewhere. They said something about hormones. I have to work two jobs just to keep buying new clothes."

Dr. Leopold tried to get some words in.

"Well, now . . ." he said.

"So if you'll just write that down on a piece of paper, I'll give it to them. That's what I need. A little form, one of those little forms you write the blood test on and a letter and I'll take him somewhere that specializes in this kind of thing because I don't know but maybe there is a pill or something and they've been talking to me about growth hormones and I don't understand but maybe there is some kind of medicine to slow it all down."

"Mrs. Spink," said Dr. Leopold. He motioned Davey up from his chair and put him against the tape measure stuck to the door frame. "You are absolutely right. He was tall before, but now he's really off the chart. We'll do exactly that. We'll get a blood test. That will be our first step."

Dr. Leopold patted Davey on his hard helmet of Brylcreem. "What do you think of that plan, young man?"

"I think it's a great plan, Stan," said Davey.

"Hush now, Davey," said Mother.

While we waited for the blood results Mother's dark heart feelings grew. Not just Davey dark heart feelings but others too. She worried I didn't eat enough. She worried that Davey ate too much. She worried that the holy trinity of warts on my knee was contagious. She worried that Davey didn't clean his teeth well. She worried that he needed glasses. I was glad that worry had passed on from me. She worried about money. She worried about food. She worried about clothes. She worried about weather. She was jangly with worries.

"Something's not right," she said to herself.

She jumped each time the phone rang.

"Why do you keep doing that?" I said.

It was only ever the Golden Living Retirement Home asking her to do an extra shift or Mrs. Gaspar with a Mr. Petersburg spotting or Mr. King downstairs asking if we needed a box of bananas.

"A box of bananas," shouted Mrs. Gaspar. "Who does he think he is? The king of the jungle? Oh, Cyn-thi-a! Mrs. Spink! He uses these bananas to get up the stairs into your house. You must not let that bad wolf in."

"Oh, he's just a friend, Mrs. Gaspar," said Mother. "He's not too bad, is he, children?"

She looked at us so hopefully that Davey couldn't help himself.

"He's a really nice guy," said Davey, staring at the first *E* issue, which contained eagles. Eagle statistics, life cycle of an eagle, four colour plates containing all the eagles of all the continents, including the golden eagle. He was almost drooling.

I refused to say as much. I flipped through my *E* issues slowly. Eggs. Egypt. The Eiffel Tower.

Electricity. Elephants and elevators.

"His fruit is full of worms," said Mrs. Gaspar under her breath when Mother was out of the room. I nodded in agreement and smiled at her. I could tell she had dreams inside her that she wanted me to know.

Mother even jumped when the phone rang and it was Nanny Flora. Even though Nanny Flora was a regular event, once a month, on a Sunday.

"How's things, Lenore?" asked Nanny Flora.

"Not too bad," I said. But they weren't. What if I told her about Mr. King?

"How's Davey, then? He still growing?"

"Yes," I said. Sometimes Davey just went to the bathroom and he came out taller. "But he had a blood test to see what's causing it. Maybe some hormones."

"Hormones?" said Nanny Flora. She said *hormones* like it was a dirty word. I glanced at her photograph on the hutch. She wouldn't tolerate vermin or germs or hormones.

"Put your mother on," she said.

Dr. Leopold phoned five days before Christmas. It was afternoon and the snow had stopped and Davey was reading the comic *Space Family Robinson*.

"What does this say?" he whispered to me. He whispered because Mother said we were too loud. We were the loudest kids she'd ever met. We needed to learn to be quiet.

I said, "A laser-spouting warship zeroes in on Tim and Tam." He looked pretty happy with that.

"Wow," he mouthed quietly. I could tell he wished he was Tim and that I was Tam. I just knew it. It was the kind of thing Davey wished for.

He wished he had the book of 101 magic tricks, which was located amid the comic book's advertisements. The Barlow knife too, the atom pistol, the sneezing powder. He wished he had the snowstorm tablets. All we needed was the lit end of Mrs. Gaspar's cigarette and we'd have a room full of snow. He wished he could join the Junior Sales Club of America and sell greeting cards and win a portable typewriter or a transistor radio or a complete archery set. He wished he could win the intercom telephones or a full-sized wooden guitar or a giant telescope with an optical finder.

He wished for Sea-Monkeys.

"Sea-Monkeys aren't real," Mother said to him one thousand times.

But they were there, a whole family on the centre spread: "A Bowl full of Happiness. Only $1.00."

On the day the phone rang, Davey had just made it to his Sea-Monkeys. He was gazing at the happy family gazing at their bowl full of happiness. I was watching him gazing and I too was wishing they were real. That they actually did grow that way, like a little miniature family with a castle to live in. A mother, a father, and a boy and a girl.

Our wall phone rang.

Mother said, "I knew it."

She leapt toward it and had it in her hand before it could ring twice.

"Hello," she said. "Yes, that's me."

There was a long pause then. She looked startled, confused, as though someone had told her a joke that she didn't understand.

"So," she said, carefully. "So," again.

Another pause.

"So do we come now?" she said. "Oh, I see, the morning. Yes."

"Yes, thank you," she said.

"What happened?" I asked.

"We have to go to see Dr. Leopold about the blood test in the morning," Mother said.

Davey said nothing. He looked at his Sea-Monkeys, flipped the page back to the laser-spouting-warship story.

"Okay, Davey?" said Mother.

"Okay," said Davey.

"I'm sure it's nothing to worry about," said Mother. But she was lying. I could tell. She was nothing but a Cindy Spink cicada shell filled up with dark heart feelings.

January 12, 1976
Apartment 15, 762 Second Street
Grayford, Ohio 44002

Dear Martha Brent,

*I'm writing because the E issues have begun arriving and still
there is no sight of the volume covers. Nor was there a reply to
my previous letter dated December 13th. Christmas has come
and gone and there has been bad news for Davey. There is
something wrong with his hormones. We are going on the night
bus to Chicago in two weeks' time to see a special doctor who
knows about these things. Davey is a good boy and very
brave. Lenore is the best big sister you could ask for. Each
day my children check the mailbox to see if the volume covers
have arrived. I don't want to have to tell them that Burrell's
Publishing Company does not deliver what they promise, which
was a* Build-It-at-Home Encyclopedia, *completely free.*
Yours sincerely,
Mrs. Cynthia Spink

The Magic Blanket

5' 3"

JANUARY/FEBRUARY 1976

t was true, the *E*s lay in a pile, volume-coverless. Davey was glued to eagles while I waded slowly through the anatomy of the ear, ecology, economics, and education. The tedium was broken only by embalming which we looked at with frequent furtiveness. Embalming contained a painting of a shadowy room and an embalmer at work upon a pale white body. It was bluish-white that body. It was something turning, something decaying. Looking at it was daring the universe in some way, but I wasn't sure how.

E contained Earth.

"Been there, know all about it," Davey said, deadpan, when he saw the two-paged illustration of our blue-green planet. Sometimes he really made me laugh.

El Salvador. The history of enamels. The Etruscans and Europe.

But the rest of Mother's letter was lies. The lies were piled on thick. We never checked the mailbox every day. We checked on Fridays, when the issues arrived. I was not the best big sister anyone could ask for. Davey was not brave. If I said Peter Lenard Spink in a scary voice he screamed out right away. In that letter, my mother's high school handwriting had grown rigid and jerky. The whole thing reeked of sadness and rage.

"It's pretty good," I said.

"They mightn't send us any more," said Davey. "When they get that."

"Oh, they'll be sending them to us, all right," said Mother, "or I'll drive all the way to Indianapolis and get them myself."

It was an empty threat. We didn't have a car.

I'll take a Greyhound bus to Indianapolis and get them myself, didn't have the same ring.

I imagined what the Burrell's headquarters looked like. I saw a dark driveway and a drawbridge. We'd have to shout out our business to the guards. "We've come to see about the volume covers." The drawbridge would lower, and our feet would be loud on the wooden floor.

Inside was half castle, half factory. There were encyclopedias stacked up high to the ceiling. In shadowy corners, authors worked by candlelight. I caught a glimpse of a woman working on beetles. She was surrounded by jars of them and she smiled knowingly at me.

Martha Brent wore an emerald green cloak. She came down the stone staircase and her cloak swirled around her.

"I need pacaranas," she commanded. "I need the history of painting. I need palmistry, I need Pennsylvania."

Her minions turned their pages in unison.

"I need beetles, I need biochemistry, I need blue jays."

I pictured vast libraries in the turrets where the information was sourced. They were large circular libraries, filled to the ceiling high above with books. Ladders reached up into the gloom.

"Lenny," said Mother. "Earth calling Lenny. Drop this in the mailbox near the bank in the morning, letters go quicker from there."

Since Dr. Leopold and the blood test, Mother asked about Davey's head each morning. No one ever mentioned the word tumour. We could say *hormones*, but not *tumour*. Mother could not even use the word tumour in her letter to Martha Brent. The word tumour would have added weight to that letter. I figured we would have received the volume covers the next day, special delivery.

Dr. Leopold had said there could be one, on account of all the growth hormone. "Your boy's got an awful lot of growth hormone," is what he said. "Could be a tumour on his brain." That's why we had to go to the special doctor. But when we got home and I'd mentioned it, when I'd said "What's a tumour?" Mother had hushed me violently.

"Don't say it, just don't say it," she had whispered in the kitchen, as though just the word might make it real, might make one burn suddenly into existence in Davey's head. As though the word was magic and I was a tumour-creating magician. "Tumour," I could say at school and give everyone one. CJ, Matthew Milford, Mr. Marcus.

We didn't have the *T* issues. The *T* issues were a long way away.

Davey kept growing. He grew at an alarming rate. His head got bigger. His jaw got bigger. His teeth got bigger. His hands grew. After the visit to Dr. Leopold a new gap appeared between his front teeth, and his two big toes burst out of his sneakers spontaneously. He said his kneecaps ached.

"What do you mean, your kneecaps?" cried Mother. She was only worried about his head. The kneecaps were a new and sinister development.

We walked to school together and puffed our breath out in front of us like dragons. Davey looked at his shoulder and I knew he was looking at his imaginary golden eagle. It annoyed me. I wanted to shout at him but I didn't in case he had a tumour. I wanted to say, *Maybe you've got a tumour and that's why you're so weird.* But I didn't. Because whatever was inside me seemed powerful. My anger and sadness, a big ball of it, felt electric, white-hot, I felt like I could cause tumours just by looking at people. I was a tumour-spouting laser gun.

We went past the bank, where I mailed Mother's letter. It looked like such a normal letter on the outside, but Martha Brent didn't know what was coming to her.

I walked Davey to his class and that took us right past Nurse Sandy's office. Davey stopped and said hello at her door. He did that because secretly he loved her. He rubbed the toe of one large new sneaker on the ground and looked at her from under his lashes.

"Well hello, Davey," said Nurse Sandy. "How are you feeling today?"

"I'm feeling just fine," said Davey.

"Well, I'm glad to see that," said Sandy Sunshine. "And how are you, Lenny?"

"Great," I said.

But I wasn't. I walked the whole way to my class trying not to think about Davey. About the black egg. About him growing so tall that he hit the ceiling. About tumours which in my mind looked like marshmallows but in a sinister marshmallow-y way, a dreadful spongey grey. I disliked Mother. I disliked Davey. I disliked Nurse Sandy. I disliked everyone dancing around the word tumour.

Yes, my mother lied about me in that letter.

"I can't believe you get to go on a bus," said CJ. She was playing the drums with two pencils on her workbook. CJ never stopped playing the drums. Her new blue Junior Ludwig Drum Kit sat in her living room at home right beside the television. And if she wasn't there with it she used anything she could find to beat out a rhythm.

"I know," I said. "At night."

"Will you be gone for weeks and weeks?" she asked.

"I don't know," I said.

"Will you write me a letter?"

"Yes," I said.

Matthew Milford said, "Wh-wh-wh-wh-wh-wh-wh-wh-why are you g-g-g-g-g-g-g-g-g—?"

"Going? Because my brother has something wrong with him that makes him too big. Maybe a TUMOUR. And a special doctor needs to see him."

It felt good to say that word out loud. I said it extra loud.

I watched Matthew's and CJ's face. Marshmallow-shaped tumours didn't suddenly erupt from them.

"Yeah, a tumour," I said again. Just for good measure.

Matthew appeared satisfied with that explanation. I could tell he had no idea what a tumour was. CJ played with her pencil drumsticks.

"I hope your brother is okay," said CJ at last.

"I'm sure it's nothing to worry about," I said.

But in bed that night I saw Davey feeling his head with his fingers. He moved them slowly, creeping them through his hair like he was looking for something.

"What are you doing?" I asked.

"Nothing," he said.

"Everything will be fine, Davey," I said.

"I know," he said.

We listened to Frank and Roger and Martin cooing on the dark sill.

"Can you tell me about Great Bear Lake?"

So I did. In this story, we walked up through the Dakotas. It was a long way but we kept going. We slept in barns and railway yards. We ate food that we found. Stuff that Timothy hunted for us. Rabbit cooked over a campfire.

"Could you really do that?" Davey asked.

"We'd have to, Davey."

"We could save for a bus ticket," he said.

"How?" I said. We hardly ever got pocket money, no matter how many chores we did for Mrs Gaspar. I sighed in the dark. "And anyway, a bus wouldn't take us all the way to the North-west Territories."

Jefferson City, Lincoln, and into the Dakotas. Just thinking of the Dakotas, I shivered.

"What?" asked Davey.

"Nothing," I said.

I could feel the cold still air there and the sky all sprinkled with burning white stars and our boots on the hard ground, tramping and our breath rushing out before us.

"Keep going," he whispered. But I couldn't. I was stumped. My eyes were tired from staring into my imaginings. Saskatchewan and Yellow Knife and Great Bear Lake shrivelled like fallen leaves. We flew backwards and our hearts lurched and landed right back in our chests. Back in our little room.

Mrs. Gaspar dreamed she found a magical blanket. She was going through her linen closet and she found it there in among all her sheets and pillowcases. It was black with colourful squares and she hadn't remembered it until she found it.

She remembered she made the squares with her sister. They had sewn them together long before the war, when life was good and there were berries in the fields and dances in the square on Saturday nights and Max Jakab had a motorcycle and she was going to marry him. Before fear. The magic blanket was made before fear.

"But how was it magical?" I asked.

"Just listen and you'll find out," said Davey. He was lying on Mrs. Gaspar's sofa, holding *Space Family Robinson*.

"Yes, just listen and you'll find out," said Mrs. Gaspar.

But her dreams were so long. She would tell me what soup she made next. How she cleaned the magic blanket with a brush made out of some kind of birch twig. I pretended to lose interest. Mrs. Gaspar didn't care.

"I carried it to the window, dumplings," she said. "Very carefully. Because I had remembered. I opened the window."

Davey had closed his eyes, listening, a smile on his face.

Maybe she was going to fly out the window on that blanket? I wished we were in the dream, but she always told us if we were.

"I took that blanket and I shook it out," said Mrs. Gaspar. She shook out the imaginary blanket in her hand. "And out came the meadow pipits."

"Huh," I said.

"Out came the sparrows and the wood pigeons and the night-jars," she continued. "They flew out the window, all the brown birds, then came the songbirds, the thrushes and warblers, out they poured, singing. All the loons and larks, all the geese and swans. I shook that blanket out until all the birds were gone."

"Cool," said Davey.

"What does it mean?" I asked. "How is it magical?"

Mrs. Gaspar ignored me. She looked at her imaginary magical blanket sitting on her lap and she began to cry.

The Night Bus

5' 4"
LATE FEBRUARY 1976

The night we went to Chicago, Mrs. Gaspar kissed us all on the heads and cried. Her lips were cool and smelled of cigarettes. Davey clutched the falcon and falconry issue to his chest, for the *F* issues had arrived. For me, fleas, fireflies, false eyes on the backs of beetles and flying ants. For Davey: falcons.

I considered falcon and falconry disappointing but Davey could find no fault with it. There was one colour plate and only two paragraphs on the ancient art of hunting with birds of prey. I wondered if Martha Brent, as well as withholding volume covers, had done it deliberately.

"Don't cry, Mrs. Gaspar," said Davey. "We'll be home in a day or two."

"Oh, my dumpling," cried Mrs. Gaspar and she sobbed against his chest because Davey was taller than her now.

Davey smiled at me over her shoulder.

"Okay, then," said Mother. "We better hurry or we'll miss the bus altogether."

Davey extricated himself from Mrs. Gaspar's shaggy tangerine bathrobe.

"Gootbye, Lenora," said Mrs. Gaspar. She was much more formal with me. "I will watch you from the window."

Downstairs Mr King called out to us from the front of his shop. "Take some oranges for the trip," he said but Mother declined. He ruffled Davey's hair and told him to behave, which was stupid because Davey was the best-behaved kid in the world. I took a step back so I was out of hair-ruffling reach.

The whole of Grayford seemed stopped by the cold, like a picture, the streets empty and iced. The air caught in my aching throat. Mother and Davey said goodbye to Mr King and we walked to the Greyhound bus station where we'd watched countless arrivals and departures. Now it was our turn.

We'd never been anywhere before.

I looked up and counted windows until I found Mrs. Gaspar's bedroom window. She waved down at us. I saw a shadow moving in the window next door and knew it was Mr. Petersburg. I looked again, eyes straining in the dark, but the shadow didn't appear again. I didn't tell Mother or Davey because they looked too nervous already.

The third window along was our own. It made me think about what it must have been like for Peter Lenard Spink looking up and how small his goodbyes were until he vanished altogether. I sighed right there in the dark.

People stared when we got on. They stared at our little mother in her good jeans and her good coat and me in my navy jacket with glow-in-the-dark toggles and six-year-old man-sized Davey with his slicked-down hair and his new good pants and shirt and tie. We looked over-dressed on the Greyhound bus, like we were going to church. Mother had a paper bag filled with food. Most of it was for Davey because he ate so much.

"That's a mighty big boy you got there," said the driver when we passed.

"He has a condition," said Mother. "We are going to Chicago to see a doctor."

She said it in her small polite Cindy Spink voice like she was being interviewed on channel five about an accident she saw.

We proceeded down to our seats. Davey and I on one side of the aisle, Mother on the other side next to a bald man.

"You look a lot like Kojak," said Davey loudly. "I'm Davey."

"Hush, Davey," said Mother.

Somewhere someone whispered, "She said he has a condition."

But then the bus engine started up and it hummed our bottoms on our seats and we were off. Mother clutched onto the seat in front of her like she was on a fairground ride. She looked scared, but the truth was that it was good to go somewhere. I couldn't stop my heart from hammering in my chest. The city became suburbs, and Second Street changed somewhere from a big street to a little street and then to a highway, and on either side the suburbs melted away to frosted fields and pastures. There were red barns glowing in the moonlight like in storybooks. Another city rose up once and then towns in the cornfields like prickle patches and we ploughed straight through them.

We were on the bus for a night, and when we arrived at our destination, we were crumpled versions of our previous selves. Davey's back ached when he unfolded himself. He said so himself and he never complained. All the way to the doctor's office I could still feel the bus rushing and swerving inside me.

The doctor's name was Professor Cole and he didn't look like the type to deal with giant boys. Professor Cole was normal sized, but old and stooped and the sleeves of his white coat were crinkled. "David Spink," he said. "David Spink."

"You say there are tall people in the family, then, Mrs. Spink?"

"Yes," said Mother.

He had gold-rimmed spectacles and he looked to me like someone who should sit at a table mending dusty clocks or building ships out of toothpicks.

"Hello, David," he said in a voice so soft that Davey had to turn his ear toward him.

Professor Cole asked Davey to bend his head forward and searched through Davey's clumps of fair hair slowly. He looked at Davey's ears. He held Davey's forehead, his brow, he looked at his jaw, in his mouth, up his nose. He muttered things: *Interesting. Epiphyseal. Scoliosis. Should be straightforward. That's quite the femur. I see. Six, you say? When did he start this growing business?*

He asked Davey to take his clothes off and Davey sat there in his small office in just his underpants while he was examined. Professor Cole examined Davey's spine and his arms and his hands. His legs and his toes. He measured Davey. He measured him from his feet up to his head and from his head down to his feet. He measured the depth of his chest. He got him to blow into a machine to measure how big his lungs were. Davey blew the needle off and it pinged across the floor and rolled to a stop.

"Sorry, sir," said Davey.

"That's fine, young man, no need to apologize," said Professor

Cole and he ruffled Davey's hair and I could tell he liked Davey. The way everyone did.

Professor Cole measured and documented every inch of Davey. He measured him like he was going to build him a suit of armour. That's what I thought sitting there. Our mother sat watching. Her hair in a fountain. Her tired face. Golden Living Retirement Home hands, red and worn, wringing over and over soundlessly.

"Mrs. Spink," said Professor Cole at last.

She jumped a little in her chair.

"I've looked after quite a few giants, you know," he said.

She shook her head side to side. It was a negative. It was a don't-call-my-son-a-giant.

"Yes, indeed," said Professor Cole, like he was going to settle back and tell us a long story. "I've stopped them growing as best I could. Children can be different depending on where the tumour is. Is it on the pituitary or is there some other extra-pituitary cause? Almost ninety-nine percent certain it will be the pituitary. Do you know where the pituitary is and what it does?"

Things had changed direction fast. We thought we were settling back for a story and now we were on a quiz show. Everyone ignored the word tumour as best they could.

We didn't have the *P* issues of the *Burrell's Build-It-at-Home Encyclopedia* set but we did have the brain one. The entry was a page long, with a large diagram of a colour-coded brain. The colour-coded brain was in the silhouette of a man's head. It looked like he was wearing a fancy shower cap. The pituitary was pink. It was small and lay very deep.

My mother opened her mouth. She was going to try and answer the question.

"It's the mastermind," said Professor Cole. Mother closed her mouth. "It's in charge of all the hormones in the body. It makes women women and men men. It makes the milk that women feed their babies. It makes little boys and girls grow or not grow or grow too big.

"It's the mastermind," he said, very softly, again, and he took Davey's head in his hand and held it like he might be able to look inside. He smiled at Davey.

"Yes, I'm ninety-nine percent sure this will be a tumour," said Professor Cole, "so our job is to see what we can do with the tumour to stop you from growing and growing, young man. Because that's what you'll do. You'll just keep growing until your head hits the ceiling and that won't stop you either."

We all thought of Mrs. Gaspar's dream.

Professor Cole took the pages where he had drawn and measured Davey and stacked them neatly on a desk.

"Can he still go to school?" asked Mother.

"Of course he can," said Professor Cole. "That's the best thing he can do. In the meantime, I'll arrange some more blood tests and the surgery and send you a letter."

He looked at my mother kindly. The kindness made her cry. A sudden eruption, all bubbly and snotty.

Professor Cole said, "I'll fetch the nurse for you."

G
Giants

5′ 5″

MARCH 1976

🦅

We caught the afternoon bus home. The new knowledge sat inside, an extra heavy piece of luggage. An unclear and murky knowledge. We were 99 percent certain something was inside Davey, but we really couldn't understand what, or how, it would be removed. If I tried to ask questions, Mother shushed me. She shushed me like a circus clown with a whistle. I just had to open my mouth and she shushed me. I snuck out words, *why, how*. She shushed me wildly. I went hard and rattled out a whole sentence—"But how do they open up?"—and she shushed me so hard I thought I'd fall over.

Mrs. Gaspar came to hear the news and Mother took her away into the kitchen to tell her. We heard Mrs. Gaspar wail. Davey raised one eyebrow at me and it made me laugh. He said he felt okay. "I feel just fine," he said.

"And how are those free books coming along?" asked Nanny Flora down the phone line.

"They're fine," I said.

"What letter you up to?"

"We've nearly finished *F*."

Feathers, fathers, firemen, fans, Millard Fillmore, the law of falling bodies. I said nothing. I gave Nanny Flora nothing.

"That all? What if you need to know something about Niagara Falls?"

I shrugged.

"Don't shrug," said Mother. "Your grandmother can't hear a shrug."

"How's school?" asked Nanny Flora.

"Good," I lied.

"And you look after Davey there, right?" she asked. "You're his big sister, remember."

She didn't know the half of it.

What if I told her?

What if I described it to her?

What if I said I was ashamed of him sometimes? Everyone loved him but I was ashamed of how big he was and how he needed a grown-up chair and how much he leaned and how he was so loud and happy when he talked about tractors. And what if I told her the shame of being ashamed was even worse than the shame? The shame of being ashamed made me feel hot and sweaty and wild, like I was growing fur, like I was a werewolf. I was a monster for thinking such things. That's what it felt like to be ashamed of being ashamed of Davey.

"And your mother told me he's having an operation?" said Nanny Flora.

"Yes," I said.

"They set a date yet?"

"Not yet," I said.

"And it'll stop him growing, right?" she asked but her voice sounded far off and clean and uninvolved with all of it.

I shrugged again and Mother snatched the phone out of my hand.

When we got home from the city, there were several volume covers waiting for us and a letter from Martha Brent. Mother read the letter out loud.

March 1, 1976
Burrell's Publishing Company Ltd
7001 West Washington Street
Indianapolis, Indiana 46241

OUR GIFT TO YOU IS
THE GIFT OF KNOWLEDGE

Dear Mrs. Spink,

We thank you for your recent correspondence regarding the Burrell's Build-It-at-Home Encyclopedia *volume covers. The Burrell's family values all of our customers and we wish to inform you that you will now receive all volume covers as part of your prize. The additional year books are not part of this plan. In addition, we'd also like to provide you with three months' free access to our triple-issue plan so you can*

see just how easy it is to build your encyclopedia at home!
That's right! You'll receive three issues per week for three
months completely free of charge! And we also send our best
wishes for Davey on his trip to the doctor's. I hope the news is
good news. The falconry issue should be by now safely in
his hands.
Yours sincerely,
Martha Brent
General Sales Manager

Mother smiled while we clicked issues into volume covers.

"I knew Martha would do the right thing," said Mother.

"She sure is kind," said Davey.

"I wouldn't go that far," said Mother.

The banished beetle issue came back out of Mother's bedroom so it could be fastened into the *B* volume cover. I was relieved to see those pages again. Something settled when I saw all those antennae and serrated legs, all the shells, big and small.

"I just don't understand," said Mother, shaking her head, but I could tell she was trying.

"I just want to know about them," I pleaded back. "I just . . . want to know."

Davey showed the covers to Mr. King when he came for Friday dinner. Mr. King rolled his eyes like he was looking at something useless. *His fruit is full of worms*, I said to myself silently, *his fruit is full of worms*. It was like whispering a curse and it made me feel calmer.

He acted familiar now, almost like he owned the place. He plonked himself down on the sofa and waited for his glass of milk. He said, "Who is the freak in the suit next door?"

"Not in front of the children, Mr. King," said Mother.

"Oh sorry, Mrs. Spink," said Mr. King and Mother giggled nervously, but distractedly, because she had a lot on her mind. Davey's brain, for instance. I imagined Mr. King getting attacked by the abominable snowman and then embalmed, all while I stared politely into space.

"Hey, Davey," said Mr. King. "How's your noggin?"

"My noggin's great," said Davey. He stood up and showed Mr. King his new pants. Miss Finny the seamstress had made them because she could put a lot of seam allowance in, not like store-bought clothes. Miss Finny liked working with Davey. She never saw him as a problem. Her little ebony face could have fit inside his hand. Miss Finny liked all the lengths of Davey, his one leg longer than the other.

"Well, you give my brain a good gallop around the park," said Miss Finny when she measured him. "You don't need no fancy tailor, now, do you, Davey? You don't need no store clothes. You just need good old Miss Finny."

"You'll be a magnet for the ladies," said Mr. King.

"Mr. King," said Mother, exasperated.

Your fruit is full of worms, I said to myself silently. *May your fruit always be full of worms.*

That night I heard Mother say, "I'm really tired, Harry."

I heard him pleading for her to stay up a little with him.

"No, really," I heard her say. "It's been . . . there's been a lot . . ."

The door closed harder than usual that night.

After he was gone, I got out of bed and knocked on Mother's door just to check on her.

"Are you okay?"

"I'm okay."

"Why'd he slam our door?" Unsaid: *Why'd he sit on our sofa, why'd he look down at our encyclopedia, why'd he eat our pot pie?*

Mother shook her head. She smiled.

"Don't worry," she said. "Just go back to bed, Lenny."

"I'm worrying," I said.

"What are you worrying about?" said Mother.

"I'm worrying about Davey's brain," I said.

"It'll be okay," said Mother. "He'll have the operation. Everything will be fine. They'll send us the date soon."

She said it like he would shrink back into the shape of a normal boy. But I knew Professor Cole never mentioned a shrink gun. She smiled again, but she was a liar. I could tell she was having dark heart feelings.

Peter Lenard Spink. Peter Lenard Spink. Peter Lenard Spink. I whispered it back in bed. Did he ever think about me? Was he lying on a bed somewhere, thinking about me? I didn't like that thought, that thought made me almost cry. I back-pedalled fast. *Peter Lenard Spink. Peter Lenard Spink. Peter Lenard Spink.*

You worry too much, has always been your problem, was what I imagined him saying to me.

— 125 —

The first three *G* issues arrived on the same day that the letter from Professor Cole came. I held the *G* issues and Mother held the letter in our building foyer. She held the letter like it contained a great and monumental secret or reward, like she might open that letter and find a cheque for one million bucks, not a date for brain surgery. She held the letter and stared.

"Seriously, just give it to me," I said and then Mr. Petersburg walked in from the street and stopped still when he saw us.

Now, I had seen Mr. Petersburg a few times before, but nothing could ever really prepare you for it. He was tall and his thin shadow fell over us staring at that letter from Professor Cole. He had pale skin and white hair but his eyes were dark. It was like those eyes belonged to the original him, the beginning him, only that had all faded away.

"Haunted eyes." That's what Mrs. Gaspar had said and it had snatched my breath right out of me.

"Why?" I had gasped. "Why are they haunted?"

It was exactly the kind of thing I loved about Mrs. Gaspar.

"Because he has seen something terrible. Or he remembers something terrible," she had whispered and then blown a plume of cigarette smoke forcefully up toward the ceiling. "Or he has done something terrible."

Davey had never seen Mr. Petersburg until that day in the foyer. I heard his gasp.

"Wow," Davey whispered. "Is that really you, Mr. Petersburg?"

"Hush, Davey," said Mother. "Good afternoon, Mr. Petersburg."

I don't know if Mr. Petersburg replied. There might have been a whisper of a word. A small desiccated *hello*. But Mother was already taking Davey by the shoulders and was bustling us away and up the stairs. Davey kept turning back and me too, of course, once, twice, three times before we went around the corner. Mother wrenched Davey by the arm when he stopped to crane his neck over the bannister.

"Stop that," she hissed.

"But he's still there," said Davey.

"Stop it," she hissed again.

"Holy Batman, I saw Mr. Petersburg," said Davey at our door, joyful astonishment all over his face.

"Shhhh," said Mother, but by then even she had the giggles.

"He's not that scary actually, Lenny," said Davey when we were inside. "He looks kinda nice."

"If you don't stop talking about him, I'm going to get real cranky," said Mother and she sat down on the sofa. She had the letter in her hand, still unopened. I felt like seeing Mr. Petersburg was an omen, but I didn't know if it was a good or a bad omen.

She opened the letter carefully, neatly, and in the voice of someone handing out a prize at the Academy Awards, read out the date of the operation. "Operation date is May 6th, 1976," she said. "Transphennoidal surgery for excision of pituitary tumours." She let out a whoosh of air.

"Transsphenoidal?" I said. It sounded bad. *Trans–sphen– oid–al*. It sounded like something a bad wizard would say holding a wand, in a booming deep voice.

And the little *s* at the end of tumours. That hung in the air between Mother and me.

"Oh man, I can't believe I saw Mr. Petersburg," said Davey.

G contained giants. It was a smallish entry as though no one could be much bothered with them. Martha Brent, in her cloak, had swirled down the stone staircase and said, "We can skimp on giants. A paragraph is all we need."

There was no illustration, although the giant buttercup had one right beneath it. There were many giant things. Giant armadillos and giant bamboos. Giant clams and giant garlics, giant water bugs and the giant tortoise of the Galapagos Islands. At least that was comforting, the rate at which nature threw up big things.

G contained all the giant things and all the great things. *G* contained wonderful things. Yuri Gagarin and galaxies. Galileo and gannets and three pages on geese. Geiger counters and gases and three colour plates filled with gems. *G* contained golden eagles.

"Imagine if you had an eagle and in the morning you opened your window and let it fly out and you watched it go flying through the buildings but you knew it would come back," said Davey on the way to school.

"You couldn't keep an eagle in our apartment," I said.

"Just imagining it," he said.

"Eagles need to eat rabbits and such," I said. "I haven't seen any rabbits lately, have you?"

"What about rats?" he said. "There are plenty of rats."

It was true, sometimes we watched them scampering across the road from the Greyhound bus station.

"We need the Northwest Territories for your eagle," I said. We hadn't mentioned it for weeks.

I could see him picturing it all the way to school: Timothy hovering above us as we walked through the forests.

At the school gate, Davey waved at some first-grade girls. The cute-as-pie types. They giggled behind their hands. I glared at them just in case they were making fun of him, and they looked afraid of me.

"You're all red again," said CJ.

"No I'm not," I said.

I stared down Matthew Milford, daring him to disagree. He knew better. He handed me a matchbox with a little yellow bug inside. It was the prettiest thing I ever saw. I went to give it back and he said, "No, I c-c-c-c-c-c-c-c-c-c-c . . ."

"Caught it for me?"

My face turned a deeper mauve. I wanted to punch Matthew Milford right on his big hairy mole. Someone giggled. I shoved it in my bag, that matchbox, and pretended I didn't care. "Trans-sphen-oid-al," I said to myself slowly.

"Maybe I should try and let your father know?" said Mother at the dinner table the next night. Davey's peas fell off his spoon, a small avalanche.

"Let him know what?" I asked.

"That Davey is having an operation on his brain," said Mother. Davey went about picking up his peas.

"How do you know where he is?" I asked. "I thought you didn't know where he was?"

There was a rising tin-whistle in my voice. I was my mother's daughter.

"He had a brother around here," she said. "His brother's family lived on ... it was either Sycamore or Maple. I think. I could try and look in the phone book. There was a sister too but she lived somewhere north."

She mentioned them casually, that brother and sister, but her hands shook. She put her knife and fork down.

"I mean, what do you think, Davey?" she asked. "Do you think we should tell your dad you're having an operation?"

Davey's peas fell again.

I knew he would say, *I don't know*.

Davey always said, *I don't know*.

"I don't know," said Davey.

"You never told us he had family," I whispered. She never told us we could just try and find him.

"Hush," said Mother. "This isn't about that."

"I have cousins," I whispered.

"Lenny," she said louder. "This isn't about that."

Davey scratched at his corn-coloured hair. Smiled nervously. I could see he had the cousins in his mind now as well. We read each other's minds across the table.

"What do you think, Davey?" she asked again.

Peter Lenard Spink. Peter Lenard Spink. Peter Lenard Spink. The incredible disappearing man.

"I don't know," said Davey.

That night, with the traffic rumbling down below and the buses pulling in and out of the station we didn't run away to Great Bear Lake in our fantasies. We deliberately did not think of the possibility of finding our father. We imagined the cousins across our little dark room instead. We imagined them to life. We imagined them in Technicolor. We imagined them with trampolines and green lawns and tennis courts. We imagined them fresh-faced, white-teethed, the *Sound of Music* Spinks in a station wagon. We imagined them with dogs and cats and canaries in cages. We imagined them bright as stars until they burned behind our closed eyes.

The Search for
The Sound of Music Spinks

5' 6"

APRIL/MAY 1976

Matthew Milford's yellow-beetle gift went round and round inside CJ's bug catcher. It was a shining leaf beetle. *Pelidnota punctata*, your typical June bug, only it was early. It had four black spots on its elytra like it had been stapled. It didn't like elm leaves or oak leaves or birch leaves, all of them new and green in the park.

So I let it out the window in our bedroom, which was against the rules. I opened the window slowly so it wouldn't squeak and Davey gasped on his bed, like I'd just unlocked the gates to hell, and I could tell he wanted to scream, *Mama, Lenny's opening the window,* but somehow he kept it in. I let the beetle go, shook it out of the bug catcher.

It stayed there for a while like it didn't know what it should do. It clung to the window in the April rain like it didn't want to go.

It needed vineyards. "Fly," I said.

I didn't like its chances on Second Street.

"Why'd you do that?" he asked.

"I studied it enough," I said.

All the numbers Mother had called got her nowhere. She had opened up the telephone book to *Spink* and started. There were several Spinks in the phone book and I couldn't believe I had never thought to look. There was a Spink who lived three streets over on Fifth. An E. Spink. Davey and I imagined names for E. Spink when we were alone. Edward. Edwina. Elvis. Esther. Eleanor. It could be the uncle or it could be a grown-up cousin. It could be a grandfather. He would live in an apartment filled with old books and smoke a pipe. That thought almost lifted me up into the air, my head was so breezy with grand thoughts. I went to say it and then bit my tongue.

"I don't think that would be one of his family," said Mother when her finger rested on E. Spink three blocks over. "He would have said if he had family so close."

But what if I had a grandmother three streets away, little and grey, with a knee rug and a round belly and cookies baking in her oven? I couldn't stop it. What if she came to the door and smiled and said, *Well, would you look at you, you're the prettiest little thing I ever did see.*

What if she had a quaint little apartment and a cat called Nefertiti?

What if she had a complete encyclopedia set?

What if she had flowers in vases and needlepoint pictures on the wall?

What if she kept her teeth in a glass at night?

My mother left a message with a man in Broomfield. He denied he was a Spink, but he said he knew the Spink man she was looking for and would get in touch with him. No one ever called back. The Spink in Sycamore said he didn't have a brother named Peter Lenard. He had a brother called Bob. He'd never heard of a Peter Lenard. He didn't have any first cousins, no. He wished he could have helped, because my mother sounded like a mighty nice lady.

"Well, we tried," said Mother when she tucked us into bed. "That's the best we could do."

"We sure did," said Davey in his pleasant Davey way.

I could tell he was itching to get started on our nocturnal saga of the cousins. Ellen and Kelly had been jumping on the trampoline and Ellen had broken her arm. Grandma E. Spink was about to enter the story. She was going to come to the hospital after a long estrangement.

"How's your head, Davey?" asked Mother. "Does it hurt?"

"No, it's okay," said Davey. "It doesn't hurt at all."

"How are your eyes?" she asked.

"They're just fine," he said.

"How are your kneecaps?"

"They feel brand-new," said Davey to get rid of her.

"Good boy," said Mother.

But the truth was, he was growing fast. He was growing like his tumours knew they were running out of time. He got blisters from his shoes that were suddenly too small. He stared at his blisters willing them away. He knew what happened when blisters appeared. Mother got anxious. She started marching up and down, talking about the price of shoes. She started looking in her money jar on top of the refrigerator.

But it wasn't just his feet. His ears grew. His nose. He looked down at himself, held his arms out, looked at his hands, as if even he was amazed.

"You've got to slow down, Davey boy," said Mother.

"I'm trying," said Davey.

"Every time I see you, you're a bigger boy," said Mr. King when he came for Saturday lunch.

"Why does it take so long for this operation to be coming?" said Mrs. Gaspar. Her chubby arm barely reached around him when they waltzed in the kitchen. She smoked her cigarettes and told us stories about giants she had known in Hungary. They lived in the mountains and at night you could hear their footsteps, boom boom boom, far away. They wanted little children to be their servants. She would never have told that story if Mother hadn't been at work.

Davey and I looked in Mrs. Gaspar's phone book while she was taking a shower, thinking hers might have been different. It was the same. All the same Spinks. I ran my finger down the list and stopped still at the E. Spink on Fifth Street.

"What if it's our grandma?"

"Or our grandpa?" said Davey.

"We could go there," I whispered.

Davey's eyes widened. It was only three days until he and Mother had to go to Chicago. I was going to stay behind with Mrs. Gaspar.

"Why not?" I said. "It's just a knock at the door. We can run away if it's the wrong person."

"Are you crazy?" asked Davey.

I was. We didn't go. The days started going too fast. Davey's class made him a giant GOOD LUCK card which was as big as him. I had to help him carry it home from school. Mr. King came out to the front of his fruit store. Mother had been distant with him, she was busy, she had things to do, Davey was sick. He tried to wheedle his way in with us. He said, "Well, here come the two best-looking kids in town." I stared straight through him. "How you feeling, Davey, how's your noggin?"

"My noggin is fine, Mr. King," said Davey, smiling.

"Not long until Davey's operation," said Nanny Flora. "How tall did you say he was?"

"Five feet five inches," I said. On his side of the kitchen door his line was ever-changing. It didn't stay stationary for months like mine.

"I'll be thinking of him here and praying to our good Lord," she said. "And you're staying with the lady across the hall?"

"Mrs. Gaspar."

"Foreign, isn't she?" she said with the same voice she used when speaking of vermin.

"Hungarian," I said.

"She feed you okay?" she asked.

"Mostly goulash," I said.

"Put your mother on," said Nanny Flora.

"No, you don't have to come," said Mother. "No, she'll be fine. We'll be fine. Lenny and Mrs. Gaspar get on just fine."

— 137 —

Mother and Davey took the afternoon bus on a school day but I was allowed to stay home and walk across the road with them. The Greyhound bus station was dishevelled in the sunlight, the plastic chairs faded and the GO OUT AND SEE AMAZING AMERICA posters weary and buckled. No one looked amazed. We shuffled forward in the line toward the bus and Mother panicked about me walking home alone.

"I walk to school every day," I said.

But there was no being rational with her when she was anxious.

In the GO OUT AND SEE AMAZING AMERICA poster we stood beside, there was a family looking very happy in a bus. The father was pointing and the children were leaning forward to see what he was pointing at.

"Go now, so I can watch you cross the road," Mother said.

"No," I said, "I'm staying to wave."

In the GO OUT AND SEE AMAZING AMERICA poster no one was catching a Greyhound bus to get their noggin sliced open. No one was leaving and not looking back. No one was running away. No men with nicotine stains on their fingers saying goodbye forever.

"Please can she stay?" said Davey. He was carrying the complete *F* volume because falconry had been clicked inside. Falconry was his favourite even though the eagles entry was much better. Falconry was about humans and birds of prey together, was how he explained it.

"Everything will be fine," I said to Davey.

"Give your brother a hug," said Mother.

"No," I said.

"Oh, you upset me," she said.

Then the bus driver was calling for everyone to get on.

"Bye, Davey boy," I said. It was the only way I knew how to say goodbye.

"Bye, Lenny," said Davey.

When they took their seats inside Mother made hand signals at me to go, to start walking back so she could watch me, but I didn't. I stared at Davey and he stared at me. I saw him make the bombardier beetle fart noise, I saw my mother look displeased. Then the bus was pulling out and he put his one great hand up against the window and I raised my hand outside. Then they were gone and I was walking back in the bright May sunshine alone.

The package was lying on the floor beside our mailbox, beside the letters for Mr. Petersburg from Louisiana State Penitentiary and Leavenworth in Kansas and Sing Sing in New York state. We liked to see those ones from Sing Sing. *Sing Sing*, Davey always said under his breath, as if it were magical. *Don't you dare touch those letters*, Mother always cried.

The package was from the Burrell's Publishing Company, addressed to Mother. I opened it. I normally wouldn't, but Mother wasn't there and maybe it was important. Maybe they had decided to give us the year books for free too. Maybe they wanted us to come to Indianapolis for a free tour of the headquarters. Maybe they wanted me to write some articles on beetles for them.

I ripped it open. It was bigger than our normal packages, bigger even than the packages with triple issues. Inside were *H* issues, six of them all together. A letter too and my heart gave a little lurch.

April 30, 1976
Burrell's Publishing Company Ltd
7001 West Washington Street
Indianapolis, Indiana 46241

OUR GIFT TO YOU IS
THE GIFT OF KNOWLEDGE

Dear Mrs. Spink,

We hope you are enjoying the triple-issue plan free of charge for the limited time of three months. I thought I would send all the H issues at once, for Davey, because I know he is sure to like hawks and perhaps hummingbirds. I do hope they make it to you before you travel. I wanted to let you know how sad I was to hear that Davey needs an operation. Everyone here at Burrell's Headquarters is wishing him a speedy recovery.
Yours sincerely,
Martha Brent
General Sales Manager

Mother must have written to Martha Brent. It was the only way she could have known about Davey's operation. I folded the letter and put it in my pocket. Mrs. Gaspar was seated on her sofa with Karl and Karla, head bowed, when I opened the door. I didn't interrupt her. I sat quietly on the floor and waited. She prayed the names of saints. She held a picture of Pope Paul IV in her hands. She kissed it several times and the glass was smudgy with all her kisses. She really needed to clean that glass. When she was finished, she opened her watery blue eyes and smiled at me sadly. Karl and Karla got excited that she was finished. They stood up and nuzzled against her.

She offered me the pope picture to kiss.

I said, "No thanks."

"What now?" she said, lighting a cigarette and exhaling forcefully.

I shrugged. I tried to act completely normal. But I had a sudden thought of Davey and Mother on their bus, going along the highway and I felt a deep sorrow because in all my life I had never been separated from them. It was like a trapdoor opening and the ground falling away beneath me and I let out a loud sob there in Mrs. Gaspar's living room.

"Oh, there, there," cried Mrs. Gaspar and she motioned me to sit closer. "My dumpling."

Dumpling annoyed me. It added a zing of aggravation to my sorrow. It made me want to cry more.

"We'll eat," said Mrs. Gaspar. "It will make you feel better. A full belly always makes you feel better."

I dried my eyes on the yellow handkerchief from Nanny Flora. I wouldn't have even minded talking to her. The day stretched inexorably. The apartment was quiet and lonely without Davey. His *Space Family Robinson* comic lay open on the end of the sofa and I couldn't bear to look at it. I looked at it out of the corner of my eye. Karl and Karla watched my every move.

I was glad when evening came. I unfolded my sleeping bag in the living room and the blanket was stiff and smelled like dog fur but it was good to be there with the light off, away from Mrs. Gaspar. I imagined the cousins, or I tried. Each time they flared to life then faded like a match in the rain. I tried to imagine them, all their scooters and bicycles, their Hula-Hoops and trampolines, but each time they fizzled and faded. Without Davey, they were nothing but embers.

H
Hungary

5′ 6″

MAY 1976

🦅

M rs. Gaspar's egg-yolk-coloured phone rang when they'd been gone two days.

"Oh goot," said Mrs Gaspar. "Goot. Tomorrow. Yes, Friday we will be praying then."

"The operation is tomorrow," she said to me. "Yes, I'll put her on. Yes, she is being a goot girl."

Mother sounded far away, much farther than Chicago. She sounded like she was calling from the moon. Her voice had an echo and I could hear the dimes dropping through the phone.

"Are you okay, Lenny?" she asked. I could tell she was nearly crying.

"Yes," I said. I wasn't. I was terrible. I was adrift. When I walked to school I felt like part of me had been amputated. I felt made of air. I could easily be blown away by the late spring breeze.

"Well, the operation is in the morning tomorrow. Here's Davey, he wants to say hello quickly."

"Hello, Lenny," said Davey. "Guess what?"

"What?"

"I saw a Ford N-series tractor out in a field on the way here. It was so good to go in the day. And hey, guess what?"

"What?"

"I think I saw a golden eagle out above the fields too, diving down."

"Are you kidding?"

"No kidding," said Davey. The coins fell through some more. He didn't say anything and I couldn't think of anything. I heard Mother say something.

"I have to go," he said.

"Okay," I said. "See you, Davey boy," I said but I think they'd already run out of money.

The next day, the day of Davey's operation, was the exact same day that CJ rocked out on the drums at the school assembly. No one expected it. CJ was so small and pale she kind of blended into things. Hardly anyone in the school would have known her name. She was just another snotty fourth grader. But all that was about to change.

Artie Sellick was the seventh grader who played the drums in the school band. There was a drumming band as well, but this was the real drum kit, the full kit, that backed up the orchestra. And that day at assembly Artie was sick.

His understudy Martin Kennedy was also sick.

CJ, who usually played the triangle in the big band, put up her hand.

"I can play the drums, Mr. Maxwell," she said.

Mr. Maxwell looked over the top of her when she said it, scanning the band crowd for Lewis Ford, who had played for a couple of years, but then stopped when he started to learn the saxophone.

"But really, Mr. Maxwell," said CJ. "I can play. I have a drum kit at home."

She was like an annoying fly in Mr. Maxwell's ear. He looked down at her distractedly.

"I'll show you," CJ said, and she ran to behind the drum set and took a seat, which was too low, and played a quick round. She had Mr. Maxwell's attention now.

"Can you do 'When the Saints Go Marching In'?"

"Of course," said CJ. She played a segment.

And so with minutes to spare before the school filed into the hall, Mr. Maxwell helped CJ adjust her seat and she took her place.

CJ played with the band and CJ excelled, but she didn't stop there. When the march was finished, CJ kept playing. All the woodwinds and brass and her triangle buddies had their instruments in their laps. The kid with the cymbals had his mouth open, astonished.

CJ went crazy. CJ went around the kit. She broke into a galloping rhythm, she crashed up and down the scales, she settled momentarily in a 4/4 beat before she was off again. The whole auditorium started tapping their feet. They couldn't help it. Finally, she came down; she smashed her hi-hat several times, did one huge flyover, and banged to a stop.

The audience went wild. Mr. Maxwell shook his head smiling. Mrs. Dalrymple, the principal, took the microphone.

"Well, I think you should stand up and take a bow, young lady," she said.

And so little CJ, wiping her watery eyes, stood up smiling and bowed.

"Why'd you do that?" I asked when she took her seat next to me.

"I just couldn't keep it inside anymore," she replied.

I looked at the *H* issues in a small pile beside Mrs. Gaspar's sofa. I stared at the phone on the wall. I sighed and picked up the first issue and began to read. The day of Davey's operation, I pretended to be very interested in hamsters and Hawaii and hair. President Harding and the two Presidents Harrison.

"What are you looking at?" asked Mrs. Gaspar who had been vacuuming dramatically, her beehive wobbling precariously. She had dusted. She had emptied her ashtrays. She had stared at the telephone too as though willing it to ring.

"Halibut," I said.

She rolled her eyes and turned on the vacuum again.

I pretended to be super-interested in halibut, the heart (with its diagram containing three transparencies), halos, harps, horsehair snakes.

Hawks. A painful lump of sadness expanded in my throat and I quickly turned the pages.

"Mrs. Gaspar," I cried. "Look what's here."

I showed her Hungary.

I thought it would make her happy, but it didn't. She burst into tears and took the book from my hands and cried over the map. I closed my eyes and wished everything could go back to the way it had been. I wished no one had to crack open Davey's head like an egg.

"Hungary," she cried. "Hungary."

And I wished I'd never shown her.

"Here, look," she said at last, regaining a little composure. "Dumpling, I will show you."

She traced her white pudgy finger over the map. She showed me the mountains where the giants lived. She showed me the river and the fields and her little village.

"Oh yes," she said, closing her eyes, "I can feel it. I can feel the stone road and I can smell the wild rose, yes."

It was exactly the type of thing that happened if you were left alone with Mrs. Gaspar for too long.

"Please now," she said and she took my finger and she put it down on her little town.

I closed my eyes and tried to feel it.

I imagined a field with flowers in it and the warm sun on my shoulders and on the crown of my head and I was only just starting to enjoy myself when the telephone rang.

After operations, people have breath that smells like metal or that's what Mother said. Not then, but much later. She said, "You had terrible breath, Davey, I'll never forget it," and for some reason it always made him laugh.

"As bad as dog breath?" he would ask.

"Much worse," Mother would say.

They did not crack open his head but went up his nose, which surprised them both. And me too, on the phone.

"Up his nose?" I said.

"His nose?" cried Mrs. Gaspar in the background.

"He's doing well but he didn't wake up for some time," said Mother.

She had hovered near him in that hospital bed. She had hovered and fussed and rung the little bell countless times. For the blood on the sponge at the end of his nose. For the one time he coughed. When he turned himself over onto his side. When he wouldn't wake up. She rang the little bell.

"He's doing well," said the nurse. "He's a strong boy."

"When will he wake up?" said Mother. She was a nursing aide but the sight of Davey lying like that with a sponge tied to the end of his nose brought out the shaky shivery Cindy Spink. The nervous, weeping, tin-pipe-whistling Cindy Spink.

"He'll wake up when he wants to," said the nurse.

"Should there be that blood on the bandage?" said Mother, fluttering. She was like a moth in a jar.

"It's just a little," said the nurse. "It's normal."

"I don't know," said Mother. "Are you sure he's just sleeping?"

"Yes, honey," said the nurse. "He's just sleeping."

When the nurse was gone, Davey opened his eyes.

He had blue eyes, Davey, very clear. His lashes were long and thick and curved up ward like an old-fashioned movie star's. Mother rang the bell like there was a fire.

"Hello," said Davey. He looked glad to be back. He looked

around the room. He smiled at Mother. He rubbed his head and the nurse took his hand and told him not to touch his nose.

"Oh," said Mother, and she began to cry against his arm.

"Have I stopped growing?" he asked.

"Hush," said Mother.

"Oh, praise the Lord," said Mrs. Gaspar. "He's goot. He's goot, Lenora. He's goot."

She did a little dance in her shaggy bathrobe. I smiled but I also wanted to bury my head in my hands and cry. I did when it was night, soundlessly, my mouth open. I cried and cried until I was hollowed out inside and just a Lenny Spink casing like a cicada shell.

I was happy. But I felt strange. The next morning, I felt stranger.

It was Saturday and I'd never had a Saturday without my mother or Davey. Saturday was cartoons on the sofa and if Mother wasn't working, she would clean in her pyjamas. She would vacuum and mop and dust and she would shout at us for our laziness during the week. I wanted to be shouted at like that again. It was overcast and threatening to rain but it wasn't my rain sadness flower. It was a listless, calm emptiness.

Mrs. Gaspar came past. She crossed herself in front of the Jesus. She smiled at me and I saw she didn't have her teeth in. And right then, at that exact moment, I decided I was going to visit my imaginary grandmother.

I told Mrs. Gaspar I was going to the comic book shop for Davey but I walked to Fifth Street. I walked slowly, pretending I wasn't going there. I looked at the street signs like I was an interested tourist. The sky was pressed down heavy between the buildings and the air tasted of diesel exhaust and rain. If Davey had been with me he would have told me to go back. He would have said, *This is bad, Lenny, real bad*, because he was a great big baby.

But I was on my own.

I turned onto Fifth Street and the buses and trucks roared past me and the traffic lights changed so that all the people crossed, and there seemed a lot more people on Fifth. They were bustling and hustling past me and I got bumped and snagged on some of them and a man in a maroon suit told me to watch my step.

But that was at the seven hundreds. The six hundreds were quieter. By the five hundreds, the crowd was well thinned and there was just an old woman walking her dog and two men looking at a newspaper together.

Four hundred they disappeared.

Three hundred I was on my own.

Two hundred and seventy-six. It was a tall grey building, narrow, only three windows across, with satiny smooth old front steps. My feet made a hushing sound as I climbed them. They'd be slippery in the rain. My grandmother would have to watch out.

Davey would have said, *Let's go. Come on, Lenny, I wanna go.*

But I stepped up to the door plate and read the names. Hugo. Fanning. Spiro. Lionel. Davidson. Petrovich. Martin. Cowell. Smyth. Ackermann. Spink.

Spink.

It seemed so strange to see it there and belonging to someone else.

"Are you okay?" asked a man and I nearly jumped clean off the steps.

He was small and wiry with thinning hair. He was neither friendly nor unfriendly. A neutral kind of in-between.

"I'm s-s-supposed to help my grandmother but I forgot my k-k-key," I stammered. I couldn't believe the words, surely they weren't mine.

"Mrs. Ackermann?" He raised his eyebrows.

"Yes," I squeaked.

He opened the door and let me through, then rushed up the stairs in front of me, two at a time, until he disappeared into the stairwell gloom. Inside that building was dark. A light bulb hummed beside me on the wall. Nineteen. Apartment nineteen, fifth floor. There was an old elevator with a metal grate but I didn't take it. I started the long walk up the steps.

If Davey was there he'd say, *I don't have a good feeling about this.*

Second floor, third floor, fourth floor. There were four apartments per floor, facing each other about the stairwell. I heard sounds. Sometimes voices. Once a door closing. Each time my heart banged a painful beat. Fourth floor. Fifth floor.

I stood in front of apartment nineteen. Even the number seemed magical. It was the kind of number a grandmother would have. I tried to calm down my breathing. It was all knotted inside me. It was quiet but in the quiet I heard music. I pressed my ear to the door and heard a violin.

A violin?

My grandmother plays the violin!

Even I couldn't have imagined something so amazing.

I pressed my ear to the wood again to hear the music. It was sad music, beautiful music, and that music and the grey rainy sky in the window above the stairwell opened the rain sadness flower in my chest as I listened. I closed my eyes, and as soon as I did, the door opened and I fell in.

Great-Aunt Em

5' 6"
MAY 1976

🦅

er skin was a story. Her face was covered in fine blue veins, as though someone had drawn all over her with an ink pen. There were bruises on her arms, some the colour of mulberries and others yellowing. Her legs were veined and dry like the bark of an old tree. But the tops of her feet in her slippers were puffed up and polished.

Her hair was cut close to her head, sparse, tufted, like a bird just losing its down. She had a yellow nylon scarf tied there in a bow.

She had blue eyes. I looked for Davey's in them. It made sense. I thought I saw them. I thought for sure I could see them. She had intelligent eyes, thinking eyes, a little sprinkle of whiskers on her chin.

"What are you doing spying outside my door?" she asked.

Every word I ever knew had been erased from my tongue. I stood there gasping like a fish out of water. In the end I managed, "Spink." I managed, "Peter Lenard."

Her intelligent eyes looked me up and down, side to side, maybe calculated ages and time. She closed her eyes, opened them just as suddenly.

"Come on in," she sighed, as though she'd expected this day to come.

I stepped into her little apartment. It smelled of cooking, bacon perhaps. I could see the kitchen and there was a frying pan on the stove and a haze of smoke still high up to the ceiling. There was just one chair in the living room. That was the saddest thing I ever saw. One single armchair. It faced a big radio on a stand. From the radio came the sound of the violin.

She said, "Sit at the table."

Down the little hall, I caught a glimpse of the corner of her bed. It was unmade, a blue bedspread, my favourite colour.

Peter Lenard Spink. Peter Lenard Spink. Peter Lenard Spink.

Her apartment wasn't messy. It was bare. A sad blue kind of bare. A stopped-still kind of bare. She sat down at the table and she looked at me long and hard.

"I can see him in you, yes, I can," she said.

She didn't offer me a drink and my mouth was so dry my words came out snagged and twisted on my teeth.

"Are you my grandmother?" I asked.

"Do you know who your grandmother is?" she fired back.

"No," I whispered.

"It's not me," she said with great force, like she was glad of it. She shook her head vehemently. "Great-aunt. I'd be your great-aunt Em—Ez has been dead years. Years and years. I can't even recall how long Ez has been dead. Yes, Ez is dead."

I guessed Ez was my grandmother. It was sad news but there was also a small kind of relief. My imaginary grandmother evaporated into a puff of smoke and here in her place was my great-aunt and I'd never expected that. A little cog moved into the right position in my body, a gear changed. I could breathe.

Great-Aunt Em said, "Your father, he never once visited me in all these years."

She pierced me with her blue eyes, as though I was somehow to blame for that. But I wondered if anyone had visited Em. There were no signs of it.

"His mother, the stories I could tell you of his mother," she said. "Now, she liked to drink, yes she did. She was good friends with the bottle."

"Oh," I said.

"Esmeralda," said Em. "She was the prettiest girl in the West at one time."

"Oh."

"But her boys had a hard life."

"So my father had brothers?"

"Why yes, he did," said Great-Aunt Em.

"Have I got cousins?" I asked. The colourful *Sound of Music* Spinks crowded around in my brain.

"Well, you probably do," said Em. "I think you probably do, come to think of it."

"My father went away when Davey was five. He never came back."

"Sounds like him," she said. "What's Davey like? Does he look like Paul?"

"Peter," I said. "Peter Lenard Spink."

"That's what I meant. I told you he never visited me for a good twenty years, since he was just a boy himself. Is Davey like him?"

"No," I said, thinking of Davey who was the friendliest person you could meet. "He's pretty different."

"Well, that's probably a good thing," she said and then she grinned suddenly giving a wide view into her vacant mouth. She had two dimples, one on either side. Just like I had. The bane of my life. I smiled back, ashamed and happy and relieved and terrified. I had never felt so alive.

I giggled nervously.

My great-aunt slammed her bony hand on the table and began to laugh too.

Mrs. Gaspar looked at me suspiciously when I got home. It felt like I'd been gone a whole day, that's how long it seemed but the hand on her mustard-coloured clock had only moved to eleven. That was all, two hours. Two hours and I had found a whole new family.

Mrs. Gaspar was watching the television when I came in. She looked at me and narrowed her eyes.

"What?" I said.

"Where is the comic book?"

"I couldn't find anything he'd like," I said.

"Pah," said Mrs. Gaspar. "In a shop filled with that many comics?"

What if Great-Aunt Em could show on me? I smiled and I felt my hereditary dimples, one hundred percent genetic. I un-smiled them.

"Did Mother call?" I asked.

"No," said Mrs. Gaspar. "I will make you a sandwich."

I'd already eaten a bacon sandwich with Great-Aunt Em. It was the best bacon sandwich I'd ever tasted, stale bread and all. So much better than Mrs. Gaspar's soup. We had laughed right through that bacon sandwich because just looking at each other made us laugh.

"I'm not hungry," I said.

"You are not hungry?" said Mrs. Gaspar. She felt my head. "Your cheeks are red. Are you having fever?"

"I don't think so," I said. "Maybe."

"I will make you a special fever tea," said Mrs. Gaspar.

"Maybe I should just lie down," I said.

I lay in my sleeping bag till noon then. I snuggled my face against the pillow and my dimples appeared. I tried to stop the smile but I couldn't. I squeezed my eyes shut and beamed.

Horse People

5′ 6″
MAY/JUNE 1976

"She was a good girl, my sister," said Great-Aunt Em, the very next day. "She was a good girl, your grandmother. After our mama died, each night she made sure I had a blanket over me. She sang me to sleep with our mama's own lullaby. 'Hush-a-bye, don't you cry, go to sleep my little baby. When you wake, you shall have, all the pretty little horses.'"

She shut her eyes and sang that song and she was the strangest creature I ever saw.

"She can only have been nine or so and I was just six perhaps. And we kept that picture of our mama wrapped up in the strip of cotton."

"How did your mama die?" I asked.

"A little sore on her leg was all," said Great-Aunt Em. "But it festered and she got it in her blood. We were a long way from any medicine, somewhere in Wyoming, Lenny Spink. We were always travelling. It's just the way my daddy was."

That made sense, maybe that's why Peter Lenard was the way he was. I sat on the edge of my kitchen chair, waiting for more story. I was shaking I wanted her stories so much.

"We were horse girls, Lenny," she said. "Our daddy taught us how to ride and girl could we ride. I could ride a horse bareback and blindfolded. We once rode all the way from Jefferson to the outskirts of Kansas City. I could ride any horse you put in front of me."

"I've never even ridden a horse," I said.

"You look like you could," said Em. "You've got the right posture. You've got the right manner. You look like a girl who knows how to talk to animals."

My heart swelled and my eyes grew foggy. I thought of my beetles. The way I understood them. I didn't tell her about them though. Beetles weren't the same as horses.

"Could my father ride a horse?" I asked and wished I hadn't almost right away.

Her eyes looked faraway, as though she were trying to remember.

"Your father," she said slowly. "I'll have to try to remember."

I waited.

"You haven't told anyone about me, have you?" she asked suddenly.

"No," I said. "My brother's away in the hospital and my mother's with him. I'm just staying with Mrs. Gaspar."

"Good girl. We don't want to do anything to give him a shock now, do we?" she said. "Not when he's just had a brain operation."

"No," I said, breathless. "I won't tell them yet," I promised.

The day after the surgery, Professor Cole arrived at Davey's bedside with his first version of the operation. He smiled when he saw Davey yet a dark heart feeling swelled and stormed through Mother's veins.

"Well, it was a tricky one," said Professor Cole.

He touched Davey's head, remembering.

"Did you find what you were looking for?" asked Davey and he smiled his big gap-toothed smile.

"I sure did," said Professor Cole. He didn't really look at Mother so much for this version, just concentrated on Davey. "They were big and a little unusual. But I'm sure I got them all."

Like he was talking about fish he'd caught.

"I would like you to try some experimental radiation," said Professor Cole.

"Radiation," said Davey slowly, his eyes wide. "Like what happened to the Incredible Hulk?"

It made Professor Cole laugh.

"We'd give you a little less than the Incredible Hulk," he said. "Aim it at the right spots in your brain."

"Holy Batman. I'm gonna be zapped," Davey whispered.

"I'll have a chat with your mother later, Davey, you need to rest right now," said Professor Cole. "Resting is good. Put your feet up and rest."

My mother told me the version for her was different. Professor Cole packed his smile away. Outside the office Mother had been taken to there was a steady procession of patients and nurses and carts bumping and rumbling. The charge nurse came and stood beside her.

"That's one fine boy you have there," was how he started.

Mother exploded into tears.

"Now, Mrs. Spink, the operation went well, but they were unusual tumours, and in fact, I'm going to be honest with you, the strangest tumours I've ever seen," said Professor Cole. "In most children I've treated these tumours look a certain way but these were different. The lab test will show us one way or other. Whatever it is, it's a rare thing we're dealing with here, I believe, and while I'm pretty sure I got it all I think some radiation would be good. We'll start as soon as possible."

Later, my mother told me all she could think was how fine her boy was. How it showed. How everyone who met him was charmed by his smile and kindness. She just couldn't quite take Professor Cole's words in.

"Yes, I'd like to try some radiation," Professor Cole said, "With your consent of course. It's a new and exciting field. We zap him with some radiation. Zap any tiny little remainders of tumour cell. Then we watch and monitor. But there are side effects. Sometimes brain damage, sometimes seizures, sometimes we go the other way with hormones, not enough, not enough of the boy hormones."

"How are you doing, sweetie?" said the charge nurse.

"I'm okay," said Mother.

"You're doing great," said the charge nurse.

"Does he really need the radiation?" Mother asked. She couldn't quite fathom it.

"I believe he does," said Professor Cole. "And then we'll see. We'll wait and see. This first year will tell us, we'll see how much he grows this year."

"How do I know what is a right amount?" asked Mother, like she was measuring a thimbleful of something.

"A little is fine, a lot is not," said Professor Cole.

"A lot of girls nowadays never get to feel the wind in their hair," said Great-Aunt Em. "Riding a horse ought to be something they teach in schools."

"Much better than math," I agreed.

We were eating bacon sandwiches and it was my third visit and Mrs. Gaspar thought I was doing her laundry at Bubbly Betty's Laundromat. I'd put her delicates in the washing machine and fed it coins and run out of there as quick as I could. I'd run through those spring streets like I was an Olympic sprint star and so that when I got there I had to bend over with my hands on my knees and Great-Aunt Em said, "Whoa, pull up a pew and catch your breath."

"Let me look at you," she said. "Yes, I see your grandmother in you. I see her there, all right. She was a pretty girl, Ez, oh, she was pretty with her golden hair, everywhere she went people saw fit to comment on how pretty she was."

I had to try and breathe over the size of my heart.

"What can you tell me about my father?" I asked on my third visit. I had to work up the courage. I tried to say it casually, like I was asking for some more ketchup. But I wanted to know things. In between Em with her dimples and me with mine, there was Peter Lenard Spink, an empty hole. I wanted to know what he ate for breakfast when he was a boy, if he rode a bicycle, if he did his homework.

"Well, I'll have to think on that," said Great-Aunt Em. "In the meantime, what do you think about running an errand for me to the grocery store?"

"Of course," I said.

I thought of Mrs. Gaspar's undies, not even dried yet.

"Your mama won't be worried, will she?" she asked.

"No, she's still away with Davey. He has to have radiation on his brain," I said. Those undies never needed long in the dryer.

"Radiation," she cried. "Oh Lord, don't be telling them about me then. They don't need any shocks, certainly not Davey."

"I won't, I won't," I promised.

Mrs. Gaspar was angry when I got home, and with her delicates still damp.

"What?" she cried. "Le-o-nor-a."

"I'm sorry, I went to the comic shop and then the time just flew," I pleaded. I'd bought a whole basket of groceries for my secret great-aunt. Mysterious things like denture adhesive and coal tar soap and powdered milk. I smiled at Mrs. Gaspar, just the way Em would, a little wicked. I felt sneaky and sneaky didn't feel too bad. Sneaky made me feel alive. "Let me make you some tea, Mrs. Gaspar. It was just an accident."

When Davey came home from the hospital, I was allowed to meet him and Mother down at the Greyhound bus station. I thought he might walk with crutches and have bandages on his head, but he didn't. I was never more relieved to see him.

He looked thinner but no taller. His head had been shaved for the radiation therapy. He came down the bus stairs a little unsteadily, but carrying his *F* volume and grinning. Mother came after him, small and rumpled-looking.

"Lenore," she said and hugged me so hard I felt winded.

"How are you feeling, Davey?" I asked. They'd been gone five whole weeks.

"I'm not too bad," said Davey, and he held out his arms and looked at them, and then down at his body, as though to check he was all still there. We laughed. I told them to look up and there was Mrs. Gaspar at her bedroom window, waving and even from there we could see her ecstatic smile. I knew there would be talk of miracles.

In the stairwell, I told them about the letter from Martha Brent.

I told them how we already had all the *H*s and that some of the *I* issues had arrived too.

"Hawks, Davey," I said.

"Hawks!" shouted Davey.

"Hawks," I said.

"Are you kidding me!" shouted Davey. I loved his face like that.

"I'm not kidding you!" I shouted back.

We were shouting and laughing so much and Mother was shushing us so much that we didn't hear the footsteps behind us in the stairwell.

It was Mr. Petersburg, *again*, one level down. He must have been moving slowly to avoid us. We mightn't have even noticed him at all if he hadn't accidentally dropped a letter on the floor. Davey looked over the railing.

"Mr. Petersburg!" he cried.

"Davey," whispered Mother.

Mr. Petersburg looked deeply embarrassed to have been discovered. Frightened too. He bent down to pick up his letter. He said something, but we couldn't make it out. He wore his powder-blue suit and his white hair was combed back severely over his white skull. The letters trembled in his very white hand.

"Hello, Mr. Petersburg," said Mother and she was pulling Davey by the arm away from the railing. She was pushing me in the back to make me keep walking. I craned my neck to catch another glimpse of him. He was pretending to look for another letter, as though he'd dropped two, not one.

"Oh man," said Davey when he'd been tugged in front of Mrs. Gaspar's door and Mrs. Gaspar was opening it and shouting out a hallelujah. Davey was being enfolded into her arms just as Mr. Petersburg made it to the landing. I looked back, before Mrs. Gaspar's door closed, to see him gliding silently across the floor.

Our eyes met for just a heartbeat and then the door was shut.

"Did you see him?" I said to Davey, to Mother, to Mrs. Gaspar.

"Oh man," mumbled Davey, from Mrs. Gaspar's shaggy bosom, "I saw him. I saw Mr. Petersburg again. I think this is the best day of my life."

Mother told Mrs. Gaspar the story in the shrine-to-the-Apollo-landing kitchen. The shrine to Neil Armstrong. The shrine to the moon. She told the story while Davey slept on Mrs. Gaspar's sofa. He fell asleep just like that, about ten minutes after he got in the door. I bit my bottom lip and watched him.

Mother picked at a piece of tape holding a newspaper article to the wall. Smoothed it down, picked again. She explained the operation to Mrs. Gaspar. She explained the tumours. "They were unusual, he said. He thinks he got them all." She explained the radiation as best she could. "They shaved his head and drew an X in marker pen, so they knew where to zap him."

"They zapped him!" shouted Mrs. Gaspar, who read *The Incredible Hulk* comics when Davey was finished with them. "Oh, Cyn-thi-a, I do not like to hear such things."

I sat listening on the floor, my back against the door frame, my legs stretched up, examining my holy trinity of warts. Davey slept on.

"Yes," said Mother, finger up to her lips. "Zap."

"I don't like this zap," said Mrs. Gaspar.

"He had three zaps," said Mother. "And he might need more. He needs his blood tested in three months. The zapping didn't affect him so much. The professor was pleased. It's just made him mighty sleepy but sleepy is normal."

The next day, Mother discussed it with Mr. King. He couldn't wait to get up to our apartment the minute he knew they were back. His eyes needed to goggle all over her. He listened absent-mindedly, holding three large Valencia oranges.

He listened to the word *tumours* and the word *operation* and the word *radiation*, but they didn't much affect him. They pinged off him like he was wearing armour.

"So we just watch and wait now and he has his blood checked again in three months," she said.

"You need me to take you out to dinner," I heard him say. "Somewhere special. You need a break from all this worrying."

I felt Mother bristle. I could feel it even from the living room. My bristle radar was highly tuned. I saw her relieve him of his oranges and put them down, rather hard, into the fruit bowl. Mother was making meatloaf. The house had a meat-loafy smell that forever after would remind me of Mr. King. Davey was looking at inventions. I was itching for insects but he wouldn't hand over the issue.

"Come on," I said quietly. "You've been on that page forever."

It made him stay on it even longer.

The *I* issues had been a mixed-up affair. *I* contained some exciting things. Igneous rock, for instance, which meant fire rock. It came from volcanoes. Most moon rock was igneous. *I* contained thundering impalas and of course insects. But mostly it was severe and no nonsense. It contained Iceland and Ireland and Iowa. Immunity. Irony. Indianapolis.

"You leave him alone, Lenore," said Mother, because she had a new fully operational anyone-being-mean-to-Davey radar. "He can stay on inventions as long as he likes."

Mr. King came to the kitchen door. He smirked under his bristle brush. I stared straight through him like he was just a speck of dust.

Davey looked at inventions: tinned cans and pneumatic tyres and thermometers. Muskets and wheels and steamboats and telegraphs. He perused them slowly, closing his eyes from time to time to think. He looked at adding machines and a spinning jenny and a rotary printing press.

"Are you messing with me?" I said under my breath. He ignored me.

The radiation had not just made him super-sleepy, it had also made him super-annoying.

"You hitting school again when summer vacation is done, Davey boy?" asked Mr. King.

"Sure am," said Davey.

"Well, that will depend," said Mother, "on how you are feeling."

"Whether I need more zapping," said Davey and he put his fingers to his head and made the sound of a *Space Family Robinson* laser gun.

He really made me laugh sometimes.

"Stop that right this instant," cried Mother.

"I can't wait for school," he said, mostly to calm Mother down. "I hope that Miss Schweitzer is my teacher again, and I'm in a class with Teddy and Warren. Even Fletcher."

Teddy had sent him a letter in the hospital. He'd included a photo of his grandpa's Golden Jubilee tractor. Davey put it on our dresser right beside my jewellery box which contained no jewellery, but the unstuck sticker my father gave me from Buffalo, Wyoming.

Peter Lenard Spink. Peter Lenard Spink. Peter Lenard Spink.

I said it quietly in bed at night. I wondered what Great-Aunt Em had remembered about him. She would remember something good about him, I knew it. She'd remember a story and she'd tell me that story. I couldn't see his face anymore but it didn't matter now because in the darkness I could see her face. I saw my great-aunt. I thought of my great-aunt. I didn't tell Davey.

1
Insects

7 years
5′ 6″

SUMMER 1976

T he *I* issues were clicked into the *I* volume cover. Iambic meter to Ivory. I gave the insects entry ten out of ten. It set out the major classifications of the Phylum Arthropoda, class Insecta: the beetles, the mantids and cockroaches, the true flies and mayflies and dragonflies, the butterflies and moths and ants and bees and stick insects.

I caught a carpet beetle in Mrs. Gaspar's apartment. I looked it up in the beetle issue, but also reconfirmed its identity in *American Beetles* at the library. I didn't want to tell Mrs. Gaspar that there were probably larvae in her closets or her linen chest munching away on her tablecloths from Hungary. I kept it in CJ's bug catcher, knowing full well it wouldn't live long.

Davey watched me watching the carpet beetle.

"What if Mother finds out?" he said.

That question made me jump inside my skin, but then I realized he was only talking about the beetle.

"She never will," I said. And Great-Aunt Em was heavy inside me. The sneakiness didn't feel so good now that Davey was home.

It wasn't that I didn't want to tell Davey about our great-aunt. I did. I had it all there, aching to tell him. It's one thing to keep a normal secret. I was a small-scale secret-keeping expert. The perfume bottle in the doll-shaped bottle sent to me by Nanny Flora that I poured down the toilet. *That* was going with me to my grave. Mrs. Gaspar's yellow tea that I'd grown adept at tossing down the sink when her back was turned, that was an easy quick secret, no problem at all.

But an entire great-aunt. An entire person, all bony and angular and whiskery and filled with cackling laughter. All nylon stockings and strange orthotic shoes. All stories and sizzling bacon fat and radio violins. That secret was huge. Each time I looked at Davey, I knew I had to tell him, but each time I went to tell him, my thoughts clogged up. The secret sat on my tongue like a spoonful of peanut butter.

CJ saw it when I went to her house for a sleepover.

"What in blazes is wrong with you, Lenny?" said CJ.

"Nothing," I said.

"You're thinking about something, all right," said CJ and she raised her pale eyebrows.

"What's up with you, Lenny?" Mother said at the dinner table and I jumped.

"Nothing," I said.

"Penny for your thoughts," said Mrs. Gaspar in her living room.

"I'm not thinking anything," I said. But I was. I was thinking up excuses for why I needed to go somewhere in the afternoon without Davey. Why I needed to be absent for two hours. *I went with CJ to the park. I needed to go to the library. I really wanted to go to the comic-book shop. Davey's asleep, I'll just go for a little while.*

Really, I was running, the moon-rock-coloured buildings flying past me. I was running and I was running and every step felt like parts of me were flying off, parts of me I didn't like, parts of me I didn't need, the wind was taking them and throwing them behind me. I was pressing the buzzer and rushing up the dim staircase and I was telling Great-Aunt Em about my day.

"Something is going down with you," said Mrs. Gaspar, using the words of Starsky, and she looked at me very suspiciously.

My carpet beetle died. When Mrs. Gaspar wasn't watching, I searched in her closet for the woolly bear, which was the name of the larvae. I didn't find any, although I found a fur coat that was so thick and heavy it must have been a real complete bear. I whispered to Davey to come see what I found. "Holy Batman," he said. "Is that a grizzly?" We'd never seen Mrs. Gaspar wear it.

While Mother was at work, we walked to the park together, even Mrs. Gaspar, and I wished I could break loose from them and see Great-Aunt Em. I tried some excuses. I said, "Maybe I'll just go to the library instead, I've got a headache."

"Nonsense, dumpling," said Mrs. Gaspar. "A beautiful summer day is good for headaches."

"I forgot my matchbox, in case I find a beetle. I'll just run home and get it."

"Nonsense, dumpling," said Mrs. Gaspar. "We will put this beetle in my handbag."

I breathed deeply and tried not to think of Great-Aunt Em, all alone.

In the park, Davey lay in the sunshine on the grass. He watched the sky. I could tell he was imagining Timothy, his eagle. "How does your head feel, dumpling?" asked Mrs. Gaspar.

"It feels just fine," smiled Davey.

"I think you have stopped growing," said Mrs. Gaspar.

Davey said, "I sure hope so."

I found a stick insect in the park and with much ceremony and concern I placed it inside Mrs. Gaspar's handbag. I didn't know if it would survive the cigarette smell in there, but when we were home I gently extracted it and placed it in the newly vacated bug catcher. It was the biggest insect I had kept so far.

"I really need to go to the library now so I can read up on them," I said.

"The library will be closed soon, dumpling," said Mrs. Gaspar.

"There's a whole hour," I said.

"I'll come too," said Davey. "I need to look up log cabins."

"No, I'll look for you," I said. "Mother said you need to rest in the afternoons. Didn't she, Mrs. Gaspar?"

Mrs. Gaspar looked at me doubtfully and I held my breath until she nodded that I could go.

I ran through those late-summer streets, all diesel and clanging traffic, green trees and dive-bombing bluebirds. And already I could feel the first cold breaths of autumn hidden on those sunshiny streets. Soon the trees would change their apparel and the sky would sweep itself clean.

"You're such a good girl," said Great-Aunt Em. "Coming all this way."

K
Kyzylkum

5′ 6″
END OF SUMMER

The *J* and *K* issues arrived and we rushed down the stairs to meet them. We considered such letters exotic and they would contain exotic things. A wave of *J*s first: Jackals and jacarandas, jack rabbits and Chinese jade. Japan and jellyfish and Thomas Jefferson. A street map of Jerusalem. Then the *K*s: katydids, Kansas and Kentucky, the Bluegrass State. King snakes and kingbirds and king crabs. Two pages on how to make kites.

Kyzylkum; the great Central Asian desert.

"Kyzylkum," I said as I fed Charlie, my stick insect, "Kyzylkum."

Kyzylkum was the most mysterious-sounding place in the world and I was glad for knowing it. Davey watched me.

"One day she's going to find out," he said, and I nearly died all over again until I realized it was only Charlie he was talking about.

"Like you can talk," I said. I knew he had filled out his application to join the Junior Sales Club of America. He'd taken that little form—*Please Sir, without obligation enroll me as a member. Send me my free membership card, free portfolio of greeting cards, along with a free prize catalogue*—and he'd mailed it. He'd done all that even though he'd been told not to.

I knew he'd also cut out the order form for the Sea-Monkeys. He hadn't filled it in yet, but I knew he would. He was going to buy those Sea-Monkeys without asking and without any thought for where he was going to hide that bowl full of happiness.

"But, Lenny," said Davey, "just think of the things I can earn if I sell those greeting cards. The nylon tent! The jumbo AF/FM radio, the Dacron sleeping bag, the walkie-talkies, the complete fishing set."

"Oh, yeah," I said, to placate him.

"We'll need those things on our trip," he said.

Great Bear Lake had not been mentioned since before his operation.

"I guess," I said.

Even though we rushed down the stairs to fetch those *J*s and *K*s, something had changed between us. It was all my fault, yet some of it was his. He was different and I was different, all in the space of weeks. He was quieter but also full of self-importance. If I went to lie on the sofa, he said, "That's my spot, I had a brain tumour." He kept the hawk issue beneath his pillow even when I needed to look at the Hercules beetle. I was so filled up with secrets I couldn't think straight.

I was dismantling our story of running away to Great Bear Lake, I knew it. I was folding up all the dusty roads. Scrunching them up, a fistful of paper ribbons. I was blowing apart our log cabin with one big breath.

"Lenny," he pleaded in our bedroom. "We need the tent."

I shrugged and stared at Charlie.

"Fine," said Davey quietly, very quietly for Davey. "I'll go by myself."

I had told Great-Aunt Em about Charlie, my stick insect. I was frightened to in case she thought less of me. It would have been better if I had a brown horse and I rode it fast up and down Second Street.

"A stick insect, you say?" she said, grinning. "Sounds like a good kind of pet. No mess I bet."

Her apartment was quiet and filled with echoes. My feet on the floor, even my breathing, which was ragged from running there.

"Put the kettle on," she said.

We talked awhile about this and that. She told me about waking up with the horses on empty plains, just her and Ez, riding someplace to somewhere else. They were always riding somewhere in those stories. There were gulches and campfires and sometimes even gunfire.

"So have you remembered some stories about my father?" I asked into a pause. I wondered if he woke up with the horses on the empty plains. I wondered where he went to school. I wondered if he had dimples, the way I had dimples and Great-Aunt Em had dimples because I just couldn't see his face right in my head anymore.

"Paul?" she said.

"Peter Lenard," I said.

"Well, I promise I will," she said. "Wondering if you could do a chore for me and run to the pharmacy before it closes?"

"Sure can," I said.

L
Log Cabins

5′ 6″
SEPTEMBER 1976

The *L* issues brought ladybugs and lacewings, larder beetles, leafwings and leatherbacks. I had dreamed of the family Lampyridae, the fireflies, and I was not disappointed. For Davey, *L* contained log cabins.

Davey drew log cabins. The log cabins replaced tractors. He drew them in the morning and at school and when he got home and before he went to bed. He didn't draw them cosy cabins in the woods with a sun and birds, he drew them with a ruler, log by log, with correct joints, like a diagram for how to build one. He borrowed *How to Build a Log Cabin* (with 56 illustrations and diagrams) from the library again and again.

He said, "First you cut down the trees. Then you measure out your clearing. You need to get your angles exact. Then you start the foundations and flooring so the cabin is above the frost. I would use dovetail notches, they look the best."

I said, "Do I look like I'm interested?"

"You will be," he said. "When I build one and it stops you freezing to death near Great Bear Lake."

"What are you two fighting about?" said Mother from the kitchen where she was making meatloaf and Mr. King was watching.

Davey went back to the *Burrell's Build-It-at-Home* log cabin entry which he must have memorized already. He ran his fingers along the lines.

"Oh, you'll thank me," he said under his breath, eyeballing me.

"Would you look at those log cabins?" said Mr. King, his shadow falling over us. I studied the entry on larvae like my life depended on it.

"Maybe you're going to be an architect," said Mother, coming in with the meatloaf. She looked tired. I could tell she was thinking about other things. Radiotherapy, for instance. A letter had come from Professor Cole reminding us of Davey's check-up appointment. If Mr. King hadn't been there, she would have slammed that meatloaf right down on the table.

"No, I'm just going to build one log cabin," said Davey.

"Where are you going to build it?" asked Mr. King.

"Way up north, in the Northwest Territories. At Great Bear Lake."

I raised my eyes from larvae. We'd never said that out loud before. Never.

"Well, count me in," said Mother, and her little busy frame materialized in our forest clearing. She buzzed about, tidying the cabin, washing our dirty clothes in the lake, scaring away all the fish.

"Dinner is served," said Mr. King. "Lenny. Davey."

Like he was the man of the house.

"Okay," I said, not looking at him.

I read: *Larvae occurs in the metamorphoses of various groups of animals*. I re-read those words. I felt my cheeks stinging. The living room filled up with the smell of singed meatloaf.

— *185* —

Mr. King slammed our door hard that night. We'd heard him say, "Please!"

"Please Harry, I'm just so tired."

"Please," again.

"Soon," she said.

I didn't like the sound of her soon. Davey must have sensed it too.

"I really do know how to build a log cabin," he said in the dark.

"Shhhh," I said.

"And when I join the Junior Sales Club of America, I can get the slingshot and the Smoky Mountain pack and frame."

"Shhhh," I said again.

"I know you'll come, Lenny," he whispered, and turned over on his side.

Davey didn't grow one inch. Summer ended and school began and we waited for him to grow. We waited and pretended to not be waiting. When my mother drew the line above his head against the kitchen door, she pushed down his hair perfunctorily and slashed the line above him, as though spending too much time focusing might make him start up again. We looked at that line briefly, as though we didn't much care.

It stayed put.

That line stayed the same in July. In August. In September. It stayed the same no matter what. When he lay on the sofa and watched *Days of Our Lives*. When we walked to the park.

It stayed the same even though he still ate the same amount. When we went back to school, the line stayed the same. Davey had his blood tested and Professor Cole phoned and said the results were good.

When school started, my new teacher was Mrs. Albrecht. She was no-nonsense but pleasant enough, and an added bonus was that she liked science. She liked people to bring in bugs and spiders. We had a classroom ant farm. She asked for volunteer ant farm custodians and my hand shot up so high I nearly hit the roof. "I see you like the insect world, Lenny Spink," she said to me in front of the whole class. "It's good to see. It's a real good thing to see."

I couldn't help my smile. I tried to cover it over with my lips but I couldn't. Another surprise that first day of school was that Matthew Milford had had his mole surgically removed, including all five feelers. Even more surprising than that was what happened. Girls started noticing him. It seemed everyone liked Matthew Milford without his hairy mole. Tara Albright picked him in Farmer in the Dell to be her wife.

I watched how everyone liked him now. He was a brand new version of Matthew Milford. A revised edition. They couldn't wait to read what was inside. I watched like an interested scientist to see if he still stuttered.

I found a chafer bug on a branch outside the art classroom. It was a dull brown with black piped edges. I watched it for a while, then took my matchbox from my schoolbag and caught it quickly. When I turned, Tara and Tabitha were giggling behind their hands and pointing at me.

"Lenny Spink is a bug lover," said Tabitha.

"Yeah, Lenny Spink just looovvvesss bugs," said Tara.

They weren't mean girls, really, they weren't, and I don't hold it against them. They were just enjoying themselves. Some days are boring in the schoolyard, and you've got to find things to interest you and giggle about.

"It's for my brother, anyway," I said.

Tara smiled and nodded. But then Tabitha said something under her breath and I knew it was about my brother. I had a radar for that kind of thing. I could pick out the words *tall* and *big* from any conversation within fifty yards.

"What did you say?"

They didn't answer, just giggled a bit more. Giggling was their weapon. It was a pretty good weapon. I felt my quills growing.

"L-l-l-l-eave her alone," said Matthew Milford. I don't know where he'd come from.

They didn't like that. They didn't like the newly de-feelered Matthew sticking up for me. Tabitha rolled her eyes. Tara looked dreadfully embarrassed to be found wanting beneath his gaze. I started walking. I kept thinking of that bug in the matchbox in my bag. I wished I was a bug in a dark matchbox. I tried to control my breathing. I tried to retract my quills.

"Don't w-w-w-w-w-w-worry a-a-a-a-a-a—" started Matthew.

"—About them," I finished. "I'm not."

"Wh-wh-wh-what, k-k-k-k—" he started.

"Kind of bug?" I finished.

I took out the box and slid it open a little.

We didn't talk. It was easier not to talk. We just gazed at the bug.

"You've got no mole," I said finally.

He nodded in the affirmative.

"I miss it," I said. "I liked it."

His smile could have powered a whole city, a big city, like New York.

I kept the secret of Great-Aunt Em inside me. I went to Fifth Street whenever I could. It wasn't so difficult once school started. *I had things to do. I'd forgotten something. I needed to get something. Leaves for Charlie the stick insect, a carefully overlooked library book I had to return. Something very important that I had to deliver to CJ.* It was all about timing with Davey. I had to wait until his favourite show was on. If that didn't work and he still wanted to come I had to threaten him. A topical threat. Relevant to the day. There were any number to choose from.

"Davey, I'm meeting CJ in the park and it's secret stuff."

He said, "I promise I won't listen."

I said, "No, I'm going alone. I promise I'll be home soon."

He said, "I'm going to tell Mama."

I said, "If you tell Mother, I'm going to let her know you bought the Sea-Monkeys without asking and that they are on their way in the mail."

"You wouldn't!" he cried.

He didn't come with me. He didn't tell Mother. I watched him at the table to see if he would but he turned his head away from me, which was almost worse than him telling would have been. His kind of hangdog-Davey ignoring.

Great-Aunt Em with her stories was always waiting for me.

"We were horse girls, Lenny," she said again as soon as I was in the door. "And, boy, could we ride, Casper, Medicine Bow, Horse Creek. Mile after long mile. We rode, Ez and I, we rode those dusty miles with our hair flying out in the wind behind us."

"Could my father ride a horse?" I asked. I was ready this time. I needed to know.

At night when I said his name in bed I pictured him on a horse as a boy. It felt good to be able to see him. I saw him kick those stirrups and gallop, and a little piece of me that was missing was filled in.

But Great-Aunt Em didn't say anything. She looked right through me with her blue eyes and continued right on with the story of her and Ez.

I ignored that but it made my nerves jangle. I put the kettle on for her and swallowed down my worries. I ran her errands. The pharmacy, the grocer, I fetched her bacon at a little butcher one street over.

"You Mrs. Spink's family?" the butcher asked me.

"She's my great-aunt," I said. I worried at his use of the word *Mrs*, but chose to ignore that too, chose to swat away that thought like a worrisome fly.

I had questions ready to fire at her when I returned from the chores. Questions about Peter Lenard but they fizzled out on my tongue as soon as I stood in front of her. I was scared to hear more of her excuses.

"You're a good girl," said Great Aunt Em. "Will you come tomorrow?"

"Yes," I said.

September 10, 1976
Burrell's Publishing Company Ltd
7001 West Washington Street
Indianapolis, Indiana 46241

OUR GIFT TO YOU IS
THE GIFT OF KNOWLEDGE

Dear Mrs. Spink,

I'm writing to let you know about a fantastic opportunity to grow your knowledge! The Wonderful World Book. *That's right, you heard it!* The Wonderful World Book *is published quarterly and each volume will focus on a particular region and its people, flora, and fauna! Are you interested yet? Hold onto your seat. As a valued customer, we can sign you up for* The Wonderful World Book *introductory offer for only $5.99 per month. Hurry! Sign up to this amazing deal and avoid disappointment,*

Yours sincerely,

Martha Brent

General Sales Manager

P.S. We're all wondering how Davey did after his operation. Everyone at Burrell's headquarters is sending him well wishes. I've enclosed a complimentary copy of The Wonderful World Book: North America, which includes the bald eagle. —Martha.

Trouble Coming

5′ 6″

EARLY NOVEMBER 1976

Mr. King saw me running home late. He was waiting at the Greyhound bus station for some boxes. "Where you been so late, Lenny?" he said, like he had a right to ask such a question. But more than anything he gave me a fright because I was running fast to get to Mrs. Gaspar's. I knew she'd already be making the dinner. I was supposed to be there cutting up vegetables, and the sun was almost setting behind the buildings.

"Nowhere," I said, my hand to my heart. "Nowhere."

"You got a sweetheart," he said, smirking. "I can tell."

I looked at the box of cherries Mr. King was holding. I needed to take something like that to Great-Aunt Em. I'd taken her a feather, a leaf, my drawing of Charlie the stick insect, but these were paltry offerings. I'd thought about taking my unstuck Buffalo, Wyoming sticker. I'd thought about my whole empty jewellery box. A handkerchief, laundered and ironed from a distant, more boring section of the family.

"Yeah, you got a sweetheart," said Mr. King.

"I have not, you wouldn't know anything," I said.

"Hey, you show a little respect, young lady," said Mr. King. "I'm going to have a word with your mother."

"See if I care," I said, and I crossed the road and didn't even look back at him.

Mrs. Gaspar was beside herself. She was praying to the patron saint of lost children and wheezing. A fine wheeze, deep in her chest, like a squeaky door.

"I just lost track of time," I said but she grabbed me by my skinny arm in her shrine-to-the-moon-landing kitchen. Neil Armstrongs and Buzz Aldrins watched the scene. She wheezed while she was thinking what to say to me. She knew more than my mother. More than CJ. Much more than Mr. King.

She put her lipsticked mouth on my forehead. I tried to wriggle my way free but her doughy hands held me tight.

"Tell me," she whispered.

Davey was watching *Wonder Woman*. He hadn't even looked up when I came in, but I could tell he was listening. He was looking forward to hearing it. I could tell it all the way from the kitchen.

"Tell you what?" I pleaded.

"Tell me where you go."

"What are you talking about?" I said and I crinkled up my forehead in mock confusion. My heart took off at a gallop.

"You know what I am talking about, Lenora Spink."

Mrs. Gaspar blasted me with her cigarette breath. I didn't like Mrs. Gaspar. In fact, I decided, I never had. I didn't like her and her big smiling Jesus and her wet blessings and her stupid dreams.

"I don't know," I said.

I thought she might snap my arm in two, she held it so tight.

"You go out the front door and you cross the road," said Mrs. Gaspar. She let go of my arm. She turned her hand upside down and wiggled her fingers like running legs. "You are running, running, running."

"No I don't," I tried.

"Pah, you think I am a fool. I watch you. And then an hour, two hours later, back you come galloping. You go to see someone and I want to know who," she said.

I looked at the floor.

"You are lying," said Mrs. Gaspar. "Little girls who lie, don't you know what happens to them?"

"I'm not a little girl," I said.

"Tell me where you go," she demanded.

"You can't make me," I said.

"There is trouble coming," said Mrs. Gaspar, shaking her head. "Big trouble coming. And it's all inside you."

Spaghetti

5' 6"

NOVEMBER 1976

🦅

The last time Mr. King came to dinner we were in the Ms. The Ms were massive. The two volume covers that were required to contain all the M things of the world read Macau to metabolism. Metal to mythology. The Ms were going to take months but already there was the Mackenzie River that led to Great Bear Lake and Davey was happy. He traced his finger along its course, imagined building his log cabin there.

Mr. King came for dinner for the last time and it was spaghetti. Mr. King's appetite for spaghetti seemed to know no bounds. That night he had three bowls like he was trying to get in as much spaghetti as he could before he was asked to leave. Like he somehow knew that was his last night in our apartment, only no one knew it yet, not even him.

He was just waiting for those words he loved to hear: "Okay, you two, go and brush your teeth."

You could tell he was counting down the seconds. It was ten seconds to blast-off.

I lingered at the living room door, looked at Mother, but she shooed me with her hand.

We lay in our beds in the dark, listening to the pigeons and Mr. King's and Mother's murmuring voices. I thought about the dung beetle which can pull one thousand times its body weight. I imagined if Matthew Milford and I had dung beetles instead of crumb-lifting ants in our Olympic stadium. I would have a beetle called Hercules and he would have a beetle called Hulk and it would be a great contest. I was bingeing on beetle-thinking so I didn't have to think about anything else.

"Lenny, where do you go?" whispered Davey in the dark.

"Nowhere," I said.

"Sisters shouldn't lie to brothers, just like brothers shouldn't lie to sisters," he said.

"I'm not lying," I lied.

He was quiet then and it was way worse than if he'd said more.

We lay in the silence listening to the murmuring through the wall. Sometimes I felt like Charlie the stick insect, completely stuck in the bug catcher of my family.

"I promise I'll tell you soon," I said.

"Do you really, really promise?" he asked.

"I really, really promise," I said.

Then we heard a shout. It was Mother, shouting, "NO!"

It was a terrible *no*.

I jumped up fast. Davey too. We ran out into the living room and Mr. King was on the floor. He was on his back like a round dung beetle that couldn't get up.

"Get out," said Mother.

He struggled there on the floor, rolled himself over onto his knees.

"Get out, I said," cried Mother because he was going too slowly. He stood up and glared at us. He grabbed the keys to his Ford Gran Torino with great effect.

He said, "You'll be sorry for this."

And that was the last time Mr. King ever came to our apartment for dinner.

The Junior Sales Club of America

5′ 6″

NOVEMBER/DECEMBER 1976

After Mr. King, Mother was calm. She brushed her teeth and brushed her hair. She tucked us in and kissed us on the heads. When we tried to talk about it, she said, "Hush, now, we don't have to think about him anymore." And in the morning, she was still calm too. She put on her pink uniform and tied up her hair and smiled. But it was a dreadful calm. An empty calm. She was like the *Mary Celeste* drifting at sea. She was the *Cindy Spink*, all perfectly in order on the outside, but empty below decks.

The next day rain came. Endless rain. Biblical rain. Rain that drenched you through in seconds. Davey and I walked to school in that rain, his imaginary golden eagle on his shoulder. We wore our raincoats, but we still got wet. That rain had a way of getting in everywhere. We crossed the road so we didn't have to pass Mr. King's "King of Fruit" Fruit Store where our mother didn't work anymore.

She stayed calm all that week. She didn't cook any of our normal dinners, as though she couldn't bear to make meatloaf or spaghetti or pot pie ever again. She made us scrambled eggs and poached eggs and once just toast with honey. The rain fell down past my window and the rain sadness flower opened up inside my heart. I thought of sad things. All the beetles clinging to leaves. All the kittens lost without mothers. Great-Aunt Em streets away with the rain falling past her window. Mother asked about our days. She scraped the leftovers off our plates onto her "King of Fruit" Fruit Store shirt lying crumpled at the bottom of the trash.

We read quietly in the evenings, whispered our way through Macedonia, Machu Pichu, magma, Manitoba. Magic, Middle Ages, medicine.

She said Davey could apply for the Junior Sales Club of America even though he had already applied. He had the greeting cards and his press-out membership card and the crummy little flag to stick in his cap.

Mother said, "I don't really like the idea of you going door to door, but Lenny can go with you."

"I'm not selling greeting cards," I said. "I'm not. I'll tie myself to my bed if you try to make me."

She didn't yell like she normally would. She said, "Please do this for me, just this once, Lenny."

We went business to business, cowering under the eaves along Second Street selling the greeting cards on Saturday morning. Davey had his heart set on the Dacron sleeping bag and nylon tent. For that he needed to sell thirty-five boxes of cards. Mr. Kelmendi didn't buy any although he went painstakingly through each and every card in the box. Davey tried his hardest to sell him a box. I knew it was going to be a long day.

Miss Finny bought one and she checked the length of his pants, even though he hadn't grown an inch, which was annoying because then Davey sat in her little changing room in his underpants, telling Miss Finny all about the sleeping bags and nylon tents and transistor radios. The wooden guitar, the butterfly net, the complete fishing set.

He sold a box at the bank.

No boxes to the Three Brothers Trapani.

He didn't sell enough to even get the field glasses, which was the lowliest of all the prizes. He was not even close to the field glasses.

"Man, I really need that sleeping bag," said Davey and he was shouting above the rain just so I could hear him. "But I can't even get to the field glasses."

"Just focus on the field glasses and working toward them," I shouted back. We were wet and shivering. "It's only our first day selling."

"But I don't even want field glasses," shouted Davey. "I don't even know what they are."

"They're glasses that help you see in fields, idiot," I said. "For a long way. Like on a prairie."

"Like in Saskatchewan."

"Exactly," I said.

"So field glasses might come in handy," he said and smiled even though his Junior Sales Club cap flag was limp and soggy. You seriously never met anyone more optimistic than Davey.

We started walking home. We saw Mr. King unloading some fruit from a truck in front of his shop. There was a new woman working there now. She was wearing the shirt with the banana on the pocket. The rain dripped down my face and I didn't know I'd even stopped until Davey pulled me by the hand.

"Come on, Lenny," he said.

But Mr. King looked right through us like he didn't know us. He looked right through us like we had never been in his Ford Gran Torino, and he had never sat at our table eating meatloaf. Like he'd never been asked to leave on spaghetti night for trying to kiss our mother. It was a strange thing and it ruffled me. It made me ruffled the way I saw Mother get ruffled. I wanted to stick out my quills. I wanted to grab a rock and throw it through his stupid fruit shop window, only his window wasn't glass, but an awning that he pulled down. And there were no rocks. I'd have to walk all the way to the park to find one. That was the bad thing about living in the city.

In Great-Aunt Em's stories there were rocks everywhere. There were ravines. There was gunfire and horses thundering down dusty streets. I winced, Great-Aunt Em a jagged secret inside me.

That rain sadness flower opened up even wider inside me and it hurt.

More of the *M*s, the *M*s never ended. Machines, Madrid, mammoths. Magnifying glasses and magnets. Mapmaking, Maine, Maryland, Massachusetts, Montana. Mantises, midges and millipedes. Music and the moon.

Davey's Sea-Monkey kit had arrived. The small package lay there on the floor beside Mr. Petersburg's letters from the Folsom State and Marion penitentiaries. Davey picked it up slowly and swallowed hard. He looked terrified. He was the world's worst liar. But Mother wouldn't have noticed if he'd built a giant aquarium in the living room and life-size Sea-Monkeys floated around right in front of her eating ice-creams. Mother lay on her bed like a statue of a lady on top of a tomb. The rain came down and it felt like we were going to be washed away.

I ran in that rain to Fifth Street. I ran in that rain wanting to see Great-Aunt Em, but frightened of it too. I didn't know how I'd find her. Sometimes she was cheerful and other times sullen. "I've got no food in my refrigerator," she said, like it was my doing. "How about you run down to the store and get us some supper?" She had a small green plastic purse and she gave it to me. She wrote a list that was more than just things for supper.

I took a prescription to the pharmacy for her. She had to take a lot of medications for her heart because it was old, she explained to me.

"Tell Mrs. Spink we're out of her pain pill, but we'll have new stock in the morning," said the pharmacist.

"Okay," I said and I wondered at the *Mrs.* again, longer this time, because to my knowledge Great-Aunt Em had never been married.

On the way home, I looked at her name on the prescription, and sure enough it said *Mrs. E. Spink*, which didn't make any sense at all. I tried to compute it right there on the street. If Esmeralda was my father's mother, she was married to someone with the last name Spink. If Em was her sister, how did she end up being a Spink too, and a Mrs., unless she also married someone named Spink? A new doubt settled in my heart and I tried to cover it over, like a dog burying a bone.

"So can you remember my cousins?" I asked her. The rain poured down past her window. I shivered in my half-wet clothes. "What their names were?"

"Well now," she said. "Let me think about that. There were two girls, I'm thinking, and maybe a boy. But it's such a long time ago. And they left town without so much as a goodbye."

"I wonder how old they are," I said.

"Well, I just don't know," she said. "I only ever met them once. They were the children of Peter, I believe."

"But I'm the child of Peter," I said and giggled, but I felt queasy too.

I told her about Mr. King and Mother. I told her about Mr. King's shop. I told her of my desire to throw a rock.

"You should throw it," said Great-Aunt Em and she cackled hard and it made me laugh too. I laughed as hard as I could so it might wash all my doubts away.

But I kept thinking of the prescription. The cousins she didn't know. How she never remembered my father's name.

"Come again soon. Please come again, Lenny Spink. You're the best of the Spink girls," she said.

I longed to know the others. I covered that doubt, I buried that doubt deep as I could. I ran home through those night-coming streets. The rain was icy and there was a new wind now. Mother said, "Where on earth have you been? What is going on, Lenore?" She rubbed my frozen hands. Her cheeks were wet like she'd been crying.

While Mother ran me a bath, Mrs. Gaspar watched from in front of our television.

"Tell me, where have you been?" said Mother.

"Nowhere," I said. "I just started walking and then it was a long way home."

"Pah," said Mrs. Gaspar from on the sofa, a plume of smoke rising from her ashtray.

The very next day the wind chased the rain away and the skies grew clear and deep. CJ's fine blonde ponytails whipped around her face. She buried my cold hands inside her mittens. I wanted to say to her, *I feel scared*. Because I did. But I couldn't because I didn't know what I was scared of. The wind banged things and caused a ruckus. It crashed against our classroom windows begging to come in.

I slept at the Bartholomews' house and CJ's drum kit filled up one whole section of their living room. She played for me. She got me so that I was tapping my feet and she smiled devilishly as she did it all. But I still felt scared.

Mrs. Bartholomew asked how Davey was doing after his operation.

"He's as good as new," I said.

"So it was a tumour in his brain?" asked Mr. Bartholomew. He was shining everyone's shoes in a long row. Girls' shoes, all of them, except his own. I tried so hard to not watch him.

"Yes," I said. "He had a brain tumour."

"Do they think that's it then, he'll stop growing?"

"Enough questions," said Mrs. Bartholomew, and she looked sternly at her husband. "You two go up and play."

Then I felt more scared. I covered it up by being funny. We read aloud from the list of the names of JC's future babies that she'd taped to the wall. We said them in silly voices. "Valerie," I squawked. "Tiffany," grunted CJ. *Jacqueline, Claudine, Pamela, Heidi.*

"Heidi!" we both screamed.

Pamela, Melissa, Lisa, Deanna, Cynthia.

"Talk about something else," I said.

"What about what you're going to be when you grow up, let's talk about that."

"Coleopterist," I said.

"Still?"

"Yes," I said.

"Drummer," CJ said. "In a rock band."

It felt good beside her. Her bony hip jutted into my bony hip. She rested her leg across mine. She smelled like apples and cold-sore cream. I tried not to think of Davey alone at home with just Mother lying perfectly still upon her bed. I tried not to think of secret Great-Aunt Em. But I was glad to be away from them all. I wondered if the Bartholomews would adopt me. I wondered if Mr. Bartholomew would shine my little shoes. The guilt that came with the thought twisted my insides into a tight knot.

"So what is your secret?" asked CJ.

"I have a stick insect that I hide from my mother," I said.

"That isn't a secret, I know about your stick insect," said CJ.

"It is a secret, though, technically."

"Please, Lenny," said CJ.

"I can't say," I said.

"Lenny, it will help to tell someone, really it will."

"Okay, I'll tell you one of my secrets," I said.

"Tell me," said CJ, lifting herself up onto an elbow.

"Mr. King tried to kiss my mother on the lips in the living room when they were sitting on the sofa and she said no but he still kept trying. So she pushed him and he fell onto the floor."

CJ was silent for nearly a whole thirty seconds.

"Holy cow," she said at last. "Is that why she doesn't work at the fruit store anymore?"

"Yes," I said. "And you want to know something else?"

"What?" said CJ, breathlessly.

"I'm going to get a rock and throw it at his shop and smash something."

"Lenny," cried CJ. "You can't!"

"Why not?"

"Because," said CJ. "What if you have to go to jail?"

My heart beat fast at the mention of jail. I tried to slow it down, but there was something else happening to me. There were hot tears on my cheeks before I even knew it and snorting out my nose. CJ was so shocked she sat bolt upright. Then she plunged into my chest so hard I was winded. She hugged me and hugged me and hugged me and told me that everything would be fine.

Igneous Rock

5' 6"
DECEMBER 1976

I might not have seemed like the type of girl who throws rocks. Great-Aunt Em would have been such a girl. She would have thrown a rock and spat after it for good measure. Then she would have twisted a finger in her good Spink hair and smiled slyly.

I wanted to throw an igneous rock because I had read about it in the *Burrell's Build-It-at-Home Encyclopedia*. Fire rock was what was needed to smash something good in Mr. King's shop. I'd smash his cash register. Or his refrigerator. Igneous rock was what I had on my brain.

Igneous rock, I said to myself, slowly and surely. Matthew Milford watched me scratching in the playground dirt.

"Wh-wh-wh-what . . ." he started.

"Igneous rock," I said.

He nodded and helped me look.

But nothing I found was right. Nothing I found was the rock I sought. I looked in the park too, with Davey right beside me. I ruffled through the winter-dead garden beds and I found rocks. Small rocks. But not the rock I wanted, a rock made from lava one million years ago.

"What are you doing, Lenny?" Davey asked.

I ignored him.

"Len-neeeeeee," he moaned in the cold. "I want to go to Third Street and sell cards."

I dug and found nothing.

"Nothing," I said. "Why is there nothing?"

"But what are you looking for?" he whined.

"Nothing," I said.

"You're crazy," said Davey.

It was Matthew Milford who gave me the rock. "Lenny," he said at school the next day. He opened his bag and he gave it to me. It was a big rock. It took my two hands to hold it. "It might be i-i-i-i—"

"Igneous," I breathed. It felt like fire.

"Thank you," I said, and placed it in my bag. He smiled at me.

"What did Matthew just give you?" asked CJ.

"Oh, nothing," I said.

"Did he just give you a rock?" asked CJ.

"What?" I said. "Of course not. Why would he give me a rock?"

CJ narrowed her eyes at me and looked terribly worried.

All day I thought of that rock in my bag. I was jittery sick with nerves and my hands trembled. I wondered if it was possible that I could do such a thing. Mrs. Albrecht taught us the poem "The Tyger", and I said those lines, *Tyger Tyger burning bright, in the forests of the night*, just like everyone else, but all I could think of was the fire rock. Davey talked all the way home, about Teddy and the tractor on Teddy's grandpa's farm, and I listened and I agreed and I nodded my head, but all I thought was *igneous rock*.

The day I threw the rock, we saw Mr. Petersburg and I took it as an omen. We came in from school and he was there bending down to pick up his letters from the floor. We both stood very still, like two children who have come across a deer in a forest clearing. He stayed very still looking back at us.

"Let me help," said Davey then, and he was down on the floor picking letters up for Mr. Petersburg, down so fast he nearly knocked Mr. Petersburg clean off his feet. "Boy, you must write a lot of letters," said Davey, gathering them all up and handing them to Mr. Petersburg.

"Yes, yes I do," said Mr. Petersburg very quietly. "Thank you."

"That's no problem, sir," said Davey. "I have to go to the post office a lot now that I'm a member of the Junior Sales Club of America. So if you ever need anything mailed."

"Well, thank you," whispered Mr. Petersburg.

"I sold two boxes of greeting cards but I need to sell seven to get the field glasses which are the first prize level I can get to and they would really come in handy in Saskatchewan."

Mr. Petersburg looked like he might disappear in a puff of smoke, like he was trying to remember the spell to do just that.

"Thank you," said Mr. Petersburg again even though Davey had only been talking about field glasses.

"Come on, Davey," I said, pushing him in the back because he would just stand there all day talking and smiling at Mr. Petersburg.

"You have a nice evening," said Davey.

It was an omen, I knew, seeing him.

"Can you believe it?" Davey whispered loudly in the stairwell.

"Hush," I said.

"But seriously, Lenny," he said. "I can't wait to tell Mrs. Gaspar."

Mrs. Gaspar said, "Pah, I see him every morning. There is nothing special about this old man."

We sat on her sofa and she blessed us. I closed my eyes and thought, *Igneous*. It was a good evening to throw a rock. Mother was working the mid shift and wouldn't be home until after dark. *Igneous*, I thought when I stood up. I said I was going down to check the mailbox. "We were just at the mailbox an hour ago," said Davey.

"But we didn't check our mail," I said. Mrs. Gaspar looked at me doubtfully.

"I'll only be a few minutes," I said.

I went to Mrs. Gaspar's tiny bathroom and looked at myself in her old vanity mirror. I looked at my solemn face for a sign of a girl who threw rocks. I was skinny and very white. My hair was thin and its colour vague. It couldn't be bothered to make an effort to be anything. It was the colour of cardboard, some cements, a certain sort of plain indistinct doorknob. I had big dark eyes. Nails chewed down to the quick. Boney knees. I didn't look like a girl who threw rocks. But ... *You want to throw a rock, then you throw that rock*, I heard Great-Aunt Em say. And I smiled timidly at myself and my dimples appeared. I took the rock from my bag and slipped it down inside my parka.

Outside the temperature had dropped low and the air was still and so cold it hurt to breathe. It was nearly evening even though it was only just four. A bluish cold evening. Blue like that corpse being embalmed in the encyclopedia. So cold it might begin to snow. I passed the "King of Fruit" Fruit Store and all the awnings were down for the day but I knew that didn't matter. There was no point throwing a rock at them anyway. I had a new idea. I went to the alley.

I knew Mr. King stayed doing his books after closing up but soon he'd be out to his car. I stood for a long time looking at the Ford Gran Torino. I thought about an escape route. The alley was a dead end. I'd have to throw and run as fast as I could. I'd have to unzip, throw, run. I found that I was strangely good at doing bad things. I was methodical. I looked at the rock. I looked at the rear window of the Ford Gran Torino. I looked to make sure there was no one passing. I touched my fingertips to the fire rock hidden inside my parka.

Merry Christmas, Mr. King

5' 6"
DECEMBER 1976

The police officer came at seven-thirty pm. "Who on earth could that be?" said Mother. "Oh my goodness," I heard her say.

The police officer came into our little apartment. I was in big trouble.

"Good evening madam, sorry to interrupt your night, but it seems a little problem has been reported to us," he said.

Davey sat at the table, his mouth open, his eyes darting, like he was watching a really good episode of *Wonder Woman*. But I could tell he was also hoping it wasn't a problem with him. I could tell he was thinking about the Sea-Monkeys.

"Well, what is it?" cried my mother.

"Perhaps young Lenore can take a seat here and tell us about it," said the officer.

That's what he said and I burst into tears like a confetti cannon for crying, just exploded, wailing.

I said, "It wasn't me."

I said, "I didn't mean it."

I said, "I didn't do it."

I said, "I did do it."

He was a very kindly police officer.

"What have you done?" cried Mother.

The police officer opened his little notepad and looked into it.

"It seems a Mr. King of a fruit shop at six sixty-three Second Street reported the back window of his Ford Gran Torino shattered and a large rock lying on the back seat."

"Oh no," said Davey dramatically. He was such a baby. "Not his Ford Gran Torino."

Then he stopped, remembering me and my talk of rocks. Me digging in garden beds. My tear party cannon exploded again.

"There was a witness, a fine lady by the name of Miss Finny, who was closing up her shop for the day and saw Lenore Spink running from the alleyway where this vehicle was parked. Is your name Lenore Spink, young lady?"

"Yes," I wailed.

"Did you do it?" asked Mother, incredulous.

"Yes," I wailed.

"Oh God, you didn't," wailed Davey and he started to cry. He hit himself on the forehead. "Why'd you do that, Lenny?"

That police officer must have never met a family like us. He must have never met a criminal who gave in so easily and confessed to everything. My mother had her head in her hands.

"Does she have to go to jail?" wailed Davey.

"No," said the police officer. "I'm sure we can work out something. I'm sure we can."

He must have never met two kids like us. One little scrawny rock thrower and a giant seven-year-old crying like a baby.

"Tell me what made you do it, Lenore," said the police officer. "You don't look like a girl who just goes around breaking windows."

I'd already confessed. My tear party cannon was spent. I felt so heavy, like I was made of lead. There was no point but to tell the truth.

"He tried to hurt my mother," I said.

Mrs. Gaspar came of course, as soon as the police officer left. "Cyn-thi-a," she lamented through the keyhole, "Mrs. Spink. What. Is. Going. On?"

She wore a mournful mantle over her excitement. She was in her pyjamas and her breasts swung low. She was wintery wheezy.

"Tell Mrs. Gaspar what you did," said Mother. She had stopped crying. She looked calm. "Go on. It's done now."

Davey was blowing his big baby nose in a handkerchief. Nanny Flora had sent him large checkered ones. *Jumbo-sized* it said on the packet, and I don't know if she did that deliberately or not. They were the type a farmer might use when he was out driving his Ford tractor. Mother would probably want me to call Nanny Flora next and tell her what I'd done.

"I threw a rock through Mr. King's car window," I said.

"You what?" cried Mrs. Gaspar in alarm. Her beehive wobbled, her breasts wobbled, her fleshy fat wings beneath her arms wobbled.

"It's true," said Mother. "She did. She has to go in the morning to apologize with the police officer and I will have to pay, no doubt."

"I'm sorry," I said and I could feel that my tear party cannon was nearly fully charged again.

"Hush," said Mother. "I think you two need to go to bed."

When we were in our beds she came in. She kissed Davey on the forehead and then me.

"I love you," she whispered in my ear. "I love you so much."

When she was gone we lay there listening to the traffic sounds and the building sounds and I felt like looking at the Greyhound bus station, so I sat up and looked. My mother's kisses were still bright on my forehead. Davey came and sat beside me. I could tell he wanted to say it. He wanted to say, *Why'd you do it, Lenny?* Or maybe he didn't. Maybe he wished he'd thrown that rock with me. Maybe that's what he secretly wished. We watched a bus pull in from somewhere and all of the people spilled out. An old man and an old woman held everyone up, the man stopping to take the lady's hand and bring her down gently, the one step, like something from an olden days movie. We watched that bus and then another until our eyes grew tired.

Our eyes grew tired and still we didn't say a word. In the living room we could hear Mother and Mrs. Gaspar. Mrs. Gaspar was probably telling her about how she saw me running all the time in the direction of Fifth Street. She would be adding that to my rap sheet. I didn't really care. *Call Kojak in,* I thought. Davey yawned beside me.

"Get into bed," I said, and he did.

I pulled his blanket up for him. His big criminal sister. He was shivering, probably from the shock of it all. I kissed him on the head.

"I love you so much," I said.

Snow

5' 6"
DECEMBER 1976

The police officer arranged to meet me the next morning before school and escort me to apologize to Mr. King. Davey asked if he could come. Everyone said no. Mother didn't have to go, on account of what he'd done to her. "But two wrongs don't make a right, do you understand that?" the friendly police officer said to me in the stairwell. "You can't take the law into your own hands, young lady." I agreed, of course, outwardly, but also thought sometimes people just keep doing wrong things and never get into any trouble for them. No police officer turned up at Mr. King's door and arrested him for trying to kiss Mother, even when she told him to stop. No one escorted him to our house to apologize even though he'd smashed a big gaping hole in our life.

"Two wrongs don't make a right," he said again at the bottom of the stairs and he smiled at me.

What about three wrongs? I wanted to say. *Or five?* I felt like I had more wrongs inside me. I was just a thin dam holding back all the wrongs.

We went to the alley to look at the mess: all the glass splinters shining in the sun. I'd smashed it good. A big glittering bullseye. Mr. King looked pale with grief over it. Really, he did. He hadn't shaved.

"Why'd you do that?" he pleaded with me. He didn't use my name, like he didn't really know me. He flung his hands up in exasperation, when I, the criminal, was brought forward. He wiped imaginary sweat from his brow. He closed his eyes, pinched the bridge of his nose like he was holding back tears. "Why would you do it?" he moaned as though it was the biggest goddamn mystery in the world that no one would ever get to the bottom of.

I myself was numb with shock at the thing I'd done.

"Why?" he said.

I didn't know if he *really* wanted me to tell him. I could have said, *well you kept sliding your eyes all over my mother and then you tried to make her do something she didn't want to do and then you got angry and then you pretended you didn't know us and that you never ate all that meatloaf and spaghetti at our house.*

That's what I could have said.

The kindly police officer poked me gently in the back.

"I'm really sorry, sir," I said.

Mr. King shook his head.

He was pretending he didn't know why. I saw it. Just a little glimmer of it inside all his misery. I should have said it. I should have. It would have been the right thing to do, I know, but it would have gotten us into more trouble.

"I'm sorry, sir," I said again. "I'll get a job and try and pay it off."

"Get her out of here," said Mr. King. He waved his hand at me like I disgusted him.

When Davey and I walked to school that morning, neither of us looked in the direction of Mr. King's shop. We crossed the road early. But in looking away, we saw Miss Finny the seamstress, so I had to look away from her too. It was getting to the point where I wouldn't be able to look anywhere on Second Street. Miss Finny, who had always been so kind to us. Miss Finny, who said, *You don't need no fancy tailor, Davey boy.*

"Great Bear Lake," I said as we walked.

"What about it?" said Davey.

"I really need to go there."

People at school had heard about my brush with the law. Maybe Miss Finny was making Tabitha Jennings's mother a skirt, or Tara Albright's mother a coat, and she just happened to mention me. Or maybe someone saw me standing with a police officer on Second Street, say Mrs. Milford who told Miss Schweitzer. But that morning at school a crowd gathered around me and it was Davey's turn to be ashamed. Kids were asking me what I did. They were asking me why I had to go for a walk with a police officer. They were asking me if I had to go to jail.

"Leave her alone," said CJ, pushing through the crowd. "Get away."

"Why'd you do it?" someone shouted out while I was led away.

CJ didn't ask me that because she knew. When Matthew sat down beside us she said, "No questions, okay?" and he nodded solemnly. Since he'd gotten his mole and feelers cut off, he'd grown his hair longer. It was shaggy around his ears, not so much a bowl anymore. He stared straight ahead, but I could tell he was upset because a pulse ticked in his jaw. If anyone came toward us he stood up and looked threatening. By *threatening*, I mean he stuck his chest out and started to speak, and that was enough for most kids. I'd never seen Matthew so agitated and then I realized he thought he was somehow to blame because he'd found me that rock.

"Sit down, Matthew," I said. "You know it's not your fault, don't you? I mean you gave me that rock but you didn't know I was going to throw it."

He stared down between his knees for a while, the tick, tick, tick of his heart in his jaw.

"But, Lenny," he said, perfect, no stutter. "I did."

The *N*s arrived in a great *N* landslide. Nails: A diagram. Naples and Nantucket. Napoleon's empire. National parks. Navy insignia. Navy warships. Nebraska. All of the *New* places: New Brunswick, New Jersey, New York, New Mexico, New Guinea, New Orleans. Newfoundland.

"New Found Land," I whispered.

"New Lost Land," said Davey.

After school, I went with Davey to sell his greeting cards. If we were going to get to Great Bear Lake we'd need the Dacron sleeping bag. Actually we needed two, which meant we had to sell every greeting card we owned and more. We needed the tent. We needed the wooden guitar so we could sing on street corners in all the towns we'd travel through. We would perform on the street corners in Grand Forks and Sioux Falls and Fargo. In Yellowknife, in Swift Current, and in Saskatoon.

I stayed a safe distance from Davey in case my criminality put off potential purchasers. He tried all the same people again. The Three Brothers Trapani and Mr. Kelmendi bought none but Miss Finny bought another box. Davey said it was a good thing he'd tried her because Miss Finny had said she was right out of greeting cards. I stood outside shivering and didn't dare look in. I saw two tellers from the bank walking home; they looked at me nervously, as though the next step up from throwing rocks was robbing banks.

When Davey came back out smiling it started to snow.

"Did she ask about me?" I said.

"No," he said, but his left leg jiggled so I could tell he was lying.

We sold two more boxes on Third Street, but we still weren't entitled to the field glasses.

"We have to save our pocket money," said Davey. "We can't spend it. I won't buy comics, okay, and you don't spend yours. We put it in a jar like Mama's jar."

Mother's jar was the one on top of the refrigerator. It was for the return trip to the city for Davey's check-up.

"Promise," he said while he fed his secret Sea-Monkeys which were really just a pile of sludge at the bottom of the bowl. I lay staring at Charlie, who was swaying pleasantly on his twig.

— 227 —

Those few dimes I used to buy little presents for Great-Aunt Em. He was asking for my Great-Aunt Em funds.

But I thought of the Northwest Territories too. I closed my eyes and thought of being far away there.

"I'm going for a walk," I said.

"You can't," he said. "Mother said you couldn't. Mrs. Gaspar too. No more walking off alone."

I said, "Davey, please, I've really got to go. I just sold all those cards with you. Cover for me just this once."

"You better not be throwing rocks again," he said.

It was nearly a week since I'd seen Great-Aunt Em and I was worried. Was she warm enough, did she have enough food? I could feel her waiting across the streets, and it made me sad as I trudged there through the new snow. But I could tell her about throwing the rock, and that gave me a little glimmer of excitement, waiting to hear what she would say to that. I bought a caramel kiss from the corner store on Fourth just in case she was angry. I ran there through the great snowflakes, through the wind.

She was angry.

She said, "Why didn't you come sooner?"

"Sorry," I said. "Things got busy."

"Oh, busy, that's what they all end up saying," she said. Like there had been other girls. My face burned in her apartment. The heating was turned up high. My nose started to run.

"I'm really sorry," I said.

I put the caramel kiss near her hand. She looked at it but didn't take my offering.

"I threw a rock through Mr. King's car window," I said at last.

"You don't say," she said. She chuckled a little.

"But I got caught," I said.

Her eyes met mine, her blue eyes, her Spink eyes, but they looked different to me. Like I hadn't met her before.

"Do you want me to run to the store for you?" I asked.

"No, not tonight, it's too late for that and cold out," she said, softer now. She took the caramel kiss, unwrapped it and popped it in her little mean mouth. Nodded at how good it tasted. "You better run a long home. Before night comes."

She looked smaller than last I'd seen her. Frailer. My neglect was killing her.

"I'll put your soup on for you," I said.

"Okay, put my soup on then," she said.

"Tell me some more about Esmeralda," I said. "Do you remember when my father was born?"

"Why, yes, she sent me a telegram of course. We were living on opposite sides of the country by then. Ez was a wanderer. She could never stay still."

That was where Peter Lenard Spink got it from. I stirred the blood-red soup, listening.

"He was a dear little boy by the time I saw him," she said and I waited for more, thought she was going to say more. I tried to imagine Peter Lenard Spink as a dear little boy. I kept getting Davey in my head. I jumped when the toast popped.

"Please tell me about my daddy," I said. "I really want to know about him."

It was an anxious rushed asking, like it might be my last chance. It felt like that kind of day. My back was to her.

"Paul?" she asked.

"Peter Lenard," I said.

"Peter Lenard," she said. "I barely remember him. Big man. Probably where your brother gets it. Why on earth do you want to know about him anyway, when all he ever did was abandon you?"

I kept stirring but I was filled up with sorrows like Mrs. Gaspar's Lady of Sorrows, like my mother. I was young and already I was filled up. The little seed of doubt broke its husk right there. All her stories, who she was. They cracked open, those stories, and all the cheap tinsel rained out.

"It's nearly Christmas," she said when I put the soup in front of her. "Less than a week."

"I know," I said, and I smiled at her. "I'll come back soon as I can."

"Good girl," said Great-Aunt Em. "You're the best of the Spink girls. You're just the way Esmeralda used to be."

That night it was very quiet in our bedroom. I couldn't hear the pigeons. I couldn't hear the trucks or the buses. The snow had covered everything over. It was monumentally quiet. That night in bed I whispered across the darkened room.

"Davey?"

I thought he might be asleep, his breathing was so soft.

"Yes?" he replied.

"I have something to tell you," I said.

Destination Em

5′ 6″
DECEMBER 1976

"**W**hat?" he spat in the dark. "Who?"

"Shhhh," I said, "you'll wake Mother up."

Then he started to cry. I couldn't see him, or hardly even hear it, but I could tell that's what he was doing. He was crying, the way Davey cried, with his mouth open and eyes shut and no noise to start off with, just jerks and ticks. He was a mechanical wailing clock. He only wailed when he'd jerked and ticked enough. I had to get to him soon.

I jumped out of my bed and took two steps across the room. I held his shoulders.

"Don't," I said. "Please don't. I didn't mean it. I've wanted to tell you."

"You should have told me," he said. "I should have come with you."

"We can still go," I said. Destination Em. "That's why I told you."

"When?" he said.

"On Friday," I said. "That's Christmas Eve."

"Okay," he said.

He didn't ask what she was like. He didn't ask how I found her. He didn't ask anything. There was just a bad silence in that room because of my betrayal. Because I'd kept such a secret from him. Finally, I heard his breathing settle and then we slept.

Wednesday he didn't talk to me. A steady rush of snow fell past our windows and I could have sat there all day and watched it because that was the kind of mood I was in. Davey stamped into our bedroom and fed his Sea-Monkey sludge and then glared at me. We walked to school with Mother. We had to cross the road so we didn't run into Mr. King. Miss Finny came out to say hello and I had to avoid eye contact. Wednesday was bad.

Thursday was even worse because of Mrs. Gaspar's wheeze. When we got home from school she was sitting in one place, breathing like breathing was the only thing she could do. She had a strange smell: urine-y, dirty, sweaty. Sometimes she lit a cigarette and had one puff, then put it out. I called Mother's work on her telephone.

"I'm calling an ambulance, Mrs. Gaspar," said Mother when she had rushed home.

"No," said Mrs. Gaspar. "Please. It. Is. The. Weather. The. Snow."

She had to take a breath between each and every word.

"Mrs. Gaspar," said Davey. He took her hand. "Please say you'll go to the hospital."

"Oh, dumpling," said Mrs. Gaspar.

"Please," said Davey again. "You're so sick."

So Mother was allowed to phone the ambulance and two EMTs came up the stairs with their stretcher. They listened to her chest and bundled her up in blankets. When she was laid down on the stretcher she turned a bluish tinge, a little like the corpse illustration in embalming which seemed a long time ago. Karl and Karla whimpered.

They sat her up and some of the blueness faded away and they put a mask on her face and she looked better. She waved her fat damp hand weakly. "I will be back," she said and then they carried her downstairs and out into the snow.

Davey was inconsolable. Even if she told me her dreams first it was him she loved the most. She had looked after him from when he was a baby. She looked after him from when she had to help him to sit up, when she had to burp him. She fed him mashed pumpkin off her mother and father's tarnished silver spoons.

They were close. They sat side by side on the sofa watching *Kojak*. They watched *Starsky & Hutch*. They watched *Wonder Woman*. They both knew everything there was to know about *Days of Our Lives*. They sat together on Mrs. Gaspar's bed and looked up at the moon.

"She'll be fine," I said to him.

"I hope so," he said.

"I know so," I said.

"What is she like?" he asked, and I knew he meant Great-Aunt Em. It was his first question.

I really didn't know how to describe her. I bit my bottom lip in the dark, sighed.

"She's not what you'd expect," I said.

"Okay," he said like he didn't much care, but he did. We were on a collision course. We were hurtling toward the end of something. I knew it.

We went through the streets in the snow. Old streets for me. New streets for Davey. "How much further is it," he asked. I said, "Quit complaining." "But Len-neeeeeee," he said. "I have sore feet." I said, "I'll leave you here then." It was Friday and we were going to the library. We had our library books in our library bags. It was Christmas Eve day and the street was bustling and busy, and the Three Brothers Trapani had on tinsel ties. Davey had the *Art of Falconry* in his library bag. He didn't really want to return it. He wanted to keep that book forever.

It was terrible that Mrs. Gaspar was in the hospital but also perfectly timed, although thinking that thought made me feel guilty. It left us completely alone all day. In the morning, as Mother got ready for work, she told us what we could and could not do. No wandering the streets, to the library and back, that was all, clean the living room, clean our bedrooms, feed Karl and Karla, peel the potatoes, play with Karl and Karla.

I must have sighed too loud.

"Don't you start sighing, young lady," said Mother.

"I didn't," I said. "I was just breathing. Can't a girl breathe?"

But when our chores were done and our library books returned through the slot in the wall off we went, trudging through the wind and snow. Evening and Mother coming home seemed so far away. There was something we had to do. We had to do it that day. I knew it without saying. I marched us both toward the ending of something.

Part of my heart wished for it to turn out well, of course.

A large part of my heart.

But I was fidgety with nerves and knowing.

Davey had drawn a picture of a log cabin and folded it neatly in his pocket. He was going to give it to Em, I knew it. He didn't say it but why else would he put it in his pocket?

It made me bristle.

I tried to un-bristle.

I tried to un-bristle for three whole blocks but I couldn't get my quills back in. I turned suddenly and asked him about it.

"Is that log cabin drawing for her?"

He put his hand over his pocket like I might just shoot laser beams out my eyes at it.

"I just . . ." he started.

"She won't like a picture of a log cabin," I said.

I was surprised to find I had tears in my eyes. The wind made Davey's hair wave on his head like a field of wheat. He squinted his eyes, looked sorrowful.

I bought the caramel kisses. One from me and one from him, at the corner store.

We walked in silence, the last blocks.

"You can give her the drawing if you want," I said.

He didn't say anything. I could tell he was nervous. He kept messing with his library bag. With his parka zipper. With his pocket. He made the farty squelch sound of the bombardier beetle when I pressed the buzzer and Em clicked us in, in return. Inside that grey building was cool and shadowy. We could hear footsteps way up, a door slamming. It felt wrong, is how I'll say it. It had never felt right but now that I had someone with me it felt more wrong than ever.

I opened her door with my key.

She was in her chair facing the radio listening to music.

"Hello," she said, didn't turn.

"Em," I said.

"That's my name, don't wear it out," she said and she laughed because she thought we were alone. Even her name sounded counterfeit.

"I brought Davey," I said.

"Who?" she said and she turned so suddenly that I thought she'd tip herself out of her chair. "What?"

For a moment she looked enraged. Her eyes bulged and burned holes into me; she bared her teeth. But then that moment passed, it was over in a flicker and she smiled and said, "Well, I'll be."

My heart was the size of a fist. I had read it in the two pages on the heart in the *Burrell's Build-It-at-Home Encyclopedia*. It beat a hundred thousand times a day. With Davey standing there, toeing the floor, it beat faster than it had ever beat before in Great-Aunt Em's apartment.

"Well, don't just stand there," she said. "Let me have a look at you."

Davey walked toward the chair. I could tell he didn't want to. He didn't like Great-Aunt Em. He wouldn't look at her. He raised his eyes once, fiercely, put them down again. I saw him feel the pocket where the log cabin drawing was. He wasn't going to give it to her after all.

She made small talk. It was brittle and stilted like someone walking on dry twigs. She crunched this way and that with her words.

"A bit like your father, yes," she said. "Or maybe Uncle . . ."

She stopped, crunched back.

"I never knew that side of the family, they all turned their backs," she said bitterly. But she was making it up. I knew but I needed Davey to be there to know it completely.

"You had an operation?" Em asked.

Davey wouldn't answer. He knew right away that he wasn't related to her. That we had no right to be in that apartment. He was angry and ashamed of me. She was frustrated by him and angry I'd brought him. But there was no going back. She kept crunching with her words. I knew it was the last time.

"You don't talk much, do you?" she said at last, and there was a nastiness that had crept into her voice. She couldn't be bothered anymore. Pretending. She was done with pretending.

"You two better run along, then. I've got things to do."

My heart pained so much then. My throat closed over and it hurt to breathe. I went toward her but she put her thin bony witch's hand up. I put the caramel kiss on her chair arm. She looked at it. I put Davey's there too because he didn't seem to want to go near her.

"Off you go," she said, louder now. "Run along now."

And that was how my Great-Aunt Em said goodbye to me.

When you are sad, you feel it in your heart, and when you are in love, you feel it too. The heart is always paining or fluttering or lurching or slowing down in misery. We ran home through the blustery streets and my heart was big as a goldfish bowl in my chest. The wind tugged at us. It pushed us. Its breath smelled of nighttime in the park and far-off snow fields. It breathed us and swallowed us and spat us out again.

We ran through the streets and Davey couldn't keep up with me. He ran like a baby, flailing his arms, his face all contorted. I wanted to leave him behind. I was one block ahead of him and I only turned once every few minutes to make sure he wasn't run over. He wasn't. But then above the wind I could hear him calling my name. *Lenny . . . Len-neeeeeee.*

The wind was loud that evening. It sounded like the ocean. It swirled and buffeted. It breathed in and all the shop awnings gasped. It breathed out and they shivered. He bellowed my name above it all.

I stopped so he could catch up to me.

Wet faces, blasted dry by the wind, wet again.

"Why'd you do it?" he said.

Why'd I run from him? Why'd I take him there? Why'd I believe her? Why'd I let her trick me?

"I thought it was real," I said in a kind of wail.

It went up and down, quavered. The wind took it, grabbed it, threw it away.

We walked the last two blocks. Mother wasn't home from work. The apartment was just the way it always was, small and cosy and tidy, yet everything was changed. Davey sat on the sofa. I started to make the dinner. My hands shook. I thought of her where she was, all those streets away. The wind washing between us like a tide. What I wanted was a hurricane. I wanted a hurricane to come and blow her away. To blow down her block. To blow down her street.

A tornado to come, to suck her up, slurp her up into the black clouds.

Mother's key in the door.

I knew he'd tell her. We were both crying. Even if we weren't both crying it would have been obvious we had been. We were crying.

"What the heck's wrong with you?" I heard her say. Followed by, "Lenny?" because it must have been my fault.

He started bellowing out the story. He started snorting it out his big nose. I peeled the potatoes carefully. He told the story his way. Which wasn't my way. His story was sudden and jagged. Great-Aunt Em just appeared like a flash, a bright witch exploding there, bang, and me saying she was real.

Bang. Her in her apartment. Far away.

I slammed down the knife. I marched into the living room.

"Shut up!" I screamed.

Mother looked mighty confused. She stood there in her

pink Golden Living Retirement Home uniform, her hair in a fountain. My secret life flowed out of me.

"There's no Great-Aunt Em," she said when I was finished.

"Shut up!" I cried.

You should never tell your mother to shut up.

"There isn't," she said. "I met his mother. There was no sister."

"His mother died when he was young," I said. "From drinking."

"I met his mother," said my mother.

We all sat down. I closed my eyes. The person I hated most was Peter Lenard Spink.

"What have you been doing, Lenore?" said Mother. She didn't say it angrily. She sounded tired and sad, that's all. Here was another problem she had to solve. First it was a rock through a car window and now it was an entire make-believe family.

I tried to speak. Really I did. My mouth was open but the words were lost.

Davey put his big head in his hands and bellowed. I sobbed into my own. She put us to bed crying, both of us. We cried and cried until I felt hollow from crying. There was no trip to the hospital to see Mrs. Gaspar. Christmas Eve shone down on the street below us and a big snow came, a white spell cast over the whole city. We cried and we cried until we fell asleep.

And overnight Davey grew an inch.

Christmas Day

7 years 5 months
5′ 7″
DECEMBER 1976

I didn't notice the inch. Nor did Mother. We woke early Christmas morning and looked out at the white streets and the pink sky. My heart hurt in a way I didn't understand, an aching for something that wasn't true at all. "Where does she live?" Mother whispered to me, beside me on the sofa.

"On Fifth." But I didn't give her the address. I couldn't bear that. Not yet.

"We'll have to tell someone," whispered Mother. "Maybe she . . ."

I shook my head and tears fell again, easily.

Davey opened up his present: a walkie-talkie.

"Are you kidding me?" he shouted with joy, as though yesterday hadn't happened.

I received a book. *American Beetles, Volume 1*. Mother had covered it with plastic like it was a schoolbook. I don't know where she got it from. I didn't know any bookstores with books like that. I shook my head slowly, trying not to drip tears on it.

"Thank you," I whispered.

Mother patted me on the back of the head.

"What are we going to do, Lenny Spink?" she asked.

"I don't know," I said.

We went to see Mrs. Gaspar. There were no buses, so we took a taxi through the empty white streets. It was the very same hospital that my mother caught the bus to all those years ago to have Davey, that perfect summer's day. But now it was winter and the streets were filled with snow. Davey fogged up the taxi window.

Davey had his walkie-talkie in his library bag. There was no way he'd part with it. He'd made me talk to him on it, unravelling the long thin cord and positioning me in the bathroom and then running back to our bedroom.

"Lenny, come in Lenny," his voice crackled through the speaker.

"I'm here," I said.

"Say 'Roger that,'" said Davey.

"Roger that," I said.

"How you doing?" he asked.

"Shut up," I said into the speaker.

In the hospital, lights blazed, doors shushed open and shut, our shoes squeaked conspicuously on the linoleum for miles. We passed room after room filled with sick people, trying not to look inside. We squeaked and squeaked and Davey said, "I don't know if I like it here."

Mrs. Gaspar was causing trouble. She was arguing over her dinner which had no taste. She said, "Pah. It is sloppy. What is it?" She complained like she was in a hotel. The nurse had her eyebrows raised and arms crossed. They had no idea about Mrs. Gaspar. She just liked to argue for the sake of arguing. I thought she must be getting better.

"David," she cried when she saw Davey, and she clutched him

down to her hospital-gown-clad bosom, where some food had dripped. Davey smiled there, all folded in two against her.

But Mrs. Gaspar noticed Davey's extra inch right away.

"What is happening, Cyn-thi-a?" she cried. "He is growing more?"

"No," said Mother, "I don't think so."

Mother looked Davey over, ignoring the inch where his ankles showed afresh. She refused to believe it.

"Let me look at you," said Mrs. Gaspar. "But Cyn-thi-a, is he bigger?"

"Well, remember Professor Cole said a little was okay but not a lot."

"Mrs. Spink," said Mrs. Gaspar slowly, but then she saw me and she lost her train of thought. She looked me up and down. She peered into my eyes, which I rolled to look at the ceiling. Tears started to fill them.

"Lenora," she said. "You are back?"

I pretended to not know what she meant.

Life is full of last times, so many of them you don't even know they are happening. The last time you struggle to tie your shoelaces and the last time you keep a chafer bug in a matchbox. The last time your mother reads you a bedtime story and the last time you imagine the water going down the bath drain is a mini tornado. The last time your friend will have a mole on his face with five feelers.

Mrs. Gaspar told us a dream in her hospital room.

"Children," she said solemnly, "you must hear what I say. I dreamed I went to my bedroom, to my very own bed and I noticed a lump in the middle."

"What was it?" said Davey. His eyes were open wide. His gap-toothed smile was expectant. "An animal?"

"No, it was no creature," said Mrs. Gaspar, stopping to adjust the oxygen tubes in her nostrils. "No, no, no."

I leaned against Mother where she was seated. She put her arm around my waist and squeezed.

"I took the blanket like this," said Mrs. Gaspar, illustrating, "and I pulled it back carefully."

"Were you scared?" whispered Davey.

"Yes," said Mrs. Gaspar, "I was scared. Then what do you think I see, under the blanket? There, growing out of the middle of my bed, was a little tree."

"Are you kidding me?" cried Davey.

"Hush, Davey!" cried Mother. "There are sick people."

"A little tree," said Mrs. Gaspar, quietly, closing her eyes. "A little tree."

"What kind of tree?" I asked. I hoped it wasn't a Christmas tree. That would be too weird.

"It was like the elm tree. It had spreading branches. I knew I would have to give it water. The moon shone through my window on its leaves. I went to the kitchen to fetch some water and when I came back, it was bigger. It was growing up, up, up toward the ceiling."

I felt Mother's hand tense upon my waist then, her whole body still, the way she was when there was mention of anything growing.

"Up, up, up," said Mrs. Gaspar softly. "The leaves touched the roof and they are rustling and then the roof begins to creaking."

"Then what happened?" Davey asked.

"Then the orderly who is a big hairy man woke me up," said Mrs. Gaspar.

We all laughed with relief, Mrs. Gaspar and Mother and Davey and me. We sat around Mrs. Gaspar's hospital bed and laughed and Mother's hand relaxed on my waist and the nurse brought us hot chocolates and we didn't know it was our last Christmas together.

O
Oceans

5′ 9″

JANUARY 1977

D avey and I were different. We didn't talk so much at night. I didn't say, *If you could be a K or J, which would you be?* He didn't say, *Definitely a J, Ks are too jagged and pointy.* I didn't say, *I would be a K. Ks kick ass.* He didn't say, *I'm going to tell Mother you said ass.* That was the kind of thing we would have said BGAE.

Before Great-Aunt Em.

After Great-Aunt Em everything was different. Life was jangled up and changed. I was trying to get used to life AGAE but it was impossible to have an entire great-aunt, small and sparky and full of spittle, shivering like a plucked chicken, and then just clean forget about her.

I closed my eyes and tried to wish her from ever existing. I pushed her away but my head filled up with ravines. They slid in; horses, dusty skirts, endless roads. Great-Aunt Em slid into my head, as a child, a young Spink wild as wild could be. Great Aunt Em, who wasn't my great aunt. I thought of her and I wanted the thoughts of her to dry up like water in a puddle but they wouldn't dry. That puddle got deeper.

I thought of her waiting in her chair. I thought of her missing me.

AGAE in our bedroom at night we listened to the pigeons walking back and forth outside. The trucks and the sirens. Sometimes Davey whispered, "Why'd you do it?" to himself but so I could hear. Sometimes I whispered, "Shut up," in return.

He grew. I swear I heard him grow each night.

Mother phoned Professor Cole's receptionist and made an appointment. She pinned the time and date onto the corkboard.

Davey dropped dimes into my empty jewellery box. One by one, eyeballing me. On top of the pristine unstuck sticker from Buffalo, Wyoming. I ignored him. As if we were going to Great Bear Lake. Still, I put my dimes in when he wasn't looking. There were no more caramel kisses to buy.

AGAE I thought I would stop feeling nervous but I was more nervous. With all my lies gone I felt empty and rattled. I told my mother. I worked up the courage and I went and stood beside her bed after Davey was asleep. I was wretched with grief.

"That lady," I said.

"Yes, Lenny?"

"I think someone's got to help her." I tried not to cry. I crumpled up my face trying.

"I told the charity people at St. Vincent's," Mother said.

"So they're going to help her? Will they get her groceries?"

"They're going to check in on her," said Mother.

"She's very old," I said.

She didn't say anything. Not anything, just looked at me. Not even a bad look. A look of exhaustion. A how'd-I-produce-such-a-rock-throwing-impostor-loving-child look.

"She'll be okay," she said at last, and pulled me against her bony chest. "I promise you she'll be okay."

I lay there awhile.

I thought of bones. I thought of Great-Aunt Em's mother, who wasn't my great-grandmother, who died from a festering sore, and I thought of her buried somewhere in hard dirt in Wyoming; I thought of her as bones which seemed wrong but I couldn't help it. I thought of her bones and then I thought of the bones of her mother even, who wasn't my great-great-grandmother, buried somewhere else I didn't even know. All these mothers, who used their soothing hands and fed their babies at their breasts. Who sometimes scolded and sometimes sang and sometimes danced, who told stories of their mothers before. Then I thought of my own mother and her stories of her mother, which were thin and threadbare, and how my own mother didn't really have soothing hands but she was good at scolding, and then, when I was sure I didn't actually love her, lying there against her chest, I imagined her as bones and just that thought made me sob and I squeezed my eyes shut and sobbed again.

"Hush," said my mother, quietly, and I swear she could read my mind. "Don't think of it anymore."

The *O* issues arrived just as Mrs. Gaspar came home from the hospital. She was newly non-smoking with nervous hands. Annie Oakley, oats, oatmeal, ospreys. *O* contained oceans, which we divided up between us. Davey took the Arctic, I took the Southern. He took the Atlantic and I took the Pacific because the beetles were better there. We fought over the Indian. I hounded him over the Indian because it was rightfully mine, being home to Malaysia and the frog-legged leaf beetle, which was one of the strangest and most beautiful beetles in the world. I bullied him into handing over the Indian Ocean to me, until he put his head in his hands and cried.

O contained the handy coloured tables on onions, owls, and office work.

"That would be a good job for you," said Mother, looking at the pictures of women with big hair typing in a row. "You are neat and methodical."

"Are you kidding me?" I said.

"Lenny is going to be a coleopterist," said Davey.

"Really, now?" said Mother.

"I'm one hundred percent certain," said Davey. His face was still puffy from where I'd made him relinquish all rights to the Indian Ocean and its seas. Even after all that, he stuck up for me. Even though he was still smarting from the disaster of Great-Aunt Em, he stuck up for me. Even though I kept changing my mind about running away to Great Bear Lake, he stuck up for me.

"A coleopterist," said Mother slowly.

Everything was different. A bunch of flowers arrived. They were from Mr. King.

P
Peregrine Falcons

5' 9"

EARLY FEBRUARY 1977

We'd gone to the counter at the Greyhound bus station on the way home after school. We asked the friendly woman how much a fare was to Saskatchewan. "To where?" she said, her look incredulous.

"To Canada," Davey said. She took out her fare schedule and her calculator and got us both as far as North Dakota for twenty-six dollars, one way.

One way.

"One way," said Davey when we walked home from the station.

"One way," I said.

In my jewellery box we had a grand total of three dollars eighty-seven. Davey re-counted it several times like the other twenty-two dollars and thirteen cents might miraculously appear. He held each coin up close to his eyes.

"Why are you doing that?"

"Because I want to," he said.

But I saw he did the same with his *Space Family Robinson* comics too. He read them with his nose almost touching the page. He peered at osprey the same way. And opals. And peregrine falcon when that issue arrived.

"'A peregrine falcon is a raptor and the fastest bird in the world," he read, his eyes pressed to the page. He stopped and examined the picture. "'The peregrine falcon can fly faster than two hundred miles per hour.' Holy Batman!"

"Why have you got your face so close to that page?" cried Mother.

She could ignore the inches but not the fact he couldn't see.

"What do you mean, you can't see? You only just got those glasses last year," she cried.

She took him back to the optometrist. She paid with some of her bus-fare money. We watched her take that money jar down from the top of the refrigerator like two hungry dogs watching a bone.

The new glasses they made him were thick, with shiny metal frames. The optometrist looked nervous dealing with us. He said Mother really should be getting Davey back to see his specialist. "I don't think this is all about Davey's eyes," he said.

Mother said, "I've got my appointment, I just want him to see. He has to go to school." She puffed herself up like a vicious parrot.

Those big silver glasses made Davey's blue eyes huge. He was as tall as a man standing there in his ankle-freezers and his shoes taped down at the ends. Leaning to one side. Smiling. He grew more. He grew every night. His feet slipped over the edge of his bed. His knees ached.

The appointment reminder to see Professor Cole was pinned to the corkboard beside the refrigerator. It read March 2, 1977, but that was still weeks away. We eyeballed Mother's bus money jar on top of the refrigerator. Every time I walked into the kitchen that money jar called to me.

More flowers arrived from Mr. King. There wasn't any apology, just the flowers and the name *Harry* written on a tiny little card.

"Oh," said Mother angrily. "Why's he doing that?"

But we saw her falter inside. She tried to hide it. She tried to hide it from us but we knew her, we knew all her small moods and her large ones too, her rain showers and storms.

"I never once got flowers," she said.

Davey grew. The number of flowers grew. He left them on our mailbox in the foyer. They were the cheap sort, the ones he sold in his fruit shop. Sometimes they were half-dead. They were the flowers that didn't sell. He left them on the floor near our mailbox like it was a shrine to some terrible accident.

I said, "Ignore them."

"Hush now," said Mother. "They'll wilt there. They'll leave a mess."

"Put them in the trash."

"Cyn-thi-a," said Mrs. Gaspar when she saw the flowers in our apartment. "Please. Mrs. Spink."

And Mother did not speak to Mr. King, it's true. She crossed the road to catch the number twenty-eight. But she took his flowers all the same. I saw her stare at them, thinking. They wilted. New ones arrived. Six bunches in two weeks.

Davey ran his fingers over and over the Junior Sales Club prizes catalogue. All the prizes that would never be his. He imagined us going with the tent and the backpack and the sleeping bag. He imagined us looking at the mountains on the horizon through the shiny field glasses. In the end we had one blanket each. We practiced rolling up that one blanket with one change of clothes inside it. We each secured the roll with one belt. It seemed a terrible insult that I had to run away with a ballerina-covered bedspread. "The belts will come in handy," I said, and Davey agreed. For what I was not sure.

We stood in our room and looked at all our belongings that we could not take. Davey looked at his Sea-Monkey sludge. I looked at my bug catcher. I knew I'd have to write a note with instructions for how Mother should care for Charlie. It would be terrible for her. Not only would she find us gone but also we'd be replaced by a stick insect that she never knew about. Davey looked at his walkie talkie. I looked at my *American Beetles Volume 1*. Our sorrow clouded the air.

I took the bus money from the jar on top of the refrigerator when Mother was in the shower. Davey held his belly like it hurt him, even that act of taking it down. I tipped its contents onto the table and the sound of the coins was so loud. He put his hands over his ears. He was such a baby. I counted out the money we needed. There was over fifty dollars in that jar. She mightn't even miss the twenty-three gone. I took the money. I was the one who did it. I was a criminal already anyway.

"I don't think we should," mouthed Davey, clutching at his heart.

I shook my head.

"She's going to marry Mr. King," I said. I had to say it. I could see Mother faltering. I could see it and Davey needed to know it. That would be our life. Mr. King would live in our apartment. He would sit in a chair in our living room and be waited upon and stare with disdain at our encyclopedia set. It would all mean nothing to him. The depths of the ocean and the thundering impala and the map of the moon. He would laugh at our mother's worries. I knew it. The way Peter Lenard Spink had. He would say, *You worry too much, has always been your problem,* just the same way. He would negate her every thought, until she was nothing, just something light and flimsy. A scrap of Cindy Spink.

"Len-neeeeeee," moaned Davey quietly. "Don't say it."

"North Dakota," I whispered. "When we've built the log cabin, we'll send word to her. All she'll need is another one-way ticket."

I let him digest that. He was thinking of our clearing. Timothy the golden eagle. Then the shower turned off and I thrust the money into my bathrobe pocket and put the jar back. We went and sat on the couch and smiled when Mother came out.

"Oh God, what are you two up to now?" she asked.

On the phone Nanny Flora said, "Your mother says he's growing again, that right?"

"Sure is," I said.

"Is he growing a lot?"

"Yes, he's growing pretty fast."

"Well, I just don't like to hear that," said Nanny Flora, and her voice did sound pained, like she'd just seen a fly on food and she needed fly spray to kill it. "Oh dearie me," she said. "That doctor will know what to do, I'm sure. He'll fix him up in no time."

"Yes," I said. And I was just a Lenny Spink robot answering her questions because I was thinking about our running-away plans. I was thinking, *what if Davey needs a doctor in the Northwest Territories?* I felt sick with that thought. I was thinking, *what if he needs new glasses? What if he grows too big for his clothes, and they split off him in the clearing like the Incredible Hulk's clothes and he has to wear pants made out of rabbit fur?* Maybe it wouldn't matter. His being big wouldn't matter up there among all the air and mountains. Everything would just be normal. I'd need a sewing needle and thread and I'd make those rabbit fur pants. I would.

"You there, Lenore?" said Nanny Flora. "Put your mother on, honey."

På Gensyn
(Goodbye in Danish)

5' 10"

MID-FEBRUARY 1977

P contained Puerto Rico, pearls and pelicans. We read these things but we were distracted. A mile-wide flock of passenger pigeons that took three days to pass and blocked out the sun, but mostly we thought of our journey. The Panama Canal. Satchel Paige: greatest pitcher in the world. Twenty-five pages on painting. We read these things but all they did was make us sad. We wouldn't see Q. Even though we hadn't set a date, we knew it. If we went before Davey's trip to Professor Cole then we wouldn't see Q. Or R or S or T. Or all the exotics $UVWXYZ$. Our mother would need to open those pages alone. It was more than sad. A speechless emotion. "Don't," said Davey, when I went to say it. The words were not even formed on my tongue but he knew, the way certain brothers and sisters do. He held up his hand. "Don't."

Setting a date seemed wrong. We'd go when we needed to go. The first of the buses we'd have to catch was the eleven-fifteen p.m. to Fargo and it left right across the road. We watched it and it was always half-empty. Buying a ticket would be no problem. We'd go when Mother worked the night shift, that was as much as we knew. We practiced getting ready. Clothes on, then pyjamas on top of clothes. We'd leave our blankets in the stairwell while Mother had her shower. We'd stuff our sand-wiches in our waistbands. These are the things that we tried to think through. It seemed hard to even get out of the apartment, let alone all the way to Canada.

Davey had a terrible headache at school again. It came on suddenly while he was taking a spelling test and all the way to the nurse's office I could hear him bellowing. "Hush, Davey," I said when I got there. "It'll pass. They always pass." But I looked at him lying there and wondered about doing that in the log cabin alone. Now I needed Tylenol as well as a sewing needle and thread to make his rabbit fur pants. My list was growing. I needed to write it down.

That night I took a piece of paper and sat on the edge of his bed. *Money*, I wrote. "Where can we get more money?" I asked.

"Len-neeeeeee," he said. "We can't steal any more."

"I know, I know," I said. "But we have to go soon and what will we eat on the way? We only have money for the fare."

"We can make some sandwiches," he said. He had his arm across his eyes.

"Is your head still hurting?"

"No," he said. But I knew it was.

Clothes, I wrote. Added *warm*.

"An axe," said Davey.

"We can't take an axe," I said. "People will notice an axe."

"How are we going to build a log cabin without an axe? Maybe we can buy one in Yellowknife. Or we'll meet someone who will lend us one."

Our plans diverged here. In my great escape we were on the

run from everyone. We were hiding from everyone. In Davey's great escape he was talking to lumberjacks and borrowing axes.

"Maybe we shouldn't take the bus," I said. "That way we've got money for food."

We'd walk out of the city. We'd walk out to where the new suburbs ended and the fields began. The places we had seen from the bus window where the sky was big. We'd leave the highway. We'd follow the little roads so we wouldn't be seen. We'd sleep through the day and walk at night. We'd sleep in barns and sheds and beneath shady trees. We'd drink from streams. We'd steal from vegetable patches. It wasn't like no one had ever done it before. A thousand feet had walked that way. We'd follow the Mississippi awhile, then the North Skunk River. What Cheer, New Sharon, Eldora, St. Cloud, Rainy Lake, Regina.

"Lenny," he said. "That would take forever, you know it. We'd be walking for a year."

"So?" I said.

He took his arm from across his eyes and looked at me very, very sadly.

We did it on the night Mother spoke to Mr. King on the phone. The phone rang and she said, "Who could that be?" but she knew, we could tell she knew. The way she always knew when bad things were going to happen. Mr. King was a very bad thing. She was cool with him. "Hi," she said, like it was nothing. Like he'd never stamped out of our apartment and said, *You'll be sorry for this.* "Yes," she said. "I wish you'd stop sending them." But he must have been trying really hard because I saw her blush. He must have told her he loved her. He must have started crying. He must have said she was a princess and he'd always treat her like one. He must have said, *I'll give you flowers every day of your life*, because her face turned foolish. She said, "Oh, Harry, I don't know." Davey looked up from peregrine falcons and frowned. I don't think I ever saw him look so confused.

She got ready for her night shift after she put the phone down. I made a signal with my hand. I nodded my head. It meant, *tonight!*

"Will you do it?" I whispered.

"Yes," he said.

He lumbered after me into our room. We took our pyjamas off and put clothes on, then put our pyjamas on over the top, just like we'd practiced, only this time I felt so scared I thought I'd throw up.

We needed sneakers then. Sneakers were a problem we hadn't thought of. We couldn't go all the way to Canada in our slippers. I took Davey's jacket and made him put it on. I thrust our sneakers up inside. He raised his eyebrows but didn't complain. He was too frightened to complain. I made him sit on the sofa in his sneaker-stuffed jacket while I took our rolled-up blankets and hid them on the stairs to the top floor, opening and shutting the door as quietly as I could.

The shower stopped just as I finished making our sand-wiches. I stuffed them and the fruit in a brown paper bag and only had time to secrete them away beneath the sofa before she came out of her bedroom. How we would get them out again was another matter. Perhaps we'd have to starve. Davey sat on the sofa, looking suspicious.

"Are you okay, Davey?" said Mother.

"Yes," said Davey, clutching the *F* volume to his stuffed jacket.

"Why are you wearing your jacket?"

"It's cold," Davey said.

"Have you got a fever?" asked Mother and she touched his forehead.

"I'm really cold too actually," I interjected. I put my jacket on and yawned.

"What is going on?" said Mother.

She shook her head and went into the kitchen and in a blink of an eye I had the sandwich bag up inside my coat. The dollar bills were in my pocket.

"It isn't that cold," I heard her say. "I'm not cold. You're both sick. That's all I need. And Mrs. Gaspar might catch it."

"It's just cold," I said. "Mrs. Gaspar always has her heating up. We'll take our coats off there."

She looked dubious. She looked like she was going to argue. She looked like she was going to demand we take our coats off then and there but then she looked at the clock.

"Oh, dear Lord," she said and she flung her handbag over her shoulder and we rushed behind her out the door.

"What? They are having fevers!" cried Mrs. Gaspar.

"I'm not sure what's going on," said Mother. We bustled past her in our coats to the bathroom and relieved ourselves of shoes and sandwiches.

"Are you sick?" she called after us.

"Just a pain in my belly," I shouted back. "And Davey too."

"I'm so sorry, Mrs. Gaspar," I heard Mother say.

But then we were back out in our pyjamas, smiling.

"I feel better," I said. "Do you feel better, Davey?"

"I feel better," said Davey.

Mother shook her head. "I don't know what has gotten into you both but it is time for bed."

"I'm so tired," I said.

Davey started to cry. It was so sudden I thought he was going to tell but he didn't. He just cried and hugged Mother, her little blonde head nestled against his chest.

"What is wrong, can someone tell me?" she asked. Pleaded.

"Nothing," we both said.

After she was gone, we tried not to think that it would be the last time we would see our mother for a long time. Until the log cabin was built and we could send word to her. I was surprised at how well Davey was doing. He got the pillows ready on the sofa and I got my little cot set up. Mrs. Gaspar fussed around us. She must have come in and out of her room at least ten times.

"Tummies goot?" she asked.

"Fine," I said.

"No fevers?" she asked.

"No fevers," said Davey.

We lay in the dark counting the minutes until we heard her snore. Longing for the snore, dreading the snore. We sat up like children possessed, slowly, pale-faced, staring at each other in the dark.

"We have to go," I said. The bus left at a quarter past eleven. We had tickets to buy.

We stood quietly, jettisoned our pyjamas. They would be a terrible thing for Mrs. Gaspar to find. She would never forgive herself. We put on our sneakers, listening all the time for noise in Mrs. Gaspar's bedroom. In our experience, she slept soundly once she took her little pills. I took the dollar bills from my sleeve and divided them, half to Davey, half to me. Davey picked up his *F* volume and we left Mrs. Gaspar's apartment, silent as thieves.

With the rolled-up blankets on our backs, we went down the stairs. I had keys in my pocket. The key to our apartment, the key to Mrs. Gaspar's. Keys we would never need again. Keys, blankets, sandwiches and an apple each. I should have left the keys behind. I touched them in my pocket with my finger tip. They were like a talisman, those keys in my pocket. I tried to ignore them.

They had magical powers.

They said, *you can always come back home.*

We opened the front door out onto the street and the cold night rushed up at us. It stung our cheeks. Somewhere in the darkness Mother was on the number twenty-eight with her whole night stretched out in front of her and no idea that we were disappearing.

Just that thought and I stopped. I was like Peter Lenard Spink. Davey too. We were disappearing. Davey rustled the bills in his pocket. There was a siren far away and then men walking in uniforms, and two women in high heels clattering past us and an old man pushing a cart piled up with bags. We didn't know there were so many people on the Grayford streets so late at night. We were in our jeans and jackets but I still felt cold. We needed warmer clothes. We'd need warmer clothes the farther north we went. As though agreeing, the night breathed a great windy breath at us, and it ruffled our hair and hurt our eyes.

The keys in my pocket called.

They said, *Come home.*

"Come on," I said angrily, and we started walking toward the bus station. We joined the small line at the ticket window. Just like that. Like we did it every day. I counted my money. I didn't make eye contact with Davey. I knew if I looked in his eyes, we'd be finished. He started to cry. It was his opened-mouthed cry, no sound.

I tried to ignore it. I shivered in the cold. I counted my money again. Twenty-six dollars exactly. He made a small jerking sound. I knew he was about to wail.

The keys in my pocket said, *It's not too late, Lenore.*

"Come on," I said. "Let's go."

We got out of the line. I could feel all the people staring at us. The two kids without luggage. One as tall as a grown man, crying.

"You're such a baby," I said to him, as we walked home.

Q
Quicksand

5' 11"
LATE FEBRUARY 1977

The bus tickets to see Professor Cole were purchased. We didn't speak of that night again. We closed up all the bus stops. All the long roads, all the forests, all the night-gleaming lakes. We folded up the quintillion stars above our campfire and stowed them away.

Quintillion was a billion billion. We read it in the Qs. Quicksand too. We memorized how to escape from quicksand. Float on your back, arms stretched at right angles, not panicking, rolling gently when you come close to the edge of your quicksand mire. I told CJ. She asked where quicksand was found, looking around her nervously. "In places like Queensland, Australia," I told her, which made her relieved. "Tropical places," I said. "Rainforests."

"Well, I don't think I'll go to Queensland," she said.

"But you never know," I said. "We're not grown-up yet. We might go anywhere." An ache in my heart the size of Great Bear Lake.

I told Matthew Milford. I said, "Matthew, I want to tell you something."

"W-w-w-w-w-w-w-what, Lenny?"

He never stuttered on *Lenny*. Not ever. Not once.

"I know how to get out of quicksand and I want you to know too, I mean, in case it happens."

"H-h-h-h-h-ow?" he asked.

I lay on the concrete in front of him and performed a demonstration. He watched. He looked interested but something else crossed his face. Something that confused me. He looked at me the way I saw all the boys look at Tara Albright, like she was a doll wrapped in cellophane that everyone wanted to touch but no one dared. Now, I knew that could not be. I must be getting it wrong. I did the demonstration again, just to see.

I was in a denim overalls with red tights, and frayed sneakers.

"What?" I said angrily, when I saw that look cross his face again.

"N-n-n-nothing," he said and smiled. "J-j-j-just . . ."

"What?" I said. I was still on my back, grass in my hair.

"You're c-c-c-c-c-cool," he said, and smiled and blushed and stood up and got busy packing his book into his bag.

I frowned at him, lying there, and I felt suddenly new in my eleven-year-old body.

Besides quicksand, the *Q* volume, a slim one, contained quasars, queens, quaking aspens, quartz. A two-page spread on quilting. I wondered what else I could demonstrate.

The truth is I was glad we didn't run away. I didn't admit it to Davey in words but he understood. He said, "The *Q*s are everything I was hoping for." And I knew exactly what he meant. We'd get to see all the letters now and he'd get to go to see Professor Cole, which he really needed. His head ached and he puffed on the way to school, not the way Mrs. Gaspar puffed, a more exhausted puff. Once, we had to sit down at the bus stop near Mr. Kelmendi's shop. His feet hung over the bed now and even with his new glasses he had trouble seeing.

"What do you mean, you can't see?" cried Mother. "Those are brand-new glasses!"

But she was the main reason that we were both glad we didn't run away. Two days after we nearly did run away, Mother, Davey and I ran into Mr. King on the street outside of our building and something wonderful happened.

Mr. King was walking from his fruit shop toward us and there was no time to cross the road. He was there and we were stuck. He had a bunch of flowers in his hand and he looked at them and then Mother.

"Cindy," he said. He looked tired. He looked worn out with all his trying. He was lovesick. Or he looked lovesick, he feigned lovesickness, because he knew that Mother was a sucker for sick and injured things. He looked like he thought he had her. This was it.

"Mr. King," said Mother very kindly.

We stood on either side of her, Davey and I.

He didn't look at us. Just Cindy Spink. Seeing if she would break. I didn't know which way it would go. I tried to feel her vibes. I couldn't feel her anxiety, which was strange. I felt something else but I didn't know what it was.

"I don't want any more flowers," she said.

I could have cheered right there but I didn't. I examined the sidewalk, the cement, the cracks.

"I'll do anything," he said.

"No," she said.

A smile tugged at the corner of my mouth. I tried to keep my frown.

"We're just fine, us three," she said.

"Cindy!" he said. Like that was the stupidest thing he ever heard. How could a woman and two kids be okay?

"Yes," she said. "Just fine."

"You heard what she said, Mr. King," said Davey.

"You keep your great big nose out of it," said Mr. King. But he didn't just mean *big nose*, he meant *big, oversized, giant body*. *Big* was Mother's least favourite word. And that was Mr. King, unclothed, and the wolf out. But he wasn't even a wolf. That would do wolves an injustice. He was mangy and cunning and he licked his lips.

"Cindy," he said, like it was all still solvable.

"No," she said.

He dropped the flowers he was carrying to the ground. He pinched the bridge of his nose again, like he was trying to keep his brain in, that's how much we pained him.

Mother seemed glad to meet the real Mr. King. She smiled.

"Goodbye, Mr. King," she said.

Davey had a monumental headache two nights before his bus trip to see Professor Cole. All the other headaches paled beside this one. This one came without warning on a Tuesday night at Mrs. Gaspar's while Mother was on her evening shift.

"Ouch," said Davey. "Ouch, ouch, ouch, ouch."

He leaned forward in his chair where he was reading *The Incredible Hulk*.

"What's wrong, Davey?" I asked.

"I've got a pain in my head," he said. He didn't sound happy.

I stood up feeling scared. He held his head in his hands, one hand on either side, hard. "Ouch," he said, long and slow, gritting his teeth.

Mrs. Gaspar took off her respirator and blamed the Incredible Hulk.

"Too much nonsense, too much excitement, too much, too much for little boys nowadays."

I touched Davey's head as gently as I could.

"Maybe lie down," I said. "See if that helps."

He lay down on his side on the couch.

"Ouch," he said and he sprang straight up again. Mrs. Gaspar went into the kitchen and came back with a glass of water and two pink pills. She looked worried now too. "Davey," she said. "Open your eyes."

"No, I can't," he said, sounding very certain.

Karl and Karla watched the events like interested spectators. I put the pills in his big hand, and he lifted them up to his mouth. He swallowed the water.

"Ouch," he said, as though even that hurt him.

"What about lying on the cot?"

"Okay," he said. He got up with his eyes closed and I walked him there.

"Gee, I'm sorry," he said.

"Don't be sorry."

"But it's just my head really hurts," he said.

"Just lie still," I said. "Stop talking."

"Ouch," he said.

Mrs. Gaspar brought a wet dishcloth. I put it on his head. He sighed.

"Is that goot?"

"Yes," he said.

"Are you okay?" I asked.

"I think so," he said.

His big hand came up into the air and I didn't know what he wanted, so I took it.

It was what he wanted.

"Just lie still," I said. "Mother will be home soon. Everything will be okay."

March 1, 1977
Apartment 15, 762 Second Street
Grayford, Ohio 44002

Dear Martha,

Thank you for the yearbook and for your kind wishes. I've been wanting to reply and thank you for so long now but a lot has been happening here. Davey did well after his operation for almost eight months but now he has had a growth spurt and we're returning very soon to see the specialist. Both Lenore and Davey helped to raise money for the bus fare. Davey gave all his Junior Sales Club proceeds and they both did odd jobs for a neighbor. Can you believe it? They have contributed nearly ten dollars and I am so proud of them. I really have the best children in the world. I don't know what this next appointment will bring, but Dr. Leopold said some children have more than one operation. We are prepared for anything and you couldn't meet a finer boy than Davey, who is so very brave. The children are very excited about the upcoming R issues.
Thank you again for your letter,
Cynthia Spink.

March 7, 1977
Burrell's Publishing Company Ltd
7001 West Washington Street
Indianapolis, Indiana 46241

OUR GIFT TO YOU IS
THE GIFT OF KNOWLEDGE

Dear Cynthia,

*We are so sad to hear of Davey's troubles. What wonderful
children you have, though, to be raising money for your
bus fares. We certainly hope that Davey doesn't need any
further operations. Please keep us informed of his progress
and we are thinking of him at Burrell's headquarters. In the
meanwhile, enclosed is a book that we think he will like very
much. It is from our Earth Series, a twelve-volume set that
takes a look at the earth's animals, plants, and minerals. This
volume contains the birds! You can subscribe to the whole set
for as little as $2.99 per week.*

We hope Davey enjoys the birds very much! There are two whole pages on falcons.

Yours truly,

Martha Brent

General Sales Manager

P.S. I'm thinking of you all so much.

Searching

5' 11"

MARCH 1977

The day Davey went on the bus, Mrs. Gaspar shed dog hair and dandruff as she blessed him. He sat on her sofa and took it good-naturedly.

"Holy Father, we are praying that the news is good, and if Professor Cole does another operation, he has steady hands," she said.

"We are praying for Mrs. Spink, for You to give her strength and courage."

"We are praying for all the nurses to be goot and kind."

"We are praying for Davey to come home quickly and safely and the bus driver is a goot bus driver."

"Okay," said Mother in a gap between all the praying. "We've got to get going or we'll miss the bus."

After they were gone, I knew all the blessing would come back onto me. When I was left alone with her, there would be a blessing frenzy. It would be like drowning in quicksand.

"Stand up, Davey," said Mother. "Say thank you to Mrs. Gaspar."

"Thanks, Mrs. Gaspar," said Davey. "Goodbye, Karl. Goodbye, Karla."

Mrs. Gaspar threw herself at him when he was up.

"You are a beautiful boy," she cried and pressed her head into Davey's chest. Her faded orange beehive hit him square in the face and he pushed it gently to one side and smiled at me. It made me giggle.

He laughed in return. The old way. The way we were used to.

"Be a good girl," said Mother to me.

"I will be," I said.

She meant, *Don't go and find a weird lady and pretend she is your family*. My cheeks caught fire with the shame of it. Mother looked away from me.

"I know you will be," she said as tenderly as Cindy Spink could speak.

Davey had his suitcase and the *F* volume under his arm.

Mrs. Gaspar let out a wail and her beehive tilted to one side.

"Goodbye, Davey boy," I said.

"Goodbye, Lenny," he replied.

Since Davey's operation, I had felt like I'd been absent in my mind and heart. I was there in all those scenes of our life, but I was a carbon copy of me, a rock-throwing automaton of me. I looked out from the window at the end of the third-floor hall and I saw them looking up. Davey waved, Mother too. Then the silver bus door closed and they were gone.

I went back through the volumes looking for where I'd disappeared. Quicksand, quasars, pilot fish, Portugal, oarfish, Annie Oakley standing there with her gun, nitrogen, the Napoleonic

Wars. Nefertiti. Nebulae. Neptune. Newfoundland dogs and Norwegian elkhounds. All the *New* things. New Hampshire, New Jersey, New Mexico. New York, New Orleans, New South Wales. All the *North* things. The Normans, nuclear energy, nutrition.

Maine.

Macedonia.

Malta.

It was earlier, I knew. It was later. It was nowhere.

I went slowly.

Libraries. Lightning. Literature.

London. Longitude. Love (*see* Emotion).

Knights, knifes, kites.

The street map of Jerusalem.

Igneous rock.

Hungary. Horsehair snakes. The human body with clear plastic overlays.

I located the peanut-sized pituitary gland.

I placed my finger there as though I could obliterate it with my anger and my sadness.

Great Britain, Great Depression, Great Falls, Great Wall of China, Great Lakes. Great-Aunt Em.

"What are you thinking of, dumpling?" asked Mrs. Gaspar.

The worst thing was, I hated to think of her alone. Sitting there waiting for something. Just skin and bones and memories. Maybe I was the last person she'd ever see. Lonely people needed care. They couldn't help themselves. They were too lonely for that. They would just sit there and fade. They would droop like potted plants without water. They would wither and dry and turn to dust.

How could I tell Mrs. Gaspar that?

"Oh, nothing," I said.

"Tell me now," she said.

Loneliness was like a town. You found yourself there. You didn't even know how it happened. And there were no buses out. No trains. People had to come in. Like loneliness rescue teams.

"That lady who said she was my aunt," I started.

"She was a wolf in sheep's clothing," said Mrs. Gaspar.

But I didn't agree. She was wild bright memories in plucked chicken skin.

"She was lonely," I said. "She *is* lonely."

"Do I steal children because I am lonely?" said Mrs. Gaspar indignantly.

I had never thought of Mrs. Gaspar as lonely. Not once, but I saw a film of tears in her old rheumy eyes.

"She is a bitter pill you cannot swallow," said Mrs. Gaspar, as though it was the final word on the matter.

She is a bitter pill you cannot swallow. She is a bitter pill you cannot swallow. She is a bitter pill you cannot swallow. I said those words. I recited those words. I sang those words but my heart answered back, *not true, not true, not true.* She was skies. She was gulches. She was horses and hair blowing in the wind. She was stars and campfires and long roads. She was long ago. She was bad advice that made me feel alive.

She was a big fat hurt. She was nothing but lies. She was a glorious blaze of big fat lies. I *hated* her. And I missed her. She was my chance to find my father, to build him up again from all his broken parts, and now that chance was gone.

It was my father going. That was when I disappeared.

My mother told me that Davey was unsteady on that bus and everybody stared. He leaned outrageously to one side. He careered down the aisle and fell into his seat.

"Sorry," he said, smiling.

"Don't be sorry," said Mother. "You're just doing your best."

These are the things they did to him:

They measured him.

They made him blow in the lung testing machine.

They tested his heart.

They took his blood.

They operated on him again. They went up through his nose.

They zapped him several times with radioactive rays.

But he grew one more inch while he was there.

They took Mother to a small room behind the nurses' station to speak to Professor Cole. He was waiting there for her, behind a desk, weary and rumpled. Professor Cole did not close the door. He waited until the charge nurse arrived, a large woman, with a steely gaze. She looked prepared, she knew what was coming, and she took Mother's shoulders.

"More than anything," Mother said once to me, a long time later. When I was grown-up and did indeed live elsewhere, when the future had spilled out of me. "More than anything, I just didn't want to be apart from him. In that office, I just wanted to be back beside him. Their words, I heard them and they were terrible, but not as terrible as being apart from him."

The nurse's hands caressed her shoulders. My mother was not the sort to be caressed.

"It's not so good, Mrs. Spink. I tried to get as much as I could but the way those tumours are, he will just keep growing. They're the strangest tumours and I've never seen tumours like them," said Professor Cole. "Do you understand?"

"No, not really," said Mother. "I mean, he would have to stop eventually."

There was a silence.

"There are lots of problems associated with growing so big," said Professor Cole.

She was thinking of his pants. Of the seam allowance. Of his bed. Of the size of our little apartment.

"It's like a tangled knot, a perfectly tangled knot. I tried as hard as I could, Mrs. Spink. His eyesight will be a problem. He was already losing some sight, right?"

"He will become blind," translated the charge nurse.

My mother stopped thinking about pants. Started thinking about blindness. She couldn't quite get there. It didn't make any sense yet.

"His heart will be strained. Heart strain and organ failure in general are the complications. He already has some heart failure. You would have seen how his ankles swell," said Professor Cole. "Do you understand, Mrs. Spink?"

"He will die from this disease," said the charge nurse.

Mother looked at them like they were from outer space.

"I've got to get back," she said. "He might wake up and I have to be there."

"We've done everything we can," said Professor Cole.

"I'd hate him to wake up and I'm not there," repeated Mother.

"Of course," said Professor Cole.

They were gone three and a half weeks. On the bus home, they had a paper bag of food that a friendly nurse had packed for them. Things stolen from the hospital kitchen because she knew that living in the small hotel across the road from the hospital had nearly run Mother out of money. And also they all loved Davey. He said things like, *That's a pretty bow in your hair,* and *you've got stand-out-from-the-crowd eyes. You look tired,* and *maybe you should go home to bed,* to the cranky ones, so that even they loved him too.

They left in the afternoon. The bus took forever to get out of the city, which was choked with traffic, but when they were on the outskirts, where the farmhouses were, and then the beginning of the fields, evening came. It came rushing toward them and the sky was filled suddenly with storm clouds and Mother said, "I hope there are no tornadoes."

Across the aisle, a woman with a breathtaking array of beaded braids upon her head said, "No, honey, you can feel them in the air, these are just ordinary storm clouds."

And Mother smiled with relief because honestly that was all she needed on top of everything else.

"How'd you get so big, mister?" asked the woman. There was no not-answering her. Her hair rattled on her head while she waited.

"I have a condition," said Davey.

The woman raised her eyebrows. The bus quietened down, all the chattering and the rustling of packets; someone shushed a small child. They all wanted to know.

"It's some tumours that keep on growing in my brain and they make me grow real big and now nothing can be done to stop it. No one's ever seen tumours like mine. They just keep growing back no matter how many times they get zapped with radiation. I'm one of a kind. I'm just going to keep growing, the Professor said. His name is Cole."

"Nothing at all to be done?" said the woman.

"No, I'll just keep growing up and up," said Davey.

He said it kind of joyfully.

The people on the bus digested that. The clouds and the sky were black. There were no stars at all. Mother longed for the stars.

The woman with the braids thought about it too.

"You seem like a very brave boy," she said at last. "Maybe you are the bravest boy I will ever have the chance to meet."

Davey smiled. His disarming charming smile. Then the rain hit the side of the bus. It slapped into the side of the bus in a great spray, and then, as the bus turned toward the east, it hit it front on, a great clattering of rain that smothered up all the other sounds. It wrapped it up in its drumming, the sound of tyres on wet asphalt, it swallowed up Davey's story, and the woman reached across the aisle and patted him on the arm. Cindy Spink closed her eyes. She couldn't keep them open a minute longer.

She slept, and Davey too, all the way home.

Growing Pains

6' 0"
LATE APRIL 1977

R was a straightforward affair. There were no surprises. I ran down the stairs every Friday for the issues and brought them back up to Davey, who lay waiting on the sofa. *R* contained ravens, the Renaissance, Rhode Island. It contained radio, radar, and radiation. "There is nothing I don't know about radiation," said Davey. I sat beside him and read from rocket ships. I read to him about the great rivers of the world. But most of all I read to him about raptors.

"'Harpy eagles have a wingspan of up to six and a half feet. They can carry a whole baby deer. Golden eagles can kill bobcats. Birds of prey have the sharpest vision of any animal in the world. Female bald eagles are bigger than males. Sometimes eagle chicks eat their brothers or sisters.'"

"Davey," said Mother, exasperated, though she didn't want to sound mad. "Maybe Lenny could read you something else. Maybe some other kind of birds."

"But raptors are the best kind of birds," he said.

He fed his imaginary golden eagle, Timothy, an imaginary crumb.

He grew steadily. A new kind of growing. His joints ached. His feet swelled. They were a long way from the top of him. He was exhausted. We stopped twice on our walk to school for him to sit down. He slept when he got home from school.

"Maybe you should take some time off from school," suggested Mother.

"But then I wouldn't see Teddy or Warren or Fletcher."

A man came from the *Guinness Book of World Records* and knocked on our door. It's the kind of thing that happens when your brother grows too big. He walked right up the steps into our apartment building and Mother was so angry that someone had let him in. She said it was an inside job. She blamed Mr. Petersburg straight off. Not only was he writing letters to federal and state penitentiaries, he was writing them to the *Guinness Book of World Records*.

But it could have been anyone. Anyone at all. It could have been Mr. King. Or it could have been a teacher. It could have been Mr. Bartholomew for all we knew.

"Who is it?" said Mother, that afternoon at the door.

It was the man from the *Guinness Book of World Records*. He said so. He stated his business. He had heard possibly the biggest kid in America lived right here. He wanted to talk about getting a measurement. Gaining an entry. Maybe Davey was even bigger than Robert Wadlow at that age. He really wanted to know. Fame awaited. He said it all. His sales pitch went on for a minute. All through the closed door. When he finished there was silence and he waited. Mother stood very still on our side. It seemed like an eternity she stood there, and I don't know what she was thinking. Then she unlocked the door and flung it open.

"You get out of here this instant!" she screamed.

Not just yelled.

She screamed. She had a damp tea towel in her hand from when she'd been drying the dishes. She smacked the man over the head with it. You could tell he wasn't expecting it. He didn't even have time to put up his hands. *Thwack*, down it came again and he was running backwards, away.

Thwack, she was out into the hall chasing him.

Thwack, she was chasing him down the stairs.

He never came back. I've since looked at the entries on the tallest people in the world and there were many. I stared into their eyes in the grainy black-and-white pictures. There was Ella Ewing, towering in the big tent, and Édouard Beaupré, lifting a horse as high as his shoulders. Sideshow giants Jack Earle and Al Tomaini. There were figures and graphs. Pictures of pants and custom-built chairs. But nothing of dreams. Nothing of love. Nothing of goodbyes.

Davey grew. I walked with him to school and his back ached. "Don't lean all over me," I said.

"Sorry," he said.

"Don't breathe your horse breath all over me," I added.

"That's a pretty mean thing to say," he said.

There was a sign for the school dance in the auditorium.

"Don't think you're going to that," I said.

Davey got new pants made for the school dance. "Special pants for a mighty special boy," was what Miss Finny said. I didn't want Mother to go back to Miss Finny, not after she reported me to the police. I said as much and Mother stared at me for a good minute, shaking her head.

"Sometimes you really make me wonder, Lenore Spink," she said.

I didn't make eye contact with Miss Finny for the whole visit. It was my mission and I succeeded. Once, she said, "And how's young Miss Lenny?" and I pretended I didn't hear her.

"She's okay," said Davey for me.

Miss Finny smiled and got to solving her favourite problem, Davey.

She had some old fabric that she was going to add to the bottom of his pants. It was a different colour but she said it would create an optical illusion to make him look shorter. Mother was impressed. Miss Finny factored in his left leg being longer than his right.

"Don't need no fancy tailor," she muttered to herself as she worked. "You just need Miss Finny, don't you, Davey boy?"

Davey smiled down at her.

He put on his two-toned pants and he oiled down his hair for the dance. He was excited. Davey liked to dance. That was the worst part. Davey loved to dance but he danced badly and I knew people would stare at him. They wouldn't stare at him because he was extra-large because they were mostly all used to that, but they'd stare because they'd never seen him dance before and they didn't know what they were in for. I wore my mint green seersucker dress. I let down my thin brown hair. I covered over my freckles with my mother's powder puff. But my hairy werewolf pelt of shame was out. I was filled with Davey-dancing dread.

"I don't think I'll go."

"You have to go and look after Davey," said Mother.

I said, "I can't. You know I can't."

"Why not?"

"You know I don't like dances," I said.

"Don't like dances?" said Mother, like it was the most stupid thing she'd ever heard. "You're going. Your brother wants to go, so you're going."

Davey couldn't stop smiling as we walked down Second Street. I said, "Stop smiling."

He tried but his smile kept breaking through. His huge face cracked open and out it came.

"Stop it," I shouted at him. He closed up his great grin and looked forlorn.

"Honest to God," I said.

"Okay," he said.

But at the school he looked at all the paper lanterns and the coloured lights strung up around the gymnasium and out beamed his smile again. He looked at all the girls and boys, a big shifting wash of pastel dresses and bell-bottoms and he leaned even more to one side with excitement, his let-down two-toned pants strained across his hips.

CJ wore denim hand-me-downs. She had on the largest belt buckle I'd ever seen and her sisters had done her hair in hot rollers.

"Wow," I said.

"I know," she replied.

Her hair seemed bigger than her.

"Hello, Davey," said CJ. "Nice pants."

"Hey," said Davey, but he wasn't really paying attention. His right leg had started jiggling to "Dancing Machine." That song banged inside my brain. I was wishing he would stop it. I was so wishing he would stop it. I was wishing it with all my heart. I hissed, "Davey," under my breath but his leg wouldn't stop. It jiggled and twisted and he smiled and then his arm joined in, just one.

"Hey, Davey's dancing," said Chad Longora who was in Davey's class and was of normal height, but oversized personality. He started dancing in front of Davey and Davey danced right back at him and I tried to work out if Chad was making fun of Davey or not and I decided on not, but then I couldn't be sure because more children were joining in and I lost Chad's face in the big skin-coloured wash of smiling faces.

Even more kids joined in, Fletcher and Warren and Teddy, and they were leading the giant boy out into the centre of the dance floor and then "The Loco-Motion" started playing and it was my worst nightmare. And there was just about every kid in the entire school dancing around Davey and then forming a train, sometimes with Davey at the lead and sometimes with him in the middle. Davey danced like he was made out of metal. Davey danced like the Tin Man. Davey jerked. He jerked and smiled. It made everyone else smile.

"That's the best thing I've seen since sliced bread," said CJ, breaking off the tail of the train and coming to stand near me.

Her big hairsprayed hair looked even bigger, she couldn't stop smiling either. I hated him. I loved him.

Matthew Milford came and asked me to dance. It took him forever. I was going to just say it for him but I didn't. I made him suffer and then I suffered while he suffered. My quills came out. He could sense them without me saying a thing but he didn't back away. When he was finished asking I just stared at him.

"Come on," he said, and he was for an instant completely stutter free. We danced. It was super-serious, like a trap door would open if we made a wrong move, but when it was done and the song was over, he smiled his New York smile at me.

I went back and sat in my dark corner when it was finished like a hermit crab going back into its shell. I watched over Davey. He danced with the boys from his class in a big circle. He danced with the girls from his class. He danced with Mr. Marcus. He danced with Miss Schweitzer. He danced with Principal Dalrymple. He danced with CJ and once even with Tara Albright. He never danced alone. Not once. My shame broke up right there, crack, into a thousand tiny pieces and it drifted away like storm clouds out to sea. Without my werewolf pelt, I felt fresh and clean. I smiled at Matthew Milford and we danced again.

I saw Great-Aunt Em on the day Davey had his first seizure. It was from a distance but I knew it was her. You couldn't mistake Great-Aunt Em, after all, although the world made her look tinier and more stooped, and the yellow scarf tied around her head was bright as a daffodil.

I stood statue-still watching her.

It was on the street behind the school and she was being helped into a car outside a bingo hall. The person helping her was a woman in a uniform and she was fussing over Great-Aunt Em. She was fussing over her in a good way, and although I was too far to hear I could almost imagine what she was saying. *Come along now, Mrs Spink. Did you enjoy that? I think you look so much better for getting out in the fresh air.* And I saw Great-Aunt Em look up at the woman, smile, and start to speak. She was probably going to tell a story. A story about horses or dusty towns.

I suddenly wanted to run toward her. To race up and to bang on that car window before she left. To say something. To say, *I wish you'd really been my great-aunt. I wish it was real.* I swear I wouldn't have shouted or sounded angry. To say, *I wish you'd known my father.* To say, *I'm glad you are outside. I hope this lady listens to your stories.* To say, *No hard feelings.*

But I didn't. I stayed glued to that spot, watching and then the car was gone.

On the day that Davey had his first seizure, he said I was spotty and orange. I said, "Pardon?"

He said, "Seriously."

I said, "Mother, Davey is saying I'm orange."

He said, "I'm not saying it in a mean way."

It was a disaster. I mean, what if that was the real reason Matthew Milford had danced with me? What if he felt sorry for me because I was orange?

"Don't say she's orange," said Mother. "Really, Davey. What would make you say that?"

"And spotty," said Davey cheerfully. He looked back at the TV.

"Everyone is orange," he said, and he chuckled. "And spotty. Even the television is spotty."

"That's it, you're not going to school today, something's not right," said Mother. "Have you got a headache?"

"A little one," he said.

"You'll stay home with Mrs. Gaspar."

Davey was devastated.

I looked at myself in the bathroom mirror. At my hair, which I tried to do attractively, tied in a ponytail to one side. At the freckles on my nose, which I had tried to cover with my mother's powder puff. I couldn't see orange. There was no orange. "Why is he saying we're orange?" I said to Mother in the kitchen. She was looking out the window, stopped quite still, at the pigeons flying and the sunlight.

"Hush now," she said, and she had her hand over her heart.

I went without him and he stayed with Mrs. Gaspar. Matthew Milford smiled at me near my locker. He just happened to be there getting books out. He was taking a long time. I was taking a long time too. "H-h-h-hey," he said. "What's up?"

"Oh, nothing," I said. I wondered if I was orange. He was kind of looking at my face as though he was searching for something. Then he looked away. Then he looked at my books. "Are you d-d-d-d-d-d-d-d-oing your . . ." he asked.

"I'm doing my assignment on the Founding Fathers," I said. It was the truth.

"M-m-m-m-m-e too," he said. "D-d-d-d-do you w-w-w-w-
want to wr-wr-wr-wr-wr—"

"Write it together?" I asked. "Yes."

I thought my *yes* was too forceful. I tried another one. I toned
it down. "Yes," I said. I shrugged my shoulders at the end like
I didn't care. I could feel my feet lifting off the ground.

He smiled.

"Okay," he said.

"Okay," I said.

"Okay," he said in a robot voice. No stutter.

He did some robot arms.

"Okay," I laughed.

Afterwards CJ said, "You look different."

"Man, why does everyone keep saying that," I said.

All the way home I didn't expect anything bad. I had seen
Great-Aunt Em, and Matthew Milford had asked me to write
an essay with him, and badness was the furthest thing from my
mind that white sunshiny day. Then I saw Mrs. Gaspar standing
at the front door of our apartment building, looking down the
street, and when she saw me, her hands went up to her face and
then into the air and she started running toward me, and it was
a terrible thing to see. She was like a little skittle, lurching side
to side, her beehive waving madly. You see, you see, you see, you
see, I didn't see it coming, not at all.

She was rushing toward me and crying out my name and
my mother's name and Davey's name until she had her arms
around me.

Mother said when he woke up his face was so serene. She saw in his face a man. She glimpsed him suddenly, tall and handsome, the sort of man who finished up his work and drove his truck home and opened his front door and picked up his children and kissed his wife. A little glimpse of another future.

And when he came home to us, when he walked in through the door and lurched himself onto the sofa, smiling, I noticed his calmness.

Davey didn't need so much care at first. It was his eyesight mainly, but of his increasing blindness he did not complain. He didn't say I was orange anymore. He said, "You're glowing."

"All of me?" I asked.

"Just your face. Like you are a jack-o'-lantern, only not orange. A body with a lantern for a head."

"Stop it," I whispered.

"I'm just telling the truth," he said.

"Can you see my face?"

"Not really, it's just a white shape glowing. I like it. Are you smiling?" he said.

"No, I'm crying," I said.

"You are not," he said.

"How do you know?"

"You only cry when things are really bad, Lenny."

He bumped into walls. I had to guide him by the hand. His hand was large and coarse, the skin thickened and dry, layer after layer, until it was hard as stone. "Forward, forward, stop. Turn to your left," I said, but he forgot left from right.

"Left?" he'd ask, confused.

"Left," I'd say, "like turn left, left hand."

"Oh," he'd say.

"The toilet is right in front of you," I'd say.

"Thank you," he'd say.

He was polite like that.

I'd hear his pee hitting the floor.

"Sorry," he'd say.

Sometimes I'd say, "Don't worry about it." Other times nothing because I'd be angry at having to clean up pee. You don't become someone perfect just because your brother is dying. You stay the person you are and all your good and bad bits are magnified.

I read to him.

I read to him from the encyclopedia, his favourite parts. Sometimes what we thought were favourite parts weren't favourites anymore. Frogs, for instance, didn't excite us any longer. I read instead to him about the Great Plains where once more than 30 million bison roamed.

"That's a lot of bison," he said with his eyes closed.

"They were nearly hunted to extinction," I said.

"That's a lot of hunting," he said.

"There's a picture," I said. "It's all these bison skulls piled up in a mountain."

He didn't open his eyes. "That's terrible," he said.

"I wonder if he'll come back," he said, so quiet I could barely hear him. Like he was thinking a thought out loud.

"Who?" I whispered, but I knew.

"It was wrong to just go and never say goodbye," he said, louder now. He'd never once said that in all his life.

"Maybe he'll come back," I said, but Davey shook his head.

"I wish I was a pioneer," he said after a while.

It made me think about our running-away plans. They seemed such a long time ago. Just like Peter Lenard Spink seemed so distant. I had a pain in my throat, all my tears stuck there in a hard lump.

"Ouch," I said.

"What?"

"Nothing."

I started to cry. He lay on the sofa with his eyes closed and I cried beside him. I did it quietly so he wouldn't know.

"How's that brother of yours doing?" asked Nanny Flora.

"Not so good," I said.

"Yes, your mother wrote me," said Nanny Flora. "I hear his eyesight is not so good and he had a seizure."

"He had three," I said. "But he's home now again. He's been to the hospital twice. They put him on pills that make him so sleepy."

"Well," she said.

It was an unusual *well* for her. I thought I heard a little chink in her clean armour.

I didn't help her out, I didn't say a thing. I wasn't scared of her anymore. I'd had a totally imaginary terrifying great-aunt. Nothing could scare me anymore.

"Well, I think it's about time I came out, don't you think, Lenore?" she said.

"Huh?" I said.

"Don't say *huh*," said Mother, from the sofa.

"I mean, I think I ought to catch a bus up, don't you? Stay for a while."

I was so stunned I couldn't speak. I imagined her arriving. I imagined as best I could with her voice and her photo that sat on the top of the china cabinet. She was tiny and wiry and stick-brittle. She'd smell like dishwashing liquid and Ajax.

"You there, honey?" she asked.

"Yes," I said.

"Don't tell your mother now," she said. "It's our secret, Lenore."

"Okay," I said. And I put the phone down and tried to look completely normal.

"What in blazes are you looking like that for?" asked Mother.

Peter Lenard Spink

Here is where he might come back. There is room in the story for him. There are a thousand roads and endless cornfields and mountain ranges. There is the big blue sky. He is not caught somewhere, trapped; he has ample turning room. He has his feet in his sneakers and they can get up anytime. He can take his money from the motel table and wash his face with his hands in the chipped sink and examine his pockmarked face.

He can turn his big rig around.

He can follow all the signs. The great eastern, Interstate 90. He can follow the freeway exchanges like ribbons until he feels the familiarity of the landscape, its yellowness, its prickliness, its openness. All that running he's been doing and there is the land, all that time, just waiting with its open arms, the wide road, the motor inns, the city, moon-rock-coloured, up ahead.

There is room in this story for him to come back. To park his rig and walk across the road, his legs shaking, see, and his hands, and his heart filled suddenly with a lurching emotion, a rusty faucet turned on, smoothing down his hair. He has room to come up the stairs. There is no one stopping him.

Peter Lenard Spink, Peter Lenard Spink, Peter Lenard Spink, I whispered in bed at night, but those words had lost their weight. He was all in pieces in my head, shattered. Was I a little girl in pieces when he thought of me? A smile, a shyness, small hands. A little thing he left that never grew bigger in his mind, but smaller, more faded, papery, airy, like confetti. *Peter Lenard Spink* I whispered, but I didn't long for him anymore. He was too light to pin down, too broken to mend. Here is where he could come back but he doesn't.

Bed-Building

6′ 3″

MAY 1977

🦅

D avey couldn't fit in his bed anymore. He wasn't comfortable at all. His calves hung over the bottom edge. Even if he lay on his side, his knees came out into the middle of the room and I had to manoeuvre myself around them. He kept growing. His growing hurt him. It stretched his skin and ached his bones.

Mrs. Dalrymple and Mrs. Oliver came to our apartment. The principal and the assistant principal. Mother said, "I just don't know why people keep knocking at that door. It's like a three-ring circus around here."

I thought it would be a *Guinness Book of World Records* situation all over again.

"Hello," said Mother, through the peephole.

"Hello, Mrs. Spink," said Mrs. Dalrymple in a cheery nervous way. "It's Lucy Dalrymple and Cherry Oliver. We hope you don't mind, but we just came to check in on Davey, and all of you, really, and offer our help. Well, the school's help, really."

Mother didn't say anything. Yes, it was going to be the *Guinness Book of World Records* all over again. My eyes wandered to her hand; thankfully there was no tea towel.

"Can I see Mrs. Dalrymple?" said Davey from the sofa. "I really like Mrs. Oliver too."

"We're doing just fine," said Mother, and she opened the door a crack.

The two ladies' faces squeezed in like little terriers looking for a home.

"The school wants to organize a fundraiser," said Mrs. Dalrymple. "And really, anyone and everyone is willing to help with anything you might need."

I could see fundraiser get under Mother's skin like a toothpick-sized splinter. If she were a horse, she'd snort and stamp and then buck. She stayed as still as she could.

"A fundraiser?" she said. The two principals' beaming faces peered back at her.

"Hello, Mrs. D.," said Davey from the sofa.

"Well hello, David," said Mrs. Dalrymple from her crack in the door.

Mother sighed. She opened the door and they almost fell in.

"We won't be needing a fundraiser," she said. "But say hello to Davey by all means."

Davey was stretched out on the sofa, his eyes closed. He had *How to Build a Log Cabin* laid on his chest.

"I can't see so well," he said.

"Oh, lovely boy," said Mrs. Dalrymple and she came and fussed over him where he lay. She took his hands and he smiled to feel them.

"Wow, you've got soft hands," he said.

Mrs. Oliver smiled at Mother. Mother grimaced in return.

I sat on the floor where I'd been listing my favourite beetles from one to ten. It was a strange thing to have your principal and assistant principal in your living room. It felt like the whole world was being dismantled and rebuilt in new ways.

"Hello, Lenny," said Mrs. Oliver.

"Hello," I said.

Davey wouldn't let go of Mrs. Dalrymple's hands.

Mother said, "Davey."

"What?" said Davey, eyes closed, enjoying the hand-holding.

"Let go of Mrs. Dalrymple."

Mrs. Dalrymple giggled like a girl. The world was indeed upside down.

"We wanted to know what we can do to help," said Mrs. Dalrymple. "Seeing as you are stuck at home, Davey. What could make you more comfortable?"

"Well, we're doing pretty well, aren't we, kids?" said Mother.

"I need a new bed," said Davey.

"Really, is your bed not comfortable?" asked Mrs. Oliver.

"Your bed's not that bad," said Mother.

"But really, what's wrong with your bed?" said Mrs. Dalrymple. It was a visit from the comfort police.

"It's just too small," I said.

Mrs. Dalrymple positively exploded with a smile. It was something concrete that could be fixed.

"Well, we can fix that for sure, can't we, Cherry?" said Mrs. Dalrymple. I had no idea Mrs. Oliver's name was Cherry. It just didn't seem right.

"What about Mr. Engelmann?" said Mrs. Oliver.

"Most definitely Mr. Engelmann," said Mrs. Dalrymple.

Mr. Engelmann taught woodworking.

I closed my eyes and waited for Mother's quills to come out.

"We will build you a bed, Davey," said Mrs. Dalrymple. She said it with gusto. Arms out. Like the main star in a musical. A chorus line should've come out dancing behind her.

I could see Mother about to say no. The *no* was being squeezed up and out of her like old toothpaste, but Davey saved the day.

"Holy Batman, that would be the coolest thing in the whole world," he said.

Mother was anti-Mr. Engelmann and the bed-building. As soon as the principals left she said, "Honestly, who do they think they are? We're okay."

I said, "But Davey's bed is too small." She waved me away and started to cry because then she was a bad mother for not wanting her son to have a good bed in his dying days. Although no one ever mentioned dying days. Ever. No one ever mentioned dying. The eventual state of all living organisms. The cessation of heart beat and respiration.

"Mr. Engelmann is really nice," said Davey. "The big boys make magazine holders and coathangers and bird feeders."

He came to the house with two boys from his high school carpentry class and stood with his hands on his hips. "Heard you need a new bed, Davey," he said.

"Sure do," said Davey and he shook Mr. Engelmann's hand from where he was lying as I read to him about Saturn.

Mr. Engelmann was tall and handsome. He had curly blond hair and a boyish smile. Our apartment looked smaller and shabbier for having him there. The pale-green walls and the threadbare sofa and the plastic fruit in the bowl on top of the television. My mother was anti-Mr. Engelmann building furniture until she saw him. It's the whole truth. Until he stood at the end of the sofa with his hands on his hips, she said, "I will not have some man I do not know in our home building a bed. I'll buy a bed." But then when she saw Mr. Engelmann, he could have built triple bunk beds for giants and she wouldn't have cared.

"I told you he was nice," said Davey.

We took him into the bedroom and he looked at Davey's bed. He had to work out a way to extend the bed, that was all, so it reached all the way to the wall. Well, that was no problem, it was a piece of cake.

Mother baked a cake for him and the boys the first day. Then she baked cookies. Her trademark cookies that you could break your teeth on, but Mr. Engelmann had very strong white teeth and they crunched right through them like a metal press. "So," he said, and stuck his tape measure behind Davey and measured him. He whistled, but not a bad whistle. He measured Davey's bed. Mother watched him, touching the fountain of hair on her head.

I read about Saturn while they brought equipment up the stairs.

"Saturn is the sixth planet and it is made of gas," I said. "It has nine moons."

"Nine moons," said Davey.

"Nine moons," I said.

"Imagine looking at the sky and seeing nine moons," said Davey.

"How many moons?" said Mr. Engelmann, carrying a sawhorse.

"Nine," said Davey.

"How many moons?" asked Mrs. Gaspar who had come to watch in her shaggy tangerine bathrobe.

"Nine," I said.

"Pah," she said. "No one needs that many moons."

S seemed an important letter. It was crammed with wonderful surprises. I sat in the sunshine on my bed and read to him. Smoke signals, for starters. Snowflakes. Shakespeare thoroughly eclipsed by snake-charming. Scorpions, the colourful plates on shells, ships and shipping, the life cycle of a salmon.

"I'd hate to end up in a can," said Davey.

Saskatchewan, Saskatoon, all the *Souths*.

South America.

South American animals. I read their names and described them to him.

Flamingos, vicuñas, jaguars, chinchillas, yapoks, swamp deer.

The Andean condor.

Davey lay in his new bed, which had brown wooden legs and pillows stacked in where the mattress ended. He lay there a lot.

"You've got to get up and keep walking," said Mother. "You'll get bedsores."

"I don't feel any sores," said Davey. "This bed is the best bed. It's so solid, don't you think?"

"So solid," I said.

"Read me something else," he said.

The Sahara, nearly as big as America, filled up with sand.

Sand and its uses.

Related articles: beach, dune, desert, glass, sandstorm, silica, quicksand.

"I'm glad I never got to see quicksand," said Davey.

That stopped me right where I was, mid-sentence.

I wanted a future. I wanted Davey's future. I wanted Davey and quicksand or Davey and no quicksand. I wanted Davey. I wanted Davey to see quicksand, to fall into it so I could rescue him. So I could drag him out with a big stick and Timothy could fly down from a tree with delight and we would walk home through the woods and he would wash in the lake and Mother would be in the cabin preparing our tea.

"Why've you stopped?" said Davey.

"No reason," I said. Great Bear Lake and all the quicksand disappeared. There was a knocking at the door. It was a sharp, quick rat-ta-tat-tat. And I knew, without even thinking, it was our Nanny Flora.

Nanny Flora

6′ 5″
JUNE 1977

Nanny Flora had a beige handbag that contained breath mints and several pressed handkerchiefs, a powder compact, and a coral lipstick, the Lord's Prayer on a bookmark, but no book. I know because I looked. I woke early one morning and it was there sitting on the table. I rifled through its contents fast as a thief and my heart jackhammered inside me and nearly lifted my feet clean off the floor.

It had been nearly twelve years from when Mother ran away with Peter Lenard Spink and me, the size of a jellybean in her belly. When Mother saw her, she looked like she'd seen a ghost. The blood drained away from her face and she stumbled forward and then backward like she was drunk.

"Hug," said Nanny Flora, waving her hand.

They embraced like two women trying to stand up on a boat and when they untangled from each other and held onto furniture for balance both their faces were wet right over.

"And this is Lenore," said Nanny Flora. I went to her. I walked to her the way one goes up to get their Communion. Very slowly. I turned my head to one side and it was pushed against her bosom with her small frail hands. She was in crisp white pants and a purple shirt. She didn't smell like Ajax at all.

She smelled like lily of the valley and laundry starch and breath mints. I didn't cry or stumble when she held me but I was glad for her. I wished they hadn't fought for so long.

I got Davey up and helped him out to the living room. You could see her face blanch at the size of him but she shrugged off her horror, like good grandmothers do.

"Nanny Flora is here, Davey," I said when I had him down onto the sofa.

"I know, I can smell her," said Davey, then added, "a good smell."

They fumbled for each other's hands. Nanny Flora kissed his cheek.

"Hello, Davey," she said. "It sure is nice to meet you."

"You've got the exact same hands as Mama," he said.

When I showed Nanny Flora the *Burrell's Build-It-at-Home Encyclopedia*, she looked at it with great interest. "It's the real deal, all right, isn't it, Lenore?" she said. She turned the pages slowly.

Davey said, "Show her falconry."

I did. I showed her Florida.

"Well, I'll be," she said. "Everything you ever needed to know."

I showed her beetles. She got agitated. I knew not to tell her I wanted to be a coleopterist. Not yet. Davey was delighted to discover she quite liked *Days of Our Lives*.

Mrs. Gaspar came. There was a tense stand-off of sorts over Davey. Mrs. Gaspar fussed over him and Nanny Flora fussed over him and they met head to head over him, small springy golden curls versus a large dishevelled beehive. They were opposites. Mrs. Gaspar so dandruffy and unravelly with a big gravelly cough and Nanny Flora so pristine and lily-of-the-valley-smelling.

"He likes his pillow this way," said Nanny Flora.

"No, he likes it a little higher," said Mrs. Gaspar. They pushed and pulled at the pillow behind Davey until Mother came and told them to stop.

Mrs. Gaspar sat at the table and glared over the steam of her tea.

Nanny Flora glared right back from her position beside Davey. The prodigal grandmother returned.

But they settled. They had to.

Davey said, "Did you have a dream last night, Mrs. Gaspar?"

"Yes, Davey, I did," said Mrs. Gaspar, insulted no one had asked her sooner.

"Tell me," he said. "Please."

So Mrs. Gaspar did. It was a short one, relatively. There were no horses or dream soups. No magic blankets. But there was the moon.

"I was watching the moon," she said. "It was rising. Only, it didn't rise far away in the sky, it rose right beside my bedroom window. It rose and it filled up my whole window and I could smell the moon, the smell of it filled my apartment. It was such a good smell. Such a wonderful smell. It made my stomach growl. Karl and Karla, they howled at that giant moon."

"What did it smell like?" asked Davey, smiling.

"Well, here is the problem," said Mrs. Gaspar. "When Karl and Karla howled, I woke up and I could not recall."

She shook her head sadly.

"Now, now," said Nanny Flora, in a most tender way. "Perhaps it will come back to you."

"Yes," said Mrs. Gaspar, in a very kind tone. "Perhaps it will."

Mother took her cup and patted her on the head.

"I'll make you more tea," she said.

"I'll have one too," said Nanny Flora.

"Have my tea, Nanny," said Mrs. Gaspar. "It is good for digestion and breathing."

"Well, I think I will," said Nanny Flora. "And you come and sit beside Davey."

"Oh, no, you keep sitting there," said Mrs. Gaspar.

And they were models of womanly conciliation.

June 2, 1977
Apartment 15, 762 Second Street
Grayford, Ohio 44002

Dear Martha,

I'm writing to tell you some very bad news. Davey had another operation and some radiation, but it isn't likely he will get better. Professor Cole said he never saw tumours like the ones Davey has and it's maybe the only one of its kind on earth. It can't be stopped and it just keeps growing and Davey just keeps growing too. He is very sick now, though, with all the strain this has put on his heart and on his kidneys, and they say he has sugar disease. The tumour has made him lose his eyesight altogether now, and when Dr. Leopold visited, he said he did not think we had long with our fine boy. I wanted you to know because you have been kind to us these last two years.

Yours sincerely,

Cynthia

June 12, 1977
Burrell's Publishing Company Ltd
7001 West Washington Street
Indianapolis, Indiana 46241

OUR GIFT TO YOU IS
THE GIFT OF KNOWLEDGE

Dear Cynthia,

What very sad news. We have been hoping and praying for
Davey here at Burrell's headquarters. We will continue to hope
and pray for him. I wish there was some way we could help.
Please tell us if there is any way we can help,
Martha

The Canada Goose

No Height Recorded
JULY 1977

Of helping there was much. There was Mr. Engelmann, who came and dismantled the bed and built it again in the living room, where there was more space. "It's nothing," he said to our mother. "Why, Mrs. Spink, that is just not a problem at all."

There was Mrs. Gaspar, who made us soups and sat beside Davey just as long as anyone else. There was Nanny Flora, who washed the sheets that filled up with Davey's sweat, for he sweated and the apartment filled up with the smell of him and it reminded me of Mrs. Gaspar's dream of the moon. There was Mrs. Bartholomew and her two oldest daughters, all nurses, who came and set things right and tended to Davey and arranged care from a city hospice: more nurses, who came to the door and left their handbags in piles and sponged him and turned him and cleaned his closed eyes with cotton balls. There was Mr. Kelmendi, who sent flatbread, and Miss Finny, who brought cake, there was Miss Schweitzer, who peered into our little apartment like a visiting ice queen and then dissolved into tears, and Mrs. Gaspar, all shaggy and dog-haired, consoled her at the table and fed her dumplings. There was CJ, who came once with her sisters and leaned over Davey's head into a gap and ruffled his prairie grass hair.

And sometimes there were so many people in those last few weeks that I couldn't get near him, and I longed for our night-times, our solitude, when we would whisper to each other across the darkness in the bedroom. When we would sit with our chins resting on the sill and watch the buses arriving and departing.

"I had a dream," said Mrs. Gaspar to Davey. She stroked his hair and I saw him smile.

"What?" he asked.

"There was a giant goose," said Mrs. Gaspar.

"Oh," said Davey, his eyes still closed. A quiet happy *oh*. "Was it a Canada goose?"

"Yes, it was this goose," said Mrs. Gaspar. "Down it flew and landed on my windowsill. It shook the whole building."

"Holy Batman," said Davey softly.

"Inside it looked with its black eye. 'Honk', it says, 'honk'."

"Was it friendly?"

"Yes, this is a very friendly goose."

"Then what happened?" His hand went up to his head. To some momentary hurt.

"You said, 'I will climb on its back.' I said, 'Davey, you will do no such thing.' But you only laughed at me."

"Did I climb on its back?"

"Yes," said Mrs. Gaspar. "I cannot believe it. Up you jump, out the window and onto the back of that Canada goose."

"Holy Bat," laughed Davey softly. He was too tired to say *man*.

"And it is waiting for this very thing. And it honks just so, and up it flies into the sky with you on its back, smiling."

"Wow," said Davey slowly, his words slurred. "I never thought I'd fly on a Canada goose."

"No," said Mrs. Gaspar, stroking his hair again, "I never thought you would either."

In this time, we received the *T* and *U* and *V* issues. *T* contained tumour, one paragraph, as dry and devoid of emotion as the entry on death. A swelling or abnormal growth of the tissue. *See* cancer. *See* malignancy. *See* neoplasm. Instead I sat beside him and told him about trade winds. Tides. Mark Twain's early life. Tarantulas, tweed, and Tutankhamen. Sometimes he smiled. Often he slept.

All the *Uniteds*. Utah: a visitor's guide. Umbrellas and Uzbekistan.

Vacuums and vivisection. Vermont, Venezuela, the Vatican. Vital statistics: birth, marriage, divorce, sickness, and death.

At the time we may not have called them good days, but afterward we would. Those days contained a type of goodness for which there is no word. Looking back, I can only see those days in fragments. My mother sleeping beside her own mother. Mrs. Gaspar's hand inside Davey's hand. Sudden seizures that woke people from slumber. Clothes that someone else had folded and left in a basket on our table. The smell of diabetic urine. Of soap. Of sunlight. Of perfect summer days that passed by outside our windows.

Nanny Flora said, "Now, sit beside Mrs. Gaspar and me, Lenny, and tell us something."

I told them about spiderlings that ballooned by attaching their spinneret to twigs and launching themselves into the wind. Hundreds of miles they flew. I told them of the Picasso beetle in Mozambique that glittered with every colour of the rainbow. I explained to them the differences between grasshoppers, crickets, and katydids, pausing to see if Nanny Flora could take it. She nodded to say she could.

"I think you should have your own book, Lenny," said Nanny Flora. "*Lenny's Book of Everything*. The things you know!"

I knew she was trying to help me. I tried to smile.

"Maybe," I said.

"Pah, it would probably only have insects in it," said Mrs. Gaspar.

I can't get to the bottom of those days. Remembering them is like deep-sea diving. But there was goodness in those moments. Each of them was bright and deep. We swam in those moments.

It felt as though we had called a cease-fire with the world. Mother did not put on her pink uniform. She did not go out the door. She filled back up with some of her old magic. As Davey grew weaker, she told him stories and slept beside him, sometimes knelt on the floor, her head on the bed. She didn't do housework. People came and did it for her. Once, I looked into the kitchen and saw the principal Mrs. Dalrymple washing dishes and Mrs. Oliver, the assistant, drying. I don't know how they got in, but afterward, they sliced a cake and left it on the table and then disappeared just as quietly.

Waiting days, being days, ending days, staying days. Dr. Leopold came and told Mother that it was time for Davey to go to the hospital. It was afternoon and another long night stretched ahead. Things were going wrong. Davey's heart was in trouble. "There's oxygen at the hospital," said Dr. Leopold. "And nurses all the time, twenty-four hours a day."

"I don't think it's the right place for him," said Mother.

Mrs. Bartholomew had said, "You are doing everything right. You are the best mother I've ever seen. Here is the place Davey should be."

"He'd go . . ." Mother started. "I mean, he'd go to the hospital to die."

"Yes, Mrs. Spink," said Dr. Leopold.

She didn't ask if he was going to die. She just knew it. The way a mother knows her baby is to be born. Like she knew all those years ago that she had to catch the number twenty-four bus.

"Well, I think that should happen here," said Mother. I don't think I ever heard my mother sound so strong.

Once there was a knock at the door and there stood Mr. Petersburg. "For the boy," he whispered and thrust a package into my hands. The package contained Junior Sales Club field glasses. I don't know how he came by them, but I felt very sad, a plummeting type of sadness, but also the beginning of a new kind of rage, just a bud that had not yet bloomed. I was glad for his kindness, I was, but those glasses had come too late, and Davey could not see, and even that small time ago when he had stuck the flag in his cap seemed such a long time ago, a country we had left behind and could never return to.

"Mr. Petersburg came," I whispered to Davey. He didn't reply. "He gave you a gift."

Nothing.

"The field glasses," I held them in my hands. No response.

Just Davey's breathing.

I took the caps from the back of the binoculars and lifted them to my eyes. I saw the walls up close, the light switch. I saw the decoration on the side of Mrs. Gaspar's tea canister, which I had never really noticed before. It was a leaf pattern, a twisted vine and in the very middle the initials Z.G. I turned my head and examined up close the spines of the *Burrell's Build-It-at-Home Encyclopedia*. I peered at Davey's hands, the lines and furrows and cracked dry skin.

"Davey," I whispered, my mouth to his ear. "Remember we didn't run away? Well, maybe we still can. I think we should."

I slipped my scrawny hand inside his own and I felt him squeeze.

"We'll go up through the Dakotas, and into Canada. We'll walk for weeks."

He squeezed again.

"Davey, we'll make it to Great Bear Lake. Timothy will meet us there. I know he's there. The real one."

I squeezed his hand. He squeezed mine back. We squeezed goodbye in Morse code.

WXYZ

Martha Brent hand-delivered the issues that remained. She had driven all the way from Indianapolis for Davey's funeral. Mother had sent her a telegram. The telegram said: *Davey passed away peacefully, Monday, July 17. RIP.*

He was nearly eight.

Somehow, those issues made it upstairs after the funeral and into a small pile pushed into the corner of the living room. I tried not to look at them. Martha Brent did not wear a cloak. She didn't swish anywhere. She was regular-sized and nondescript. She wore brown-framed glasses and she smiled at me sadly and burst into tears.

"It's okay, Mrs. Brent," I said.

I saw her looking at our encyclopedias which were on the bottom shelf of the china cabinet. I saw her eyes rest on the space where the *F* volume should have been. She smiled at me again and took her glasses off and wiped at her eyes furiously. I knew she wouldn't replace it because she was smart like that. That volume went with Davey and she would leave things as they were meant to be. Mother came to Martha and talked, but I couldn't hear what they were saying.

Our apartment was filled with people. There were teachers from school and the Bartholomew family. Nanny Flora was seated beside Mrs. Gaspar on the sofa holding hands. There was Mr. Engelmann who came and put his hand on my mother's shoulder, and I saw her smile sadly at him. Our apartment was full, but very empty. That's how it felt. I kept waiting for him to come in. To arrive. I kept waiting. Waiting was the feeling I had.

CJ touched me on the elbow. We went and sat on my bed and looked at the empty space where Davey's bed had been. The pigeons cooed on the ledge: Frank and Roger and Martin. Charlie the stick insect swivelled his head slowly, watching us. The Greyhound buses arrived and departed and the whole world moved outside. The sky was blue, but there would be a storm.

I was waiting. That's how I felt. My veins, my nerves, my everything was waiting. CJ didn't say anything. She just sat with her hipbone pressed into mine. She slung her arm over my shoulder.

"Oh, I nearly forgot, Matthew Milford wanted you to have this."

She took a matchbox from her cowboy shirt pocket

"What?" I opened it to find a tiny red ladybug with seven glossy black spots. "*Coccinella septempunctata*," I said. "That's kind."

"One day you're going to be a beetle expert," said CJ.

One day. All the *one days* I got that Davey didn't. That sadness rose up in me like a giant wave and I was going to be drowned. CJ kept her arm around my shoulder so I didn't drown.

— 330 —

"I'll discover a rare beetle and name it after him," I whispered above the roar of that wave.

"I know," said CJ. "You're going to be the best beetle expert in the world."

She held me and didn't let go even when we went back to saying nothing, just sitting there waiting.

My feeling of waiting reminded me of when my mother felt something was about to happen all those years ago, when Davey was just a baby and my hand was tiny upon her heart. How she had told me we would have to wait to find out if it was something good or bad or in-between.

But now we knew. It was a good thing. All of Davey, in all his time upon the earth, was good.

WXYZ contained mostly *W*, which was a letter of wonders. Whales and Wales. Washington and wagons. Walkie-talkies. Warfare. Warsaw. Winnipeg. Watches, counting, counting, counting our seconds. Wind. The polar easterlies and the prevailing westerlies, and the trade winds. The chinook, the foehn, the sirocco, the simoom. I let these things fill me. This information fell down inside me like coins into a moneybox. Clink, clink, chink, chink. *W* was like swallowing the world in those first few days after he was gone.

X contained X-rays and St. Francis Xavier. Y contained yaks and the Yangtze and yellow fever. Yellow-jacket wasps, Yonkers and Yale and *Yankee Doodle Dandy*.

And then *Z*. The last letter.

Author's Note

Why did I write the story of Lenny and Davey? I always find the process of story creation quite mysterious. I have the embers of so many stories smouldering in my brain, and I'm never quite sure what makes one start to burn. The story of an encyclopedia set and a boy who kept growing had been in my head for many years, but it wasn't until I was writing *A Most Magical Girl* that it flared to life. This Lenny and Davey story called to me incessantly like no other story. "Everything will be ok if you can just write me," the story said. When I finally sat down to write it, Lenny was there waiting for me. I felt immediately comfortable in her voice. *Lenny's Book of Everything* felt huge: Davey growing and growing and growing, all the knowledge in those encyclopedia pages, the big friendships and the big love. It felt like I was trying to fit the universe inside a shoebox, but Lenny's voice kept me calm.

While story-writing is about creating a world, breathing characters to life, and enticing readers on a journey, it is also, for me, just as much about sorting stuff out in my head. While I wrote, I was thinking a lot about loss and grief, about ill-health, and about caring for someone who is dying, because

I had experienced all these things in recent years. I was also thinking about love in all its forms: sibling love, motherly love, neighbourly love, the love between friends. I wanted to sort out in my head what it means to love someone who is different, how that feels, and the emotions that go along with that love. But mostly, through it all, I think I was really trying to shine a light on what a cracker of a miracle it is to be alive, and how everywhere, even in the darkest hours, there's always hope. Writing this story certainly gave me hope in many ways.

Acknowledgements

M y mother and father purchased an encyclopaedia set for our family when I was a young girl. It was a pivotal moment in the history of my childhood household and I'm so very thankful to my parents, both now gone, for instilling in us a love of knowledge and a great passion for "looking stuff up".

Parts of the *Merit Student Encyclopedia* still remain on my bookshelf, spines bound in masking tape, because we quite literally loved those books to death as kids. When "looking stuff up" for this story, I turned to these pages, as well as the pages of the *World Book Encyclopedia* (1971), the *Childcraft How and Why Library* (1980), *The Encyclopedia of the Animal World* (1977), Arthur Mee's *The Childrens' Encyclopedia*, and the online *Encyclopedia Britannica,* to name just a few.

Regarding the medical detail in the story, I must stress that Davey's condition, while loosely based on pituitary gigantism, is one of my own making. I have used considerable artistic licence in creating a disease that baffled Davey's medical team in the 1970s. I sincerely hope that in doing so I have not offended anyone. As a nurse, I have cared for people for nearly thirty years and I am thankful for all those hours and the many wonderful nurses I have worked alongside, all of which have taught me much and informed many of the pages in this story.

I'm grateful for all the help given to me in writing this story and there was much. My daughter Alice, who is so patient with my writing life. My sister, Sonia, for being first reader. Catherine Drayton, as always, for her invaluable insights and pep-talks. Erin Clarke for her detailed and wise consideration of my words and all her guidance. And much thanks to Anna McFarlane and Radhiah Chowdhury at Allen & Unwin.

The writing of this book was also greatly assisted by the Queensland Writers Fellowship program, an initiative of the Queensland Government through the State Library of Queensland and Arts Queensland.

About the Author

Karen Foxlee is an Australian author who writes for both kids and grown-ups. Her first novel, *The Anatomy of Wings*, won numerous awards, including the Dobbie Literary Award and the Commonwealth Writers' Prize for Best First Book in 2008. *Ophelia and the Marvellous Boy*, Karen's first novel for children, was published internationally to much acclaim, while her second novel for younger readers, *A Most Magical Girl*, won the Readings Children's Fiction Prize in 2017 and was shortlisted by the Children's Book Council of Australia in the same year.

Karen lives in South East Queensland with her daughter and several animals, including two wicked parrots who frequently eat parts of her laptop when she isn't looking. Her passions are her daughter, writing, daydreaming, baking, running and swimming in the sea.

PUSHKIN CHILDREN'S BOOKS

We created Pushkin Children's Books to share tales from different languages and cultures with younger readers, and to open the door to the wide, colourful worlds these stories offer.

From picture books and adventure stories to fairy tales and classics, and from fifty-year-old bestsellers to current huge successes abroad, the books on the Pushkin Children's list reflect the very best stories from around the world, for our most discerning readers of all: children.